# Familiar Strangers

ANNA GRACE

# Familiar Strangers

## Anna Grace

Cover Design by Hannah Noelle Gibson
(@cartoons_bynoelle on Instagram)

Edited by Rachel Reed

# CONTENT WARNING

This book contains topics such as grief and familial issues. There are brief mentions of blood, infidelity, and alcohol abuse. Please keep these things in mind while reading.

To anyone who has ever believed that they feel too much.

Also to Hannah, who read the first copy of this book two years ago. Thank you for always suffering through my rough drafts and encouraging me, regardless of how bad they are.

# **PLAYLIST**

The Alcott (feat. Taylor Swift)- The National
The Night We Met- Lord Huron
Vienna- Billy Joel
Sad Beautiful Tragic (Taylor's Version)- Taylor Swift
Ghost Of You- 5 Seconds of Summer
Save Me- Noah Kahan
Livin' On A Prayer- Bon Jovi
Paper Houses- Niall Horan
(what i wish just one person would say to me)- LANY
Till Forever Falls Apart- Ashe, FINNEAS
New Perspective- Noah Kahan
Dancing Queen- ABBA
Mess It Up- Gracie Abrams
Graceland Too- Phoebe Bridgers
the 1- Taylor Swift
Just A Girl- No Doubt
Ventura Highway- America
Evergreen- Ricky Mitch & The Coal Miners
Silver Springs- Fleetwood Mac
Call Your Mom- Noah Kahan
Wonderland (Taylor's Version)- Taylor Swift

# OCTOBER 10, 2008

A warm hand grabs mine, right as the wind whips my hair in my face.

"Ben," I say with a smile. I know who it is, who I want it to be.

"Celia," he says back, his voice soft.

"What is it?"

He lets out a sigh as he turns to face me. Amusement brightens his green eyes, but his expression is more solemn than I've seen in a while. "We should get married."

I laugh, the sound spilling out of me before I can control it. "We're seventeen."

"It worked for Romeo and Juliet."

"Actually, it couldn't have gone worse for Romeo and Juliet. Have you even read it?"

"No," he says matter-of-factly. "But still. There's no time like the present."

"We have plenty of time to worry about something like that," I say. "All the time in the world."

Ben sighs. "Probably true."

I grab his hand, lacing my fingers through his. "The park isn't a great place to decide on a marriage, anyways."

He smiles, and it's all dimples. "It could be worse."

"I know." I lean over and rest my head on his shoulder. The wind has stopped blowing my hair around, but the clouds above us darken suspiciously. "It could always be worse."

# CHAPTER ONE

## March 13, 2009

*He wouldn't want a visit.*

I shake my head, correcting only myself.

*No. He would, just not from you.*

There.

I stand before the rusty metal gate, willing my thoughts to stop. They don't, of course. They never do.

It's been exactly six months since those gates closed behind me, and I haven't been inside them again. Today clearly isn't the day to change that.

The rain has soaked my clothes, as well as the notebook in my hand. I came here to write, but the downpour started as soon as I arrived. It's certainly no use now—I'll be shocked if the pages are still intact.

I tuck it under my shirt and start the walk down the street, kicking every single pebble out of my way. It's thundering again, but that doesn't make me pick up the pace. The pullover I'm wearing is already drenched and my shoes are squelching in every puddle. Rushing won't change a thing.

The *Greene's Grocery* sign is hardly even visible through the rain. When the actual door is in sight—blurry sight, but nonetheless—I break into a halfhearted spring and burst into the lobby. The smell of window cleaner and day-old coffee grounds greets me, and oddly enough, it's comforting.

"Hi. You're soaked," Marcus states from behind the counter. His dark hair is slightly wet, so I doubt he's been here for long. Our shift just started.

"Thank you, I couldn't tell." I turn my head enough to glare at him, and he laughs. Marcus may be my cousin, but that doesn't stop him from attempting—and succeeding—to get on my nerves. "Busy schedule today?"

He shakes his head. "Not bad. Inventory and tidying. The usual."

I set my notebook on the counter, then wring my hair out onto the ground. Marcus winces as the water hits the grimy tile. I wait for him to bring it up, but he doesn't. Instead, I catch him gazing at the dripping notebook.

"You're writing again?"

"No," I say, twisting my hair around my hand. "The rain didn't want me to."

"Oh, C. You've got to defy nature."

"I think the pages are mostly dead now," I murmur, lifting the front cover. The entire first page is shriveled up, and it looks like it'll tear if I try to turn it.

"I'll get you a new one," he says, putting his hand over his heart. "Cousin's honor."

I grin. Marcus, alongside being my cousin, fancies himself my life coach. He's been telling me to write again for months, begging me to scribble down a singular word. I told him I would, but I just haven't.

It isn't for lack of trying. I just think that my words are lost, and I haven't found them yet.

Deciding *not* to say any of that, I tuck my notebook under my arm and make my way around the counter, slipping through the tiny door behind Marcus. He grumbles when my hair drips on his clothes, but that can't be helped. I look and feel like a wet dog.

"Sorry," I tell him. "I'll be back after I change."

"Change the attitude, too," he mumbles, flicking the wet patch on his shirt. "You seem like you're in a mood."

I let out the smallest, driest laugh, then head upstairs.

The corner store has been family owned on my step-dad's side for years. It's directly under our apartment building, so we've got an easy way in. I unlock the first door with the key around my neck, then walk up a small set of stairs until I see *our* front door.

When I get inside, I wait to be bombarded by my little siblings. They're normally bouncing around the hall, toys in hand as they run up to me. Today, though, no rugrats appear and wrap their arms around my thighs.

The house is empty and I'm not sure why. It's Friday— no one is ever working elsewhere, especially not in this weather. I walk through the house in hopes of finding them.

All I find is a note, penned in my mom's flawless hand-writing:

*Cici, we're out with your Nina. She called and asked us over to her house. Wanted to see the twins, I guess. We'll be back around three.*

*-Mom*

I bite the inside of my cheek and read over the note once more.

Nina, Nina, Nina.

Yes, I'm sure she wanted to see the kids. That's all.

I crumple the note between my palms and toss it into the trash, shoving it out of my brain. Nina is my grandmother, but I don't call her family. Between her lack of contact and my lack of desire to speak with her, the word doesn't fit.

She was around when I was younger, always the mysterious type—the one that showed up on her terms. She didn't bother with holidays or birthdays or anniversaries. Anything that was not directly tethered to her was unimportant.

Recently, though, she's been trying to weasel her way back into our lives. Marcus and I don't trust it, but Mom is open to it. I wonder if that will be put to rest after this visit.

My wrists randomly begin to itch, and I'm suddenly reminded of my wet clothes. I've been standing in the kitchen for much too long, given that a puddle of water has accumulated around my feet.

I grab a dirty dish rag from the counter and toss it onto the ground, vowing to clean the mess up before I go back to the store. If someone slips, it'll be my throat. I yank off my shoes and place them on the towel as a reminder, then run upstairs.

The second I fling open the bathroom door, I toss my book down. It's as good as garbage now; there's absolutely no reason to try and salvage it.

I peel my clothes off, hating the sticky fabric against my skin. They're too wet to leave on the floor, so I toss them into the tub. Only one towel is left on the rack. I mentally thank whoever didn't take a shower this morning and wrap it around me.

I smell like outside.

I *hate* smelling like outside.

A shower would be lovely, but I'm already late to my shift. Technically, I could get a break from Don. He wouldn't mind it, but I can't take more of Marcus complaining about my punctuality.

My bedroom door is latched like I left it—a good sign that my siblings didn't raid the place. I tiptoe to my closet and change into the comfiest clothes I've got before flopping facedown onto my bed.

"I want to be *clean*," I mumble into my pillow, complaining only to myself.

And then somebody clears their throat.

*No, they don't.*

They don't, obviously. I'm alone in this room.

Still, I can feel my entire body seize up with fear. No one is here, though. I'm being insane. Totally, completely insane. The door was latched, and nothing was out of place, so—

"Please don't kill me," I hear myself say. I don't recall deciding to speak, but I'm not in control of anything at this point. I could be wearing an ax as a headband in six seconds if I don't play my cards right.

"Celia," a quiet voice says.

My stomach bottoms out.

*That* voice. That familiar, low voice, so soft that it threatens to bring tears to my eyes.

My head pops up, and the first thing my eyes land on is a boy who I never thought I'd see again. Ever.

Mainly because he died, and I'm responsible for his death.

# CHAPTER TWO

I used to find the phrase *'my past haunts me'* a bit dramatic. A little over the top, especially for mundanities.

But now, my past is sitting by my window. Haunting me.

Literally.

"Bennet," I try to say, but nothing comes out.

This isn't real. How do you address a hallucination, anyways? He—*It*—has to be a hallucination. That's the only possibility.

He's *dead.*

"Celia," he repeats, lower this time.

I never thought I'd hear my name on his lips again.

Which, I'm not. Still. This isn't real.

But he *looks* real. He looks exactly like my Bennet, only…fainter. There's no other way to explain it. Like if I stare too hard, I'll be able to see the window right through him.

His clothes are just as they were the last time I saw him: black sweatshirt, blue jeans. He's got the same blond hair I always teased him for dyeing, even though it was natural. The same pale green eyes I was hideously jealous of.

I haven't seen him like this since his death. I've dreamed of him, of course; more times than I can count. But I've never seen him in my room, sitting across my beanbag chair, looking ready to start a conversation about the weather.

"You aren't real," I say.

He'll disappear if I take my eyes off him, so I don't.

"I am, I think."

"No you aren't." *Go, girl. You're arguing with a hallucination.* "I watched you die. I'm practically at fault! You aren't real."

His brows draw together, an expression so real and vivid and *human* that I feel faint. "You aren't at fault, Cici," he says quietly. "And I am real. I must be. We're talking, aren't we?"

I shrug. "Well, I'm delusional, then."

He laughs, and I feel my stomach drop.

Suddenly, instantly, I'm overwhelmed with the urge to reach out and touch him. I don't even know if I can do that, but I want to know if I'm crazy or if he's really here. If he isn't, and I'm actually this far gone…I can't handle that. Not with the voices I've put up with every day since I lost his.

*I am real. I must be.*

I suck in a breath and lift my hand. It's shaking, presumably from adrenaline or fear or both. Ben's hands are the only part of him exposed, other than his face.

If I feel nothing, good. I've lost it. At least I'll be aware.

Squeezing my eyes shut, I lower my wrist.

And then I feel his hand. Stiff and cold as ice. Faint, but *there.*

I swallow. "Uhm."

"Don't scream," Ben says as I pull my hand back.

*He's alive he's alive he's alive he's—*

"You're here," I say, panic rising in my tone. "You're alive?"

A ridiculous thing to say, but it's all I've got.

He scratches the back of his head. "That's the thing. I don't think I am."

I blink. "Okay, so you're not. But you're sitting in front of me and talking to me. I just touched your arm. You're here."

Ben nods. "Yes, I'm definitely here. But I'm not alive. You…you did watch me die."

I feel the blood drain from my face, the excitement from seconds ago leaving with it. Of course I did. I watched his funeral. I watched them lower his casket, and I watched the life leave his eyes.

"Hey," he says, drawing my attention back to him. "You can't laugh at me when I say this, okay?"

"I'm on the verge of a conniption."

He ignores me. "I think I'm a ghost or something weird."

I rub my temples, aware of the headache building behind my eyes. "So let me get this straight. You died. I watched them put you in the ground."

"*If* you did, yes," he answers, smiling so one of his dimples shows.

"And now you're just a ghost? Are you here to haunt me? I didn't think you'd stoop so low."

Ben shrugs. "I don't know what's going on, but I'm kind of here again, I guess. At least for a little while. I'm not even sure what happened. I just kind of…appeared. Which brings me back to the ghost thi—"

"Can you walk through walls?" I blurt, my face blank.

That may be insensitive, but there's simply no better question to ask. I'm still halfway convinced this is a hallucination, and you can't offend a hallucination.

Ben chuckles. "Cici, c'mon now. Don't be ridi…" His voice trails off. "Actually, I have no idea. Let's see."

He stands from my beanbag and walks to the nearest wall. His face is full of curiosity as he reaches out to touch the wall, but it doesn't do anything out of the ordinary. At least not to my eyes.

"Maybe I have to like, will it to become walk-through-able."

"Totally makes sense," I agree mindlessly.

Ben closes his eyes and takes a confident step forward. That confidence is disrupted in mere seconds by his face hitting the wall. Hard.

"*OW*," he breathes, prodding his forehead. "Okay. That's a thing in movies."

"Plus, there's the fact that I can touch you." I swallow a laugh, but it's barely hidden. "Untouchability must be a movie-ghost thing, too."

"You're laughing."

"Of course I'm laughing. You just ran into a wall."

He flashes me a glare, but it holds no weight. He's still smiling underneath it.

Silently, he sits back on the beanbag chair.

"There's no way," I say to myself, just as a reminder. "I'm going insane, right? Maybe I've got a disease or something. One that messes with the brain, like flu or—"

Ben laughs again, and the sound completely disarms me.

I shouldn't be hearing it.

To say that I'm unsure of what to do now is an understatement. Part of me wants to hug him, and the other part of me wants to run out of this room. No matter how '*okay*' I'm trying to be about this, it's weird. It's impossible.

And yet, I hold his eyes as I ask, "How long have you been here?"

"Since this morning," he admits. "I climbed the fire escape and came through your window. For once, it wasn't stuck. I assumed you'd be here, but you weren't, so I just waited. I don't know where else to go. You're the only one I can explain this to."

For a moment, I sit and think. Then I gasp so loud that Ben jumps.

"DID YOU SEE ME IN MY TOWEL?"

He gapes. "*That* is where your focus lies?"

"DID YOU?"

He raises his hands in defense. "I looked away! I didn't see anything. Gosh. You'd think a dead guy could get a break."

I shake my head, feeling a smile on my lips. "I can't hide you here forever, Ben. If anyone sees you…"

"I know," he says. "I only want to stay until I can think of a solution, or at least figure out what's going on."

I exhale. The odds of this going well are slim to none. Ben knows that I can't keep my family out of my room, but I can't keep *him* anywhere else, either.

"That's fine." My voice is thick. "Obviously. I'll do my best to keep you hidden."

"Thank you," Ben says. "I can't go anywhere else."

I nod because I know.

Ben stares at the windowsill, and I watch his eyes follow the raindrops as they drip down the glass. He really does look the same, at least mostly. A bit paler, sure, and his hair and eyes are a bit duller. But he's the same Ben. He has to be.

I close my eyes, willing my senses to come back.

*Open them on three. If he isn't there, you're taking a trip to the looney bin.*

I open them.

He's still in front of me.

Fine.

"Look," I start. "I've got my shift at the store—"

"I figured," he says. "I'll stay here if that's alright. See if I can remember what happened."

Without responding, I take a step into my closet and shut the door behind me. Now, my focus is on getting to work before my parents or Marcus find Ben. It doesn't matter that there are bigger things to deal with. They'll have to wait while I stock inventory.

Besides. I need to think a little clearer, and that isn't going to happen in this room.

I quickly change into old jeans and a sweater, then yank on a dry pair of tennis shoes. They rub my ankles weirdly. I understand now why they were tucked behind a box in my closet.

"My family won't be home until three," I say in response to Ben's earlier comment. "You can go to the kitchen and eat, or whatever ghosts do, I guess. Do you get hungry?"

I almost laugh at my own statement. What am I even saying?

Ben just shrugs, not giving it a second thought. "I'll stay here to be safe."

*So. This is really happening.*

"Suit yourself." I tie my *Greene's Grocery* apron around my waist. "There are books and puzzles in the closet and under my bed. The disk player is in my dresser drawer." I pause. "Can you like, pick stuff up? Is that a thing?"

Ben looks around, probably for something to grab. He finds a broken pencil on my desk and lifts it, then flicks it around on his fingers like a baton.

"Well." His face is painted with surprise. "It appears so."

"Alright," I say, mildly amused. "DVDs are in the bottom left desk drawer. You should watch—"

"If the next thing out of your mouth is *Twilight*—"

"*Twilight.*"

Ben rolls his eyes and grins. It's the last thing I see before I leave my room.

# CHAPTER THREE

Marcus is waiting for me at the store, thrown over the counter in the most relaxed manner I can imagine. I try to match his nonchalant composure, but I know I'm failing. My entire body is tense and my face isn't hiding a thing.

"Took you long enough," he says, not giving me a second glance. "Did you fall up there?"

"What?" I reach into the supply closet for the mop and try to figure out what he means. I didn't fall, didn't drop anything. All I did was change, and—

Oh, right. Ben walked into a wall at my request.

"Wait, yeah, I did," I lie. "My shoes were so wet from the rain that I slipped."

"Ah." Marcus nods as I drag the mop across the floor. When he's sure that I'm working, he grabs a *Glamour Bi-Weekly* magazine from the rack and flips through it. The thing is upside down, but that doesn't seem to faze him. He stares at a page and doesn't bat an eye for a good while. "And were you talking to yourself?"

I stop short.

*The paper thin walls. Gotta love the paper thin walls.*

"Yes," I lie again.

I look up at him to see if he's buying it. The answer is definitely no, but he doesn't bother asking anymore questions.

After I finish cleaning up the mess on the floor (including mud and dirt people have tracked in), I put the mop away and join Marcus behind the counter. Few customers have come in since I got here, so we do the only thing one *can* do on a boring shift: play Headbanz.

"You're like something to sit on—no! Not really. Actually, yeah, kind of. Only if you're like, five years old, I guess."

I blink. "A school desk? Like the little fold out ones?"

"No!" Marcus huffs. The timer is almost up, and he's extremely determined *not* to lose. "Okay, uhm. I think it has a little seat buckle thing so they don't fall out and crack their skull."

"What the heck? A car seat?"

"*NO!*" He opens his mouth to try yet another explanation, but it's too late for him; the sand has already run out of the little plastic hourglass.

I yank the card off my head and scoff. "It was a high chair. You couldn't describe a high chair?"

"That's exactly what I described!"

I look at him in disbelief. "Five-year-olds don't use high chairs. That's something for two-year-olds!"

"How was I supposed to know? I don't even like kids. Do I seem like the caring type?"

"Not particularly, no," I say. "In fact, I find you rather abrasive."

He waves me off before grabbing another card.

"Okay, your turn." He puts the card on his headband and turns back to me. I'm relieved when I see what it is—a guitar. It shouldn't be difficult to explain, given that Marcus is the musically inclined one in the family.

"This is easy," I say as I flip the timer. "You play this."

"Girls."

I stare at him, stifling a laugh. "Marcus."

"I'm kidding. I am a *gentleman*. Is it an instrument?"

"Obviously."

"A bass."

"Close. Six strings."

"Guitar?"

"Bingo."

He takes his card off the band in a victorious manner, then sets it on the discard pile. "You up for another round?"

I look at the clock. It's almost three already, which means my family should arrive any minute. I've already prepared myself for the stories I'll hear. If Nina comes back *with* them, though, then we have a different problem.

"Let's not." I take my headband off. "Mom and Don are gonna be back soon. They went to visit Nina."

"Ah," he says, not bothering to mask the disgust in his tone. "You just know she's up to something."

"I know. But we aren't going to know *what* until she wants us to."

He eyes me. "Do you think it's about the divorce?"

I shrug. I want to say no, but I can't.

When I say 'Mom and Don', I mean my mom and stepdad. My real dad—Nina's son—divorced my mom a long time ago. It's very rare that we see him, and rarer still that we see Nina.

She pretty much quit talking to us after the divorce. If this visit was important to her, I'm guessing it stems from that.

Marcus doesn't keep the conversation going, and neither do I. We just sit in silence until the front door opens.

"Cici!" My siblings yell when they catch sight of me. I grin and step out from behind the counter, letting them attack my legs with their tiny hugs.

Jace and Maisie are my step-siblings. Step-*twins*, they prefer to be called. They're eight and absolutely manic at times. I'm willing to bet that they're sugared up right now.

Mom and Don step in the door, undeterred by the squealing as they shake the rain off their umbrella. Mom is grinning until she catches my eye, and it's instantly clear that she has something to tell me.

"Your Nina said *hi*," she says by way of greeting.

I nod before turning back to the twins. They're still standing by me, limbs wrapped around each of my legs. I think I can *feel* them jittering.

"Why don't you two go tackle Marcus?" I whisper loudly, pointing at him. "He beat me in Headbanz, so we aren't on good terms."

They let out a chorus of giggles before bolting around the counter and grabbing Marcus. He laughs, but I'm fairly sure he's in pain. Maisie is not a gentle one.

I'm watching them, laughing along when Mom grabs my arm. "Cici," she says.

And that's *all* she says. Her eyes that normally look youthful and happy have a different look today, one that thoroughly concerns me.

I look at Don, trying my hardest to read his expression since Mom gave nothing away, but there's nothing on his face either. No look in his eyes that tells me a thing.

He must know I'm trying to get a read on him, because he looks past me and locks eyes with Marcus. "We're closing the store early tonight."

The twins seem to take that as a signal to quit playing around. They stop climbing Marcus and run to a stand of sunglasses, looking but not touching.

"It's only three," Marcus says. "Are people going to be cool with that?"

Don nods. "I think it'll be alright for one day. We'll open back up in the morning, but the rain is probably cutting us down on customers anyways."

I'm not buying it, and neither is Marcus. He can always see through our facades, which is why it's going to be *extremely* difficult to hide Bennet from him.

Instead of asking questions, as usual, Marcus just nods and agrees.

"I'll lock up the register," he says, untying his apron.

Don gives him a quick smile. "Much appreciated."

I turn to Mom. "What's all this about, exactly?"

"Celia." She says it in one of those scolding mom voices. "The rain. It's too stormy outside. The power could go out."

Her face tenses, and I decide arguing anymore is pointless. Maybe that really is the reason; maybe nothing happened with Nina. It isn't likely but it's possible.

I take off my apron and set it on the counter, then walk to the apartment. Mom rounds up the twins and follows. I'd love to get a real answer out of her, but right now, there's no use in trying.

# CHAPTER FOUR

I waste no time going to my bedroom. My family will be up here any minute, and my mind is spinning wild circles.

What's going on with Nina? Why did Mom look so concerned? And Don never closes the store early. Never. The rain is a stupid excuse to start.

Regardless, I close my bedroom door behind me, taking a second to think. This door does so much for me, really. It's the only thing between my family and me having to explain why my dead boyfriend is sitting in my room.

I lock it for extra security, even though there's no point; Mom will ask me to unlock it, and I will. Still, it makes me feel better.

Ben is still sprawled out on my beanbag, only now, he's got the disk player propped open. When he lays eyes on me, he pauses the movie. "Edward is creepy and Bella is kind of dumb. What even is this?"

"Art," I say solemnly. "You're witnessing art."

"I'm frightened."

I laugh, then remember not to be loud. If Marcus could hear me from the store, then my family will *definitely* hear me from the living room. They won't take to my excuses as easily as Marcus.

As if on cue, I hear the door in the entryway open. I drop to the ground and stare at the space between my door and the carpet, watching for someone to walk by. Nobody does.

"What is it?" Ben asks.

I stand and walk to the end of my bed. "I don't know. Something is going on with Nina, I think, but that's nothing new." I take a seat. It feels ridiculous going on about Nina when Ben is sitting right in front of me, probably with his own things to say. "Did you figure anything out?"

He shakes his head. "No. I'm sorry. I can't remember anything."

"It's okay. Hopefully you will in due time. Maybe it will help us know what on earth is going on."

He leans forward, elbows on his knees, and asks, "Are we absolutely positive I can stay here?"

I swallow. No, I'm really not, because my family will find him in days. Mom comes into my room all the time. I've got nothing to hide, and she likes my perfumes. But I don't say that, because he has nowhere else to go.

Instead of worrying him for no reason, I say, "It should be fine. I've got some of your clothes in my closet."

Ben looks a little confused, and that expression makes me grin. "*My* clothes?"

I nod, not even caring that he might find that odd. "Remember the time you left a full suitcase here after a school trip? I never gave it back. Never got the chance before things happened. So I just kept it. Sorry if that makes me creepy, but…you know."

He doesn't seem to find it creepy. His face stays blank, right until it breaks into a beautiful smile. "Did you take my books, too?"

"Don't ask questions you know the answers to."

"Books are expensive."

"My point exactly!" An obnoxious laugh bubbles out of me as Ben tosses a throw pillow at my head. I would retrieve it to do the same, but my family is right below me. I'm still trying to keep quiet, even though I've mostly failed so far.

It takes me a few seconds to actually contain my laughter. When I do, Ben peeks at the door. "We should be quiet."

"And he still has his smarts," I tease. "But yeah, Marcus thought I was talking to myself up here. He also thought I fell."

"From when I ran into the wall?"

I nod. "The walls are stupid thin."

"Apparently so," he says, grinning. "Gosh, he still works at the store with you?"

"He's the only thing that keeps me there," I admit. "He used to drag me to my shifts. I was counting on Don to fire me before Marcus forced me back to work."

Ben chuckles under his breath, as if he expected that from Marcus. My face softens, and I'm about to laugh with him, but his expression sobers in an instant. At first, I assume he's just trying to be quiet, but then he gets an idea face. And that usually ends up concerning me.

"What is it?" I ask slowly.

"Do you think we could trust Marcus to know that I'm here?"

I blink. "What?"

"Think about it, Cici. Do you think everyone can see me, or just you?"

"I don't have the slightest clue," I say. "Haven't thought about it. But I don't see why they couldn't."

"Well, can we trust him to verify that for us?"

I tilt my head in thought. "I'm sure we could. He's the one person I've confided in over the past six months. I think he's pretty much sworn to secrecy."

"Then I think that's what we should do. Just to see…the limits, I guess."

I nod, but a nagging in the back of my head disagrees, and I'm not sure why. Maybe I just want to keep this—*him*—all to myself. What happens when other people find out?

Then again, this isn't 'people'. It's Marcus.

"We can ask him tomorrow," I say.

Ben lets out a sigh that seems relieved. I take it as a positive.

Mom and Don still haven't come to find me, so I decide to find them first. I walk to my door with zero plan. They're quite used to my curiosity—it often gets the better of me. Anytime I suspect something is up, I go looking for them. I see no need for that to change.

Just as I go to unlock the door, Ben stands. "I'm going to raid your closet. For my clothes, obviously. Though I'm sure I could pull off some of your things."

"I'm sure you could. I got some new tank tops last week." I laugh, but it's weak. Distant. My mind is already elsewhere, downstairs with my parents. "Finish *Twilight* while I'm gone."

Ben shakes his head. "The Charlie guy is my favorite."

"Impeccable taste."

I unlock the door and step out of my room. I'm still not really thinking, and because of that, I nearly slam into my mom. She must have been about to knock. If that's the case, I guarantee she heard Ben and I talking.

"Mother," I say as a greeting.

She doesn't respond. Just grabs my arm and walks me to her room, then sits me down on the end of her bed. Her face is more serious than I remember, and it sparks anxiety in my gut. It's probably something minimal, something that I shouldn't be thinking so heavily about, but still. I can't handle waiting anymore.

"Just tell me, please," I say.

Mom takes her hair down from the tight clip it was in. "Your dad has been around again."

*Ah.*

I tug at a loose thread on her comforter. She notices and swats my hand away. "Didn't we get some sort of restraining order on him?"

Mom looks halfway confused, halfway annoyed. "No, we didn't. At the time, we still wanted him around, remember?"

"And what about what happened with the twins?"

Her jaw hardens as she recalls. The twins aren't my dad's kids, they're Don's. A few years ago, when my mom got remarried, my dad came back and tried to be present in all our lives—my step-siblings included.

To put it simply, he didn't make the best impression on a couple of five-year-old kids. And they only needed sugar to be impressed.

Mom shakes her head, as if trying to rid herself of the memory. "Look, I don't want to deal with that again. It's been years, and it's over. But he wants back in your life. It's your decision if you're going to let him."

I feel my shoulders slouch a bit, and I suddenly remember what I *want* to know. "What does this have to do with Nina?"

She holds her breath for a few seconds before answering. "It's your decision because he's living at Nina's house. And since we don't want to get the twins involved again, you'd stay with them for a little while."

At that, I fully flop back onto the bed and cover my face with my hands. Mom grabs my knee and rocks me back and forth, making me laugh. Only a little, given that the chaos in my mind outweighs most things. I've got seven different trains of thought and it feels like they're all crashing into each other.

"How long would I stay?"

"A month or so," Mom says.

*Four weeks. Thirty days.*

I think about what could go wrong with that.

The cons of the situation are pretty clear. One, my dad isn't exactly the best guy around. He never treated my mom or me with any sort of love or respect, despite what I thought as a child. Leaving that behind was something I looked forward to.

Two, *again*, I'm kind of hiding my once-dead boyfriend in my closet, so I don't really know if that's a great idea.

Mom is staring at me, waiting for an answer, but I don't look at her. I close my eyes and move on to the pros of this.

It's possible that I can use this to my advantage, as well as Ben's. If I can somehow get him to Nina's house without Mom knowing, it fixes a lot. For a month, anyways. All I'd have to do is come up with Ben's origin story (boyfriend, best friend, or hardened criminal I met on the train), then send him off before I come back home.

Nina and Dad don't know what he looks like. Contact with them ended before I met Ben. They didn't know about his death, funeral, or general existence.

"I'll go," I say, trying not to sound overly enthusiastic. I'll tip her off in seconds if I'm not careful. "But just for a month."

Mom looks almost relieved at the words. "Thank you. Thank you, Cici." She hugs me, and I wonder *what* about this is so important. I never saw it as a big deal.

When she pulls back to look at me, I sigh. "When would I leave?"

"Sunday morning," she says. "We'll skip service to see you off. That gives you all of tomorrow to pack and spend time with everyone."

"And how am I getting there?"

"You can take the bus. We'll pay the fare."

I'm trying to focus on the details she's giving, but all I can think about is the fact that I've got a month. One single month to figure things out.

*Four weeks. Thirty days.*

"I'll start packing," I say.

Mom nods, gives me one more big squeeze, and tells me 'thank you' before letting me leave.

I walk out of her room and back to my own, closing and locking the door behind me. To my surprise, Ben is still raiding my closet. I clear my throat to get his attention, and he pops his head out from behind the door. Doesn't even look stunned to see me. It makes sense, I guess. I'm the one who's *supposed* to be here.

"You kept so much of this stuff," he says, holding up one of his old hoodies.

"Yeah," I say, picking at my thumbnail. "Hey, quick question. How would you feel about taking this circus out of town?"

He stands straight. Looks me over like I've gone insane in my absence. "What?"

"My Nina and my dad invited me to stay at her place for a month. I accepted. If you're good with it, I think it'll buy us some more time to figure things out. It makes most sense."

He doesn't respond, so I keep explaining my half-cooked plan. "We'll talk to Marcus tomorrow and explain everything. Then, on Sunday morning, we leave. If we happen to see someone we know on the way, we'll just have to deal with it. But I can lie. Quick, too. I think it can work."

Ben pauses. "You planned that in the hallway, didn't you?"

"Every word."

He crosses his arms. "Well. I think it can work."

My eyes widen. "So you're alright with it?"

He nods, stepping out of my closet to stand across from me. "It's going to be challenging, getting there and all. Plus, we'll have to think up an excuse as to *why* they didn't know you were bringing someone. One that won't get back to your parents. If they find out…gosh, I don't even know what would happen. Nothing good."

"Surely we can think of some excuse," I say. I hear the insane amount of hope in my voice, but I think it's okay. The exact same thing is in Ben's eyes.

This seems to excite him in some way. As if everything isn't on the line. As if this isn't the most ridiculous thing either of us have ever dealt with.

It excites me too.

"Surely we can," he says quietly.

I lean back against the wall, nearly on the door handle, and chew the inside of my cheek. Thinking isn't going to work in this situation. Can you really think through a plan when the situation *itself* makes no sense? Going at this completely blind may be our best bet.

"So," I start quietly. "That's a yes?"

Ben looks up at the ceiling. "Yes."

# CHAPTER FIVE

Ben falls asleep on my bed while I'm rummaging through my room, gathering things for the trip. All I've got so far is a pile of casual outfits, but I doubt that's what Nina has in mind. Her house is *nice*—I know that much. I'm willing to bet that her outfits are, too.

Then again, I really couldn't care less.

I throw in an extra ratty sweater just to spite her.

Everything is shoved in one suitcase because I only *have* one. It's stuffed to the brim, nearly too full to zip, but it's functional enough. I throw the disk player and a few DVDs in my backpack, along with a few random books. If Nina and Dad think I'm spending time with them twenty-four seven, they're sorely mistaken.

Surely they can't think that, though. That would be the most assumptive thing I've ever heard. It would also make me mad in record time, and I'm trying to be more positive.

It isn't really working yet.

I'm going to have to ease myself into this situation, but that's alright. I haven't seen either of them for longer than an hour at a time in years. There's no way I can just go back to being okay with them.

Besides. If I'm that irritable, I'll leave.

Neither my parents nor my siblings have come upstairs while I've been packing, so I feel better about Ben napping. I don't even know if he *needs* to sleep or if he just doesn't want to be awake.

Ghosts don't come with an instruction manual. Should be a given.

I toss the last pair of socks into my suitcase, then sit on my mattress beside Ben. Blatantly, I just stare at him, like I'm a creepy stalker or something.

Staring is allowed, though. Probably. It *should* be.

Hesitantly, I run a finger along Ben's shoulder, the touch featherlight. My breath catches at the contact, at the fact that he's still in front of me. On this level, it's no different than it used to be.

*No*, I think to myself. *It's the exact opposite.*

I never tried to hide him, not once. And now that's all I can do.

Ben startles awake suddenly, glancing up at me with a sleepy expression. "You're still here?"

I laugh, just a little. It feels strange that he's the one asking that question. "Yeah, I'm here. But I'm going downstairs. I'll lock the door behind me. You can unlock it when I come back up for bed."

He props himself up on his elbows. "Give me like, a special knock or something so I know it's you."

"I don't think anyone else would knock if I'm downstairs. They don't know you're here."

He frowns. "You're no fun. Just do something different to change it up."

"Alright," I say. "Uhm, I'll knock three times, wait a second, then knock once more."

"Perfect," he says, fluffing my pillow. "Thank you."

I laugh softly as he closes his eyes again, seemingly asleep in seconds. I leave the room and check the lock twice before going downstairs. Jace and Maisie are both sitting on the living room floor, their eyes glued to the TV. It takes them a few moments to notice me.

"Cici!" Maisie greets, motioning for me to come closer. I stand between them and stare at the show, hands on my hips. They're watching *SpongeBob SquarePants*. As one who was never allowed to watch this, I'm mildly entertained. Also equally insulted. How badly could this have fried my brain? He's a sponge.

Unfortunately, I'm not here to watch cartoons. I walk through the living room and into the kitchen to find my parents at our table. Mom doesn't look as tense or worried anymore, which eases the knot of anxiety in my stomach.

My agreement must have been vital, at least to her.

Don looks up from his newspaper when he hears my footsteps. "You leaving for a month, kid?"

That catches me off guard. "Uhm, yeah. Is that alright with you?"

"Sure is," he says, his tone soothing. "They're your family, after all. Your dad only wants a chance to know his daughter again. I can't blame him."

The knot in my stomach tightens again.

"Thank you," I say, instead of voicing the apologies that flood my mind.

Don nods and goes back to his newspaper, so Mom takes over. "Who were you on the phone with? We heard you talking."

My. Gosh. I hate these walls. If the walls at Nina's house aren't *slightly* more soundproof, this is going to be impossible.

"Marcus," I blurt out. It's the first thing that pops into my head, but it's valid—I wouldn't be calling anyone else, and she knows that.

The lie works until it doesn't.

As if I've summoned him by saying his name, Marcus walks into the kitchen from the laundry room. He's nonchalantly sipping a juice box, no phone in sight.

"What about me?" He asks.

My jaw threatens to drop clean off my face, but I try to keep my expression cool.

"Marcus has been here the entire time." Mom's tone becomes more inquisitive. "We didn't want him to walk home in the rain. He hasn't been on the phone at all."

I refrain from stuttering. My parents would never suspect me of hiding someone in my room—that just isn't something I'd do, nor have I ever done. Until today.

I'm caught, and I know it.

But I don't have a save for this one.

"She was answering a voicemail I sent this morning," Marcus starts, eyeing me as he shakes his juice box. "I just felt my cell buzz in my pocket. I asked her a few questions earlier today, but they aren't important anymore."

"Yes," I say instantly. "That's what I meant."

"Oh," Mom says, her brow furrowed. She doesn't believe it, and it's obvious. I catch her glance at Don, like she's waiting for him to object, but I stare directly at Marcus.

The look he's giving me clearly says: *'You liar. You were not talking to yourself earlier. You'll explain this to me in an instant or suffer.'*

"Come help me pack," I say suddenly, grabbing Marcus by the wrist and dragging him upstairs before anyone else can speak.

It's a miracle that he doesn't protest.

As soon as we're out of earshot—even though that isn't a *thing* in this house—he rips his arm away. "I don't know what's going on, but I'll figure it out. Or you could just tell me and save me the energy."

We're right outside my bedroom door. The only thing between us and Ben is a scraped-up piece of plywood. He's probably on the other side, waiting for me to do my special knock.

"Okay, listen." I take a breath. "You cannot scream. Promise me you won't scream."

"Be serious, C. It's not like there's a zombie or something in your ro—" Marcus gasps and wiggles his eyebrows. "Wait. You're hiding a boy in here, aren't you? Oh, I cannot *believe* you—"

I cut him off by knocking on the door. Three times, a pause, then a final time.

"You sly fox. Who's in there?" Marcus asks, his voice lowered.

The door unlocks, and I exhale. "You aren't allowed to scream," I tell him again.

"Stop being stupid, C. I won't snitch." He doesn't wait for me to open the door. No, he turns the handle and walks inside, right before freezing in the doorway.

Ben is sitting at my desk now, flipping through a book. "Oh. Hey, Marcus."

"Celia take me to a hospital," Marcus whispers.

"Marcus—"

"Celia. Louise. Greene. Call 9-1-1."

"That answers our question." Ben snaps the book shut and kicks his sock-clad feet up on my bed. "How've you been, Marcus? Did you miss me?"

I think Marcus might start crying.

"You see him?" He asks me weakly.

"Yeah," I say. "I do."

He stumbles toward my bed and sits on the end, making sure to avoid Ben's legs in the process.

"This isn't real," Marcus says, pointing toward Ben. "We watched him be buried. In the *ground*."

"I know that. Which is why we need to figure out how he's standing in my room right now."

"Sitting," Ben corrects.

If Marcus weren't hyperventilating, I'd laugh. "Not now."

"So you can see me?" Ben asks, deciding to ignore Marcus's lack of air. "Like, the second you walked in, you saw me?"

"I wouldn't be on the verge of hysterics if I couldn't," Marcus snaps, covering his face with his hands. "You were just lounging over there, and I felt like I was going to pass out. *Feel,* actually. Present tense. Please call an ambulance, C. I wasn't kidding."

"You're fine," I say, though he's being very rational about this. How would most people react to a dead person sitting at a desk? The whole *'I'm going to pass out'* thing is much more logical than my initial response.

Marcus looks up at me through his fingers. "So, uhm, anyways. You're leaving for a month?"

I nod. "And Ben is coming with me, somehow."

Marcus exhales. His breathing has slowed, thank goodness. I thought he was a goner, and his inhaler refills expired last month.

"Well," he says, turning to Ben. "Can you like, walk through walls?"

*Appalled* isn't even the right word for Ben's expression.

"You people are all the same," he mumbles, crossing his arms. "No, I cannot. The first attempt resulted in the loud noise you heard earlier."

"That sucks." Marcus frowns. "You'd think it's part of the deal."

Ben shrugs. "I didn't get a rule book. We're going to have to write our own."

At his words, Marcus clasps my shoulder, startling me. His eyes are wide and his face is overly expressive.

"Ow! What is your deal?" I ask.

"Uh? Besides the obvious?" He frantically gestures at Ben. "This is *it*, C!"

"This is *what?*"

"Your inspiration." He does jazz hands around my face. "Surely this'll fix your writer's block, right? Think of it as a story."

"You still write?" Ben asks.

I shake my head, hoping this topic can be shut down quickly. "No. Don't let Marcus fool you."

"She does still write," Marcus says, giving my arm a squeeze. "We're working through this rebellious streak."

I pluck his bony fingers off me. "Whatever. Can you come back tomorrow, please? We need to hatch some sort of plan on how to get Ben out of here."

He nods. "Yeah. I mean, we have a shift from eleven to five tomorrow, but if we get some time off, I'll help."

"I have a feeling Don will end up closing the store since it's my last day home. One more day isn't going to hurt."

"Probably not." He sighs. "That's fine. I'll meet you up here. If I can't get past your parents inconspicuously, then there's always the fire escape."

"I'll leave the window unlocked," I say, aware that it's technically a lie. The thing usually locks back on its own, but he'll pound on it loudly enough that it won't matter. "We should go back downstairs."

"Do I get a guest-of-honor's invite?" Ben asks, grinning.

"On all logical accounts, no."

He nods. "Then I'll be right here."

# OCTOBER 10, 2008

The slow drizzle of rain turns into a full thunderstorm within the hour. Ben forces me to wear his jacket, even though I'd much rather it stay on him. I'm not cold.

"We're going to have to get out of here," he says, his face to the sky. The rain has already drenched his hair. Our clothes are still mostly dry, save for the now-communal jacket.

I wring my hair out onto the ground and twist it into a ratty braid. The ponytail around my wrist does little to keep it intact, but it's better than wet hair sticking to my face.

Before I get the chance to wipe the rest of the water from my cheeks, Ben grabs my hand and spins me around. I squeal as I almost slip on the concrete, the rain making it slick as ice.

"What are you *doing?*" I ask. "It's pouring!"

Ben shrugs, pulling me closer to him. "You said you wanted to dance in the rain."

His left hand takes my right, and the other goes to the small of my back, warming my skin through my clothes. I laugh as he spins me around again.

"When did I ever say that?"

"A few times," he says shyly. "Once, you were talking to Marren in class about it. You said it was romantic."

I stop swaying with him and stand straight. His hands move to my waist as I process the words, and he seems almost embarrassed to have remembered. "I haven't been friends with Marren in…years, actually. I didn't even know you back then."

"Yeah," he says. "But I knew you."

Well. I'm grinning like an idiot.

Ben laughs. "I liked you back then. If you talked, I listened. I had forgotten about it until the other day."

I can feel the heat on my cheeks, probably caused by his stare. "You sap."

"Don't mention it," he says, smiling as I go up on my toes to kiss him. "But you know that we're going to get sick, right?"

I nod, still fully supported by his arms. Still trusting him to hold me up. "Yeah. We are."

Neither of us make any move to leave.

# CHAPTER SIX

Marcus and I stay with my parents for the rest of the evening. His apartment is directly across the street, so he stays until it's almost dark. When he's gone, I give my family the 'I'm really tired' speech so I can go back upstairs. They don't question it.

I open the bedroom door, and my eyes immediately scan the room for Ben. But he isn't here.

"Ben?" I whisper-scream as quietly as I can. He isn't in my chair, or on my bed, or in the closet. "Ben!"

Nothing.

I flop down on my bed, defeated. I shouldn't be shocked. I should actually feel ten times saner than I did an hour ago, but somehow, I feel worse.

"This is better," I say out loud. "This is so much better."

I repeat this to myself over and over for minutes. A grounding exercise, or whatever it is that tricks your brain. Something psychological.

Right when I'm at the peak of fooling myself, I hear a tapping on my window.

The color drains from my face. I *hate* fire escapes. Anybody can just stroll up here and tap on the window, which is what—

"Cici."

Oh. Never mind.

I look out the window. Ben is standing there with his arms crossed tight over his chest. His hair is blowing around his face, looking almost white in the fog.

"I am kindly requesting that you let me inside." He's shivering, I can tell. "It's cold."

"C'mon, Ben." I unlatch the window and step aside so he can walk in. "I've told you a million times. The window locks automatically."

"It wasn't locked earlier today, so I thought maybe you'd changed them." He picks a piece of fuzz off his sleeve and looks at me. "So…how's Marcus? Has he admitted himself yet?"

"No. We made a pact that he can't go without me."

"Ah. Good." He pauses. "What are we going to tell your dad and Nina?"

I was sort of hoping we'd glaze over that detail, since I don't have a plan for that part of the trip. There are multiple excuses we can use, but I think all of them would get back to my mom.

First, logically, we have the *'this is my new boyfriend'* excuse. Mom knows I haven't talked to another boy romantically since Ben died, though, so that one is extremely dangerous. Then, there's the *'this is my old friend from school'*, but that would be problematic as well. I haven't stepped foot in that high school since December, and I kept in contact with no one.

So really, we only have the criminal option.

"I don't know," I finally admit. "I say we just wait and see what the moment presents us with."

"So, along the lines of, '*I picked him up on the road because he was hitchhiking*'."

I forget that he knows my unused book of excuses. "It's better than the alternatives."

He laughs, and it startles me. I'm still not used to hearing the sound.

I redirect my focus back to the situation at hand, then quickly decide it's pointless for now. We have a day to figure it out, which certainly isn't enough time, but my ideas aren't improving.

Instead of thinking more, I walk to my closet, change into some pajamas, and sit on the edge of my bed.

Ben takes a seat beside me. "Can I make one request before we leave?"

I nod.

He wrings his hands together, looking nervous. "I think…I want to see my grave."

*What?*

I blink, completely caught off guard. That was the last thing I expected to come out of his mouth. I was thinking along the lines of shopping or something—not a *cemetery*, where he's supposed to be right now instead of beside me.

"Why?" I ask breathily.

Ben gives a loose shrug. "I don't know."

That's a completely valid answer right now.

"I haven't visited your grave since the funeral," I admit. Saying it out loud makes me feel like a horrible person, but I *couldn't*. It's been six months, and I haven't made it past the sidewalk. I don't know if I can.

It seems harder with him here, somehow.

"I never brought you flowers or anything," I continue. "Your dad did, though. He went multiple times. I saw him. He'd kneel by your tombstone, almost like he was praying, then leave a single flower and walk back home."

Ben's face is pained at the mention of his dad, and I'm instantly filled with regret for bringing it up. I'm fully aware that I should shut my mouth, but I *can't*. I have more to tell him. I don't want to lose that chance so suddenly again.

"He's doing well, by the way." I look at him until he looks back, and when he does, it makes my stomach twist. "He misses you more than you can understand. I haven't seen a day go by where he doesn't visit you."

Ben frowns and looks at the wall, almost like he's trying not to think about it. "I wish I could talk to him," he says, his voice strained.

"I know," I whisper.

There's no possible way he can see his dad without giving the man a heart attack. Ben knows it, I know it. That's why he came here first.

But if that can't happen, his first request must.

"We'll go tomorrow," I say. "To the cemetery. If you want to."

He looks away from the wall he's staring at and meets my eyes. "Really?"

"Yeah. Before my family is awake."

"Thank you," he says.

He isn't looking for a response, so I stay quiet.

We fall into a comfortable silence for the better part of an hour before I decide to get in bed. Very reluctantly, I set an alarm for six. Since it's a Saturday tomorrow, my family should at least sleep until seven. I flip back the sheets and fix the galore of pillows before crawling into bed.

As soon as I get comfy, I look up to find Ben standing over me. His arms are crossed, and he's shaking his head in a teasing manner. "You didn't offer me any pajamas."

I pull the blankets over my head. "They're in the closet. Find something and let me sleep."

He lets out a quiet laugh before disappearing into the closet. I'm still hidden under the covers when I feel the mattress dip. I poke my head out to see Ben lying beside me, facing the wall. He must know that I'm looking at him, because he says, "I'm not sleeping in the beanbag chair."

I grin before turning the lamp off. "Night, Ben."

He sighs contentedly, pulling the throw blanket he's claimed a little tighter around him. "Goodnight."

# CHAPTER SEVEN

"No, no, no, *no*. Shut that off right now."

Ben covers his head with a pillow as my alarm blares. I agree with him; I'd like the alarm to be quiet as well. The only problem is that I can't find my phone.

"I'm trying!" I launch a BB-8 stuffed animal across the room while digging through my blankets, and it spills a cup of water on my rug. I can't even tell which direction the noise is coming from—it's too early, and my brain is foggy. "Why does it do this? Doesn't it know we're awake?"

Ben grumbles and untangles himself from the blankets before standing. The noise increases as he does so.

"Where is it?" I whine. The longer this goes on, the more likely my family is to hear it, and I'll have zero explanation as to why I've woken up so early on a Saturday. I don't even do this on weekdays.

"Oh," I hear from behind me. I turn to see Ben holding my phone. "I rolled over on it. My bad."

"Say you're sorry."

"For *what?*"

"For blaming me."

"That *was* your fault." He rubs his eyes, barely grinning. "Put it on your nightstand next time."

I wave him off and walk to my closet to change. Based on the temperature in my bedroom, it's freezing outside. I pull on a pair of jeans and the thickest sweatshirt I own. My hair looks like someone purposefully tangled it up in my sleep, but I don't care enough to fix it. I tie it back, run a brush through my bangs, and call it good.

Ben changes after I do. While he does, I carefully—and I mean *carefully*—sneak to the bathroom to brush my teeth. One tipped hairspray bottle is enough to blow this, so I make sure not to bump anything.

Ben is dressed when I return. He's wearing nearly the same thing I am: heavy sweater, light jeans, white shoes.

We matched on a normal basis.

"Are you ready?" I ask.

"I think so. Do you think we'll run into anyone?"

"Not this early," I say. "Town itself doesn't wake up until eight."

He nods in response. "Alright. Fire escape?"

"Fire escape," I confirm, undoing the latch. Climbing out of the window isn't the ideal exit strategy, but it's the most discreet.

Once we're both on the ground, Ben pulls his hood over his hair. I know he's trying to hide his face, even though nobody is walking the streets. Paranoia is an extremely valid thing under these circumstances.

The cemetery is only a five-minute walk from my place. I expect Ben to ask a few questions as we walk, but he doesn't say a word. Not until we reach the gates.

"Whoa," is all he says. Silently, he surveys the headstones. Most of them are caked with flowers and dried mud.

Only one is remotely new. Clean. Untouched. And Ben walks right to it.

I force myself to follow, even though my feet feel glued to the sidewalk.

"So. This is it," he says calmly, approaching the slab of stone. The engraving itself makes my stomach churn.

### Bennet Stanley March
### 1991-2008

I bite down on my lip, hard enough to draw blood.

The flowers that have been tossed around it are dead. I'd guess the rain drowned them, just like the rest. Flowers really don't work here, considering it rains almost every day.

Ben's dad must not have come here yet today. There are no fresh flowers.

"You guys got me a boring tombstone," Ben jokes, but his face is entirely blank.

He isn't wrong—the stone is understated. Nothing extra, nothing flashy. Nothing that isn't *Ben*. Mr. March spent an insanely long time choosing one, my mom told me. Days.

"What are you thinking right now?" I ask.

He shrugs. "It's just kind of…surreal, I guess. Not in a good way."

I nod as he crouches down in front of the inscription. It guts me, watching him run his fingers along his name, then the dates.

All I can think is, *His name shouldn't be there.*

Ben's face is mild as he stands straight and shoves his hands into his pockets. A part of me longs to reach out and touch him, still, but I'm hesitant. Now doesn't seem like the time.

"I still can't believe my mom let Dad pick my middle name." Ben's mouth twists into a painful smile. "Who picks 'Stanley'?"

I laugh, just a bit. The fact that he's able to find humor in *something* here makes me feel better, though it certainly holds no weight. "I like it."

"Well, thank you. It gets you laughed at when you go to the DMV, believe it or not."

"Stanley isn't that uncommon of a name. Laughing doesn't seem very professional."

"It isn't at all," he says, his cheek dimpling. He takes another look at the grave, and I wonder how he can keep so neutral. So calm.

It's a complete contrast to me. I'm beginning to feel everything I should have felt in the past year, every emotion that I buried down inside me. My eyes sting with the tears that I've held every time I pass the gates, and nausea hits me, a little worse with every breath.

It's guilt, really. That's all it is.

That stone—that name and date—is a reminder. All one big flashing sign that *he is not here*. I can't let myself forget that.

Ben looks at me, quickly realizing something is wrong. I blink my eyes to stop the forming tears, but it's no use.

"Cici, it wasn't your fault." He shakes his head. Not in a condescending way, but more like a '*Hey. I'm back even if I'm a ghost, so you should totally believe me*' way. But I just can't.

I wipe my eyes with the back of my hand and avoid his gaze like it's my only talent. "We should get going. Before someone else shows up."

Ben doesn't press and ask what's wrong. He already knows, and even if he didn't, he wouldn't push it. I'll talk when I'm ready, and he'll listen all the same.

I stay behind him when he walks out of the cemetery. The few pebbles on the sidewalk get kicked into the grates as I walk. Ben does the same a few steps ahead of me, kicking one behind him every now and then so it hits my shoe.

I'm kind of spiraling out right now. Seeing his tombstone, it put things into perspective. Of how odd and eerie and futile this all is. The fact that we're walking the streets right now doesn't make me feel better. Granted, nobody walks this particular street before seven, but whatever. It's still risky.

I'm still trying to quiet my thoughts when a cool hand grabs mine.

It doesn't even startle me; I know it's Ben. He's hesitant in touching me, just like I was with him. It takes him a second to even lace his fingers with mine, even though that's what he'd always do. I grip his hand as we walk back to the house, my gut twisting at the feel of his skin. So natural, so logically *real*, but impossible on all accounts.

The corner store isn't unlocked yet, so we walk around to the fire escape again. I climb the rusty old steps to my window, hardly breathing the entire time. Ben is a few steps below me when I reach my room.

I push up on the frame. Wait for it to open.

Per usual, it doesn't. Per usual.

"I forgot," I mutter, sitting back on my heels. "I completely forgot."

"How the tables have turned," Ben says, laughing under his breath. Normally, I'd laugh too, but I'm slightly more worried about freezing to death outside my own house.

"Not the time, Ben." I fiddle with the hinge. It doesn't budge. "Where do we go now?"

He shrugs. "I don't know. But there are other windows in your house."

"None that we can get into."

"Hm. And the store?"

"Alarms."

"Well, then. This is really bad for us."

"No kidding." I pull my knees up to my chin and curl up on a step, trying to think of where we could go. Cafes, libraries, stores, any of those would work. But somebody would recognize Ben—I just know it.

And then, a genius thought makes its way into my mind, as they often do. "Marcus's house."

Ben furrows his brow. "Won't that cause suspicion? You know, with his mom?"

"No." I shake my head. "He's living by himself now. He got a cheap apartment on the block."

"He can afford an apartment?"

"*Cheap* apartment," I repeat. "That's probably why he spends lots of time at our house, but he needed an out. He wouldn't stay with us permanently, though. He wanted to be all independent."

"Understandable," Ben says. "He should welcome us with open arms."

I grin, knowing that absolutely will *not* be the case on a Saturday morning. "Absolutely he should. I mean, he won't be awake, but I've got a key."

Ben hums. "You stole it, didn't you?"

I fish my keyring out of my pocket, thankful that I remembered to grab it. "Of course I did."

# CHAPTER EIGHT

I send a text message to my mom and let her know that I'm visiting Marcus. A multitude of details are left out, but that's fine. As long as she forgets that he doesn't wake up until noon.

Ben and I sneak up the stairs in Marcus's apartment complex instead of taking the elevator. He keeps his face as hidden as possible, but it's unnecessary. The halls are empty.

When we reach Marcus's door, we go in and lock it back behind us. I walk to his bedroom to make sure he's still sleeping, because I didn't close the door *all* that quietly. He's out, though—snoring in the twin-sized bed, blankets thrown on the floor.

His AC is making the room feel like an ice box. It makes perfect sense as to why he's sleeping in sweatpants, a sweatshirt, *and* socks.

"Do we wake him?" I ask, looking back at Ben. He's staring at Marcus from the doorframe, his brows drawn together.

"No." Ben crosses his arms. "We can just stay here until your parents open the store. Talk and try to figure things out."

So that's what we do.

The apartment isn't very big, but it has separate kitchen and living areas. We sit at the small table, moving the stacks of paper plates and cups to the side. Marcus desperately needs to clean this place.

I take a deep breath, wondering how long I can prolong the silence. The answer is *not very long*, because I'm too curious for my own good. "Are you remembering…anything? At all?"

Ben tips his head to the side, focusing on the wall. "Slowly. Everything before yesterday feels like a really vivid dream."

I squeeze my eyes shut.

*How has it only been one day?*

"Okay," I say. "Do you remember where you were when you, like…realized you still…I don't know, existed?"

Even the wording of that question confuses me. What am I really asking? *Where do you remember re-appearing*? He isn't a bunny in a magic routine.

Ben nods, surprising me. "Actually, yes. That's the only thing I can remember."

I rest my head on my hands. "Okay. That's great. Well, better, at least. Where were you?"

He swallows and looks away from me.

It only takes me a second to guess what he means. Where he was.

"Oh," I say.

Ben frowns, and my lungs feels heavy. I get it now—he isn't just remembering where he was yesterday. He's remembering *everything*. How he died, exactly what happened.

I wish I hadn't said a word.

"I'm sorry." My words barely come out. "I'll stop talking. I shouldn't have asked that."

"It's okay," he says, trading the frown for a soft smile. "Really. I'd be asking too."

Despite that, I don't say another word.

We sit quietly for a while, just thinking and sneaking glances at the other. It's a comfortable silence at first, but it turns into something more rigid with time. I still want to talk and ask questions, but I hold myself back. The saddened look on Ben's face is burned into my mind; I don't want to see it again.

It isn't until I'm fidgeting from the tension that Ben kicks my foot under the table, forcing my eyes to his. He smiles, and suddenly, the pain melts away from my chest.

"What?" He asks. "You look distressed."

I chuckle. "I'm not. What is it?"

"Well, it's almost eight," he says, standing from his chair. "Your parents should have the store unlocked by now."

I stand as well, careful not to let the chair scrape up the floor. The tile is already scratched and grimy, but still. I have morals.

Marcus's front door is right beside me, but I don't turn that way. Neither does Ben. Instead, he gets this mischievous smile on his face, and I know exactly why we haven't moved an inch.

A grin spreads across my face. "Say it."

"Shall we wake Marcus?" Ben raises a brow. "In a kind, *loving* way, of course."

"We shall indeed."

He steps around me and walks to Marcus's room. I tiptoe behind him, though I know there's no chance of waking Marcus by accident. He's still fast asleep in the same spot as earlier.

Ben gives me a look out of the corner of his eye. I take it as, *'You do the honors.'*

I do. Obviously.

Carefully, I lean over Marcus, holding my breath to steady myself. I'm on the verge of laughing, but I bite the inside of my cheek to keep it contained.

*3…2…*

"MARCUS!" I yell as loud as possible *without* waking the whole building.

A blood-curdling scream leaves his mouth, and he jumps off the mattress wielding a purple flip-flop. "WHAT IN THE NAME OF—" He opens his eyes. "Oh. You. I hate both of you."

Marcus discards the flip-flop before pinching his nose bridge. "Leave me, Celia. Just—leave. Leave your key, too."

"I'm keeping the key."

He rolls his eyes but makes zero effort to take it from me.

"See you later, Marcus." Ben flashes a bright smile, then turns toward the living room. I give my cousin a pat on the back before leaving.

When we make it back to my block, Ben goes straight up the fire escape. I casually walk into the store, thankful that they opened today. The floor is still dirty from the rain, and the rugs need to be shaken out, but no one is here.

I sneak behind the counter and go up to the apartment. There's a singular pancake on the kitchen table but nothing else. No sign of Mom or Don or the twins.

Very quietly, I go upstairs. Ben practically falls into my room when I unlock the window. He catches his balance and stands straight, surveying the room with tired eyes.

"This was a fun morning," he says flatly, crouching down to untie his shoes. He slips both off and sets them neatly inside my closet, then closes the door. A few seconds later, he returns, wearing sweatpants and a new t-shirt.

"It was interesting, to say the least." I take my shoes off and set them next to his. No reason to track mud back through the house, though I definitely did that when I came up here. "I should go back downstairs. If not to work, then to find my family. You—"

"Can hide in the closet if I hear footsteps," he says, nodding. "I've got it down."

I tilt my head. "What if you're asleep and don't hear anything?"

"Well, it would be rude of them to wake me."

"Mm," I hum. "Lock the door."

"Do you agree to the special knock?" He lifts his hand, holds a pinky out.

I grin and lock mine around his. "I do."

"Good." He nods, satisfied. "See you later, then."

# CHAPTER NINE

Saturday passes at light speed. Before I know it, it's Sunday morning and I'm running around the house, trying to pack my bags before the train leaves.

My family always makes a big deal of trips, even when they're only for a day. Since this is a *month*, it's worse. I've been asked seventy times if I'm finished packing. The answer is always, '*No, because you won't give me a chance*'.

I only need more socks. But still.

"Do you have toothpaste?" Mom asks, reading the receipt of the store we just left.

"Yes. I had it the first twenty-three times, too."

She swats my hand away from the bag with cookies in it. "I'm just checking, honey. You don't know if Nina will have a stocked guest bathroom."

"I don't understand why we're making such a big deal out of this. Nina lives half an hour away with traffic. I could walk home—or, to a *store*—if I need something that badly."

Mom stops in the middle of the sidewalk and turns to me, staring as if I've spoken in a foreign language. "Cici.

Nina doesn't live half an hour away. The trip is four hours by train."

My mouth drops open. "What? Did it walk away or something? You guys went to see her just the other day!"

"No, honey. We visited her weekend home a few towns over. *That's* half an hour."

I forgot that Nina has a weekend home. I also forgot Nina can afford multiple houses. What even is a weekend home?

"You're staying at her *all-week* home," Mom emphasizes, and I revel in the sarcasm covering her words. "That's why we're making a big deal out of it."

I start to make fun of her clarification, but then I realize this is a thousand times better. Nobody will know Ben in a town four hours away. I mean, assuming he's never *been* there. But the chances are much better.

"That makes sense," I say, not sure what else to respond with.

Mom just hands me the bag of cookies I keep pawing at.

When we get home, I attempt to open the door quietly. It's mainly to keep the children away from the groceries, but it doesn't work. They find me almost immediately.

"We're going to miss you, Cici!" Maisie squeals, wrapping her arms around my hips. Jace joins her, squeezing me so hard I let out a dramatic yelp.

"I'll miss you guys too. I'll be back before you know it, okay?"

They both nod and release me from their grip, already distracted with something else.

Instinctively, I look around for Don. He hasn't really said much to me today, and he isn't waiting in the entryway, so I'm starting to wonder if he regrets letting me go. I pray that isn't the case, because his opinion matters *much* more to me than my real dad's.

Don was the one there for me when my cat ran away. When I broke my ankle at the park.

When my boyfriend died.

"Help unload the groceries," Mom says, handing me a single bag. I wordlessly put the chips in the cabinet, the bread on the counter. The stuff that I'm taking with me is in a different bag, so I don't have to bother separating it.

Just as a box of Cocoa Puffs falls on my foot, Don walks into the kitchen.

"Hey, guys," he says, looking over the mess of groceries on the table. "You packed, Cici?"

"Yeah," I tell him. "Almost done."

Don gives me a smile—a genuine one—and I decide he isn't mad about my going. It's likely that he would have voiced any negative feelings, but he also knows I like to make my own decisions. He wouldn't have tried to sway mine.

It doesn't matter now, though. He's fine. I'm going. It's settled.

"I've got some forms to fill out at the store," he says, pressing a kiss to my mom's head. "I'll see you before you leave, Cici."

I give him a wave in response. He walks out.

Mom hands me the bag that I stuck my things in and tells me to finish packing before Don gets back.

✳✳✳

"You know the plan, right?"

Ben laughs as he shoves a pair of his socks into my bag. "Yes, it's a simple one."

"Repeat it to me."

He stands straight up. Clears his throat like he's about to give the speech of the year. "You leave from downstairs, then I catapult out of the window—"

"Not what I said."

"—and make it to the station before the train leaves. All while avoiding your family."

"Sure. And then?"

"*Then* we find some genius way to sneak me on the train."

"Right. We'll just do what we did yesterday." I zip my backpack. "I think I've got enough money for an extra fare."

"So that should work."

"It *should*," I repeat. "But what do we do if it doesn't?"

He shrugs, like the idea never crossed his mind. "We'll figure it out. We always do."

Somehow, that's enough to calm me down.

I take my luggage downstairs, knowing I'll be bombarded with hugs again before I leave. I'm alright with it, of course. I'm leaving for a month, and it's not like I hate the rugrats. Being tackled simply isn't at the top of my list.

The twins get me first, squeezing me and mumbling their goodbyes into my shirt. Then it's Mom's turn. She turns on the tears, which I never know how to handle. I awkwardly (yet sincerely) pat her back and hope it does something.

Don gives me a tight hug. "I'll take care of your mom," he whispers, and I laugh. Nobody can actually make her stop crying, but he's the best at trying.

When he releases me, I pick up my bags and walk toward the door.

A proud smile spreads across my face.

I've done it. I've pulled it off. I'm getting out of here with no questions, no chance of being—

"Cici, what are you doing?" Mom asks, having already stopped crying. This is record time. "We'll drive you to the station."

I bite back the urge to roll my eyes, then instantly feel bad. She just wants to see me off before I leave. It isn't her fault I have a literal hidden agenda.

I smile, hoping it's convincing. "It's okay. I'll walk. The station isn't far, and you guys have to open the store."

"We were actually going to close for the day," Don tells me.

My smile tightens uncomfortably. I want them to see me off, but they *can't*. They'll see Ben too. "It's okay! Really. I'd prefer to walk, especially since I'll be on a train for hours."

Mom and Don swap a knowing glance, though they don't *truly* know. They just think I'm hiding something. The subject is unknown. "Okay," Mom says. "I guess that's fine."

I let out a sigh of relief before I can catch myself. "Good. The store doesn't need to be closed for another day, anyways."

Don shrugs in agreement. Mom elbows him.

We say another round of goodbyes, omitting the tears this time. I promise to call as soon as I arrive, and they promise to keep Marcus fed and out of trouble.

It takes a bit for me to get out of the apartment. When I do, I turn the street corner and find Ben sitting on the bottom step of the fire escape. He stands and joins right at my side.

"You got away, huh?" He says, starting toward the station. It's only a couple minutes by foot—everything here is a couple minutes by foot.

"I did, somehow."

The station isn't as busy as I'd expected for a Sunday morning. I see it as a good omen. There's an older couple, a younger mom and her child, and a large group of men and women traveling together. Besides the kid, I'd guess we're the only ones under the age of thirty.

I pay for my ticket with the money my parents gave me, then hand the conductor cash for another. He gives me a quizzical look and hands it right back.

"Just one?"

"Hm?" I ask.

"Just one," he repeats. "You've already paid."

"Oh. Uhm." I look at Ben, expecting him to have disappeared, but he's still right beside me. Maybe the conductor thinks he's paying separately?

Assuming that's the case, I slip the money to Ben before stepping aside. He holds it out to the conductor and says, "Same train," but the man doesn't respond.

Doesn't even look up.

"Have a good day, miss," the conductor says, sounding confused as to why I'm still standing there.

I stammer. "Uhm, yeah, you too."

He nods to me before I walk away.

Ben steps right past the toll booth. The conductor never glances his way.

"Well," Ben hums. "That was…"

"Odd," I supply.

"Maybe he just hates his job and wants to feel a sense of rebellion."

I practically snort. "Yeah. Alright."

We board the train, still trying to stay out of sight. I sit down and tuck my bags under the seat. Ben sits to the right of me, pressing his leg against mine. "I'm just saying. He acted like he didn't even see me."

Before I can respond, one of the older ladies I saw in the station walks up to me. "Excuse me," she says, pointing to Ben. "May I sit here?"

I blink and look at Ben, then back at the woman. I do that a few times to make sure we're seeing the same thing. The longer I take to answer, the more confused she seems.

Ben eventually gives me a frantic look and mouths, '*NO SHE CAN'T SIT ON ME*'.

"I'm sorry, but I'm saving it," I say, ignoring how thin my voice sounds. "A friend of mine is supposed to show up. He's late…"

Ben glares at me for my pun. I have to fight to keep a straight face.

"If you can't find another seat, you can sit here." I make a show of looking around the train. "He might be catching the next one."

Again, Ben looks at me like I'm ridiculous for saying so, but I can't flat out refuse. To this woman, the seat is empty, and it will be empty for the rest of the ride. I've got no good reason to turn her away.

"That's okay!" She says, smiling sweetly. "It's an empty train, hon. I'll get another seat. I just prefer an east facing one, you know…"

"Oh, yes, I know." I have no idea what that means.

The woman walks away, dragging her pink suitcase behind her. I watch to make sure she finds another seat before slumping back in mine. "That was weird."

Ben drags a hand through his hair. "You can like, still see me, right?"

"I can."

"Can you still touch me?"

I poke his face, and his cheek dimples at the contact. "Yes."

"Okay. Good." He crosses his arms. "So why couldn't she?"

"Maybe she's just got super bad eyesight. Your shirt is the same color as the seats."

"I am a *person*."

"You're a ghost," I correct. "And anyways, it's fine. We don't have to deal with it right now."

"Yeah, I know. But don't you think it's strange?"

I exhale. "This is all strange, but we can worry about it at Nina's. Besides, if people really *can't* see you, they're going to think I'm talking to myself. Don't be worried about the old lady, be worried that they'll send me to a psychiatrist."

Ben chuckles, slouching back in his seat. "And if Nina is one of the lucky few that *can* see me?"

"We've got our cheap excuses, remember?" I nudge him with my elbow. "That's all we've ever had."

"Cheap excuses and too much determination."

"Livin' on a prayer, baby."

# CHAPTER TEN

During the train ride, Nina calls to say that she'll pick me up from the station. I told her I'd walk, but I don't know where her house is and she didn't give me the address, so that plan went to ruins pretty quickly.

I am not excited for this in the slightest.

The last time I saw Nina, we had it out. She spoke her mind. Told me I was the problem in my parents' marriage, that I drove my dad to do what he did. So I spoke mine, because if there's one thing I do well, it's run my mouth.

I told her that she only 'loved' us because my dad told her to. That it was clear the second her gifts and visits ended. Her actions were solely based on what information he relayed to her. If he liked us that day, so did she. Nina is a *very* independent woman, and saying that her opinions were threaded through someone else's perspective set her off.

Yes, we had a screaming match. No, it didn't need to happen outside the courthouse after my mom and dad's custody hearing. But it did.

I was slightly less reserved at twelve years old.

"Train stopped," Ben says, pulling me out of my thoughts. My head snaps up and I peek out the window. This station is more packed than the first, but still empty enough that I'm not worried. Ben seems to be going unnoticed anyways.

We hop off the train and speed right through the platform. Silence blankets us while we keep an eye out for Nina, and I appreciate it. It gives me a second to clear my mind, to focus solely on finding them.

I'm zoned in on that task until someone walks into Ben.
*No.*

No, they don't walk into Ben. They walk *through* Ben.
"Uhm," I say.

He stares at his feet for a few seconds, frozen as I am.
"Do you think something is up *now?*" He asks.

"Yes." I nod. "Something is up."

He looks up at me, brow furrowed. "Can you walk through me? Is that something we should have tested?"

"Well, I'm certainly not going to try." I look around to see if anyone noticed, but no heads are turned our way. If someone saw, they gave it no weight.

This wasn't supposed to happen so early on. We expected curveballs, yes, but not *that.* I didn't even know that could happen.

I add that to the mental list of things to figure out.

*Can't be seen by an old lady. Can be walked through by a frat boy.*

"Okay. Well." I look over my shoulder, still finding no sign of Nina. "Maybe you were right, and we should've figured this out before Nina's."

"That gives us no time," Ben murmurs.

I frown. "Hm?"

"CELIA!" A shrill voice materializes behind me.
*Ah.*

I force myself to smile before turning around. Nina is standing there, arms wide, a similar look to mine on her features—a false smile and dull eyes.

"Hi Nina," I say, returning the hug she wraps me in. It's awkward and forced on both accounts, and when she releases me, I take a generous step away. She looks me over, no doubt evaluating me. Her expression is disapproving and she doesn't try to hide it.

Nina looks the exact same as she did when I last saw her. She's got the same face, only more *glitzy Hollywood starlet* now. Her dark hair still isn't streaked with gray, and it's pulled into a tight ponytail at the base of her neck.

Meanwhile, I'm wearing my stepdad's college crewneck and jeans that I had to unbutton when I sat down. With zero shame, might I add.

"Are you ready to go?" Nina asks, flipping her sunglasses up on top of her head. They must be for decoration because it's cloudy out here.

"Yes." I glance over at Ben. He's just standing, observing.

She still hasn't noticed him. Good.

"Great! My car is this way," Nina says, turning to her left.

We walk off the platform in a sticky sort of quiet, one that I'd rather be filled with noise. I'm tempted to ask where my dad is, why he didn't come, but I don't bother. He's probably just at the house.

"I'm so glad you agreed to stay, Celia," Nina says, throwing a smile over her shoulder. "We've got so many things planned for your visit—oh! I'm so excited. We have a formal gathering in a couple of weeks that I hope you'll attend, and—"

"Formal?" I ask, because *what?* Nobody told me about this. The most formal thing I have is my good pair of jeans—as in, the ones I *don't* have to unbutton when I sit down. "Like…a gala or something?"

She laughs. "No no, not *that* formal. It's a work thing."

"Oh," I say. Work. Of course.

Sometimes I forget that Nina is a decently well-known person, especially around here. She's a small fashion designer, big enough to have more than a few shops and *way* more than enough money. That might explain why she's wearing a fancy suit to pick me up. Probably something from a new line.

"Your dad is excited to see you," she says, slipping into the driver's seat of the car.

I open the back door and shove my suitcase in the far seat, then wait for Ben to get in before I close the door. If Nina notices a boy sitting in her car, she doesn't mention it.

She really can't see him.

"I'm excited to see Dad, too," I lie, climbing into the passenger seat.

Nina gives a stiff little '*hm!*' before starting the engine.

I stare out the window for most of the ride. The trees are dead, but some are beginning to bloom already. My fingers itch to turn on the radio, to calm the nerves buzzing inside of me at the environment, but I don't.

Nina goes on and on about work and how she's been doing for the past years. I've heard lots of the stories before—they're all variants of each other. I stay focused on the view outside and keep quiet.

Ben receives a few exhausted glances in the rearview mirror. He just laughs to himself.

Anxiety washes over me the second I see Nina's house. It's huge—basically a mansion, at least in these parts. It's also extensive, considering only her and Dad live here. It works in my favor, though. I can hide somewhere when I want to. Maybe she has one of those home theaters or something.

Right before we pull into the drive, Nina asks me how I've been, shifting the focus from her life to mine. I'm not shocked that it took her this long to ask. Honestly, I was hoping we wouldn't have time to discuss me.

"I've been okay," I say. "Not much has happened lately."

A lie. I've got lots of those today.

"How are the twins?" She asks.

"They're good. You saw them a few days ago, didn't you?"

"Oh, yes." Nina smiles. "They're just adorable. How's Don?"

She saw him a few days ago too. "He's fine."

A content nod tops off the conversation. She won't ask about my mom, and I know that for a fact. Mom is the last person Nina cares about—another thing that came to light after the divorce.

I shake my head at the reminder as Nina pulls into the garage. It's way too fancy for a garage, in my opinion. It's larger than my bedroom, and the car is the only thing in here, save for a few storage bins.

Carefully, I exit the car and tug my suitcase out of the backseat. Ben cautiously steps out and glances over his shoulder a few times. The look on his face implies that he thinks Mom or Don followed us here.

Nina gets out of the car last and closes the garage. "You've *got* to remember to close it," she says pointedly. "Anyone could just come in here otherwise. The other night, we had someone wandering around the house."

"Did you call the police?" I ask as she unlocks the door. We step inside the house, right into a dining room. At least, I *think* it's a dining room. No need for a chandelier and mahogany table elsewhere.

"Yes, we did," Nina says. "They claimed it was nothing, but I made your dad install cameras the next day. You can't be too careful."

"True," I say blankly. "Can you show me to my room?"

Her eyes flash with offense, just for a second. I tell myself I imagined it—she's got no reason to be offended. I'm *tired.* I want to change out of my train clothes and nap.

Still, though, I try to backtrack for the sake of peace. "I only meant—"

"Sure can," Nina answers, walking right past me. "Just follow."

I nod as I drag my clunky suitcase behind me. She takes me through the dining room, then a room with a sofa and coffee table, *then* down a flight of stairs. At first, I think she's sticking me in a dusty concrete cube, but it turns out to be a half-underground basement with windows and a glass door.

"The whole floor is mostly yours," she says, opening a door to the right. I peek inside to find a small bed and dresser, along with a bathroom to the left of my closet. "All I've got down here is a storage room for some fabric and sewing machines. You can stay down here if you'd like, but your dad should be back soon."

"Where'd he go?" I assumed he was here already.

"Just to the grocery. We needed a few more things for dinner."

I give a final nod. "Okay. I'm probably just going to nap, if that's alright."

She smiles. "That's fine. Just be up for dinner, please."

"I will."

Nina sticks around my room for a few seconds before leaving, then stalls even longer by wandering around the basement. When she finally goes upstairs, I throw myself down onto the bed. The spring makes an awful creaking noise.

"That was awkward, annoying, and unnecessarily tense," Ben says, sitting on the rug instead of the bed.

I roll over and look at him without a response.

"She really expects you to be fine, doesn't she?" The amusement is drained from his voice.

"She wants people to cater to her life and needs, despite themselves," I respond. "So yes."

"Well, that's ridiculous."

I begin to respond, but my phone rings in my pocket. I grab it and answer without checking who it is.

"Hel—"

"Celia." Marcus's voice is loud and clear on the other end of the phone. "You left."

"I did. And guess what?"

"No."

"We've run into a problem."

"Oh, goody." He sighs. "I definitely called to hear about your problems."

"Marcus. People can't see Ben."

Silence. I'm assuming he takes a moment to process, because he just says, "Oh."

"Yeah."

"I have an idea of why that may be," Ben cuts in. He taps his chin in thought, and I can't even tell if he's doing it ironically. "What if it's because you guys know me? I mean, think about it. People don't get haunted by people they *don't* know."

I blink. "You're haunting us?"

"No. But I'm the ghost. I know these things."

I wave him off with a grin, turning my attention back to the phone. "Any other suggestions, Marcus?"

"Nah. Ben's probably right," he says. "That would make most sense. Why would people see a ghost of someone they've never met? It would just be another person to them. Kinda takes away the magic. The pizzazz. The pixie dust, if you will."

"I won't. But I guess that does make sense."

Ben sighs and rests his chin on his fist. "So, basically, we're going to be just fine here for the next month. No one will even see me."

"Maybe we *are* geniuses," I muse.

Marcus says something or other, probably to the contrary, but I don't catch it. A voice outside my room gets my attention first.

"Celia?"

I freeze. My dad's voice carries through the basement, and I hesitate to even acknowledge it.

"Dad's here," I say to Marcus, halfway through a mumble.

"Yoinks," he says. "Good luck. You'll do great. Say nice things and nice words."

"I'll try."

He cackles at nothing and hangs up.

I toss my phone onto the armchair before poking my head outside the door. Dad isn't in the basement, which means he's upstairs with Nina, which means I'm not going up there.

"Hello?" I call.

Nobody answers, but a few seconds later, he comes barreling down the stairs. He's wearing jeans and a pullover, and he looks ten times more put together than the last time I saw him. Happier, even.

A smile completely takes over his face when he sees me. My gut twists—it's an expression I've so rarely seen him wear before.

"Celia," he says, grinning even wider. "How have you been, kid?"

"Hi," I say. "I've been alright. You?"

"I've been great." His voice is uncharacteristically soft. "How's the family?"

"They're good."

"That's great," he says. For a second, I think he's about to hug me, and I take an involuntary step back. His face drops and regret sinks deep into my stomach.

*I'm sorry*, I think, but I don't say anything out loud.

Dad recovers quickly, scratching behind his ear before speaking. "Well, uh, Nina said you were going to nap before dinner, so I won't bother you anymore. I'm just glad to see you."

I smile, hoping it looks genuine. "I'll be up in an hour or so."

"Okay. See you then."

The second he's gone, I let go of the breath I was holding in my chest.

"Hey," Ben says quietly, walking up behind me. "That was…okay, right?"

"It wasn't what I expected," I admit. I press the heels of my hands to my face and lean against the wall. "Everybody here thinks I'm just…normal again, right? They think I'm fine."

Ben shakes his head. "They aren't expecting you to be *normal*. They're just expecting the girl they knew five years ago. It isn't any better, but that's who they're waiting for."

I slide fully down the wall and sit on the floor.

"They don't know you've changed," he continues. "That you *had* to change. But you have to show them."

I tuck my knees under my chin. "It's their fault, too."

"Halfway."

"It's just annoying, you know?" I hate how whiney my voice sounds. "Because it's not that I don't *want* a relationship with my dad. I'm willing to work through things—slowly—if he is. But I just…" I swallow hard. "I think that I have limits, and I'm not ready to break them yet. That's okay, isn't it?"

"It is," he says. "I promise you. It's completely okay."

I exhale and curl myself into a tighter ball. Ben joins me on the floor, puts a hand on my shoulder. A silent show of comfort. Something I desperately need.

Despite my kneecaps digging into my cheek, I doze off a few times. Ben never moves away from me, and neither of us say a word.

We stay that way until dinner.

# OCTOBER 10, 2008

Our pent-up laughter erupts the second we walk through Ben's front door.

Mr. March walks out of the kitchen, shaking his head at the sight of us dripping wet. "You kids, I swear. Go change before you catch a cold. Toss the clothes in the washing machine, and don't worry about getting the floors wet. I've got to clean anyways."

We do as we're told. Ben leads me up to his room and throws a shirt and basketball shorts at me, then grabs some clothes for himself. "Wear that until your clothes are out of the wash."

I run to the bathroom and change, then put my laundry in the washing machine. Ben has already changed by the time I'm back in his room. He's practically wearing the same thing I am.

"So. What now?" I ask, taking a seat on the end of his bed.

Ben considers this for a few seconds, studying me with a mischievous glint in his eye. I raise an eyebrow, and that seems to be his cue. He tackles me back onto the bed and plants kisses all over my face, making me giggle obnoxiously loud.

"I asked a question," I say through laughter.

He still doesn't answer. Instead, he jabs his fingers against my ribs to tickle me. I make a horrible screeching noise and try to get away, but it's no use. We're both laughing anyways. If I run out of oxygen from being tickled, I'll pin it on him as murder.

Ben suddenly stops and pushes himself up on his arms, which have somehow ended up on either side of my head. He smiles down at me, and I want to reach up and poke the divot in his cheek, but I keep my hands at my sides.

"So," he starts. "You know the band 'The Adolescent'?"

"No."

"Me neither. Anyways, they're playing downtown at a bar. And before you ask, *no,* it is not a normal bar. I mean, it is, but it's like, a teen thing. One night a month or something. I don't know, but I got tickets. You want to go?"

I perk up, because that sounds a lot more fun than being home and doing the dishes. "Yes. Absolutely. I'll call my parents."

He rolls over to lay beside me, hands crossed over his stomach. "Good. Otherwise, I would've had to go with my dad."

"Excuse you, Ben. I have marvelous music taste," his dad calls from downstairs.

I grin. "So this evening?"

"Yep. Starts at eight."

I whip out my phone and call my mom. She agrees before I even give the details, saying I need to get out more. I disagree, but whatever. As long as I've got permission, the *why* is unimportant.

"She says yes," I tell Ben, then laugh when I see him. He's already curled up in his bed, the stuffed frog he stole from my room tucked under his arm.

"Wonderful," he says, closing his eyes. I wait for further explanation, but a few moments of silence pass. Then I hear soft breathing, which eventually turns into ear-splitting snoring.

I smile and crawl up beside him, staying on top of the blankets. It's no time before I fall asleep, noting that his breathing is perfectly in sync with mine.

# CHAPTER ELEVEN

I don't know what I expected to stumble upon when I walked upstairs. Maybe some form of circus, or crime scene, or wedding shower for Nina and her fourth husband.

But that's not what I find. I haven't found *anything* yet, technically, besides the sound of faint voices. Nina carries the conversation, and Dad cuts in, and then…there's a third voice, one I don't recognize it.

"And he died only a few months ago?" Unknown says, making me raise an eyebrow. "That poor, sweet girl. She probably hasn't had time to process it all. Has she been in therapy?"

Well. That's gonna be fun to deal with.

Nina has no doubt shared the story about Ben. I'm sure my mom told her a few days ago. Probably told her *not* to mention it, but what can you do?

Hands shaking, I walk in the room. Dad is seated at the gigantic table, opposite end of Nina. The third voice belongs to a blonde woman, maybe a few years younger than my dad. She gives me a warm, kind smile, but I can't get past the fact that I don't know her.

"Hello," I say, slowly making my way across the room. "Who are you?"

The woman looks at my dad, as if she's asking for approval to answer me. He nods, and she smiles. "Hi, I'm Katerina. You can call me Kat—most people do."

"I'm Celia. You can call me Cici."

She keeps that smile on her face. "I'm technically here for a quick meeting with Nina, but I'm your dad's…friend." She settles on the word after a few awkward glances at him.

I give her a smile back, though I know mine isn't as inviting. "Nice to meet you."

"Mom, did you not tell Cici that Kat was coming?" Dad asks, looking aggravated. He stabs something on his plate with a fork. I think it's salmon. It's an odd assumption, given that I've never once seen salmon.

I turn my head toward Nina. She feigns an innocent look, but it does little to sway anyone. "Well, no. Didn't you, Carlos?"

"Clearly not," I mutter. Unfortunately, that turns all eyes back to me, but I ignore them and take a seat. I make myself a plate, still unsure of what the food is. There are at least five forks, so I grab the first one and begin eating. After I've had a few bites—it *is* salmon, or at least fish—I look at Kat. "So. What do you do for a living?"

I stifle a laugh at my own question. This feels like adults making small talk at work, when in reality, I'm just trying to interview my dad's girlfriend.

Kat swallows a bite of food before answering. "I work with Nina, sort of."

"Oh, fun, fun," I say, stuffing another bite in my mouth. It takes me a second to realize I should ask her to elaborate, just for the sake of being nice, but Nina talks before I can act on that thought.

"Celia, we were telling Kat what happened last year. You know, the *incident*." She mouths the word, like I don't know what happened. Like I'm not fully aware, even though I'm the only one who saw it happen.

I swallow and push my plate away. Who would bring something like this up in front of a virtual stranger?

"Okay," I start. "Why are we bringing that up now?"

"Mom," I hear from my left. Dad is shaking his head, scolding her. "Not now."

Nina sighs and scoops some pasta salad onto her plate. "I don't see why it's a secret. It's been a while, Celia. You should be able to talk about it now."

"It's been six months," I say thickly. "And time has nothing to do with it. *And,* regardless of secrecy, why would we talk about it here? With someone I've never met?" I pause. "No offense, Kat."

"None taken," she says softly, dabbing the corner of her mouth with a cloth napkin. She somehow manages to leave her red lipstick intact.

Nina's jaw tightens, which I assume means that I've offended her. But I don't really care. I scoot my chair back and stand from the table, willing my hands to stop shaking as I clasp them together. "I'm finished, but thank you for the dinner. Kat, it was so nice meeting you."

"You too." She gives a small wave before I walk away.

I leave the dining room, but I don't go downstairs. Given what I overheard earlier, I want to hang back. See if anything else is said. I stay tucked behind a corner, just barely poking my head around the wall.

"I just don't understand it." Nina huffs, and I hear a fork clatter. I can almost picture her throwing the silverware down. "Carlos, she's acting so spoiled."

It stings, just a little. More than I want it to.

"Mom." Dad takes a heavy breath, and I'm suddenly eager to hear his next words. "It's not something that should be brought up over dinner. Telling her she should be over it is insensitive, and it isn't your place."

I blink in shock. That's the first time I've heard him defend me in my life.

"She *should* be over it," Nina says. "She can't stay hung up on a freak accident for life. She should be in school, getting a degree. Living on her own."

"She's a child," Dad says firmly. "She's seventeen years old! And she doesn't have to be over it. End of story. Do not bring it up again."

I stop listening after that. I don't want to hear anything else.

Watching my dad vouch for me after all these years is a strange experience, but I can't dwell on it. Honestly, I'm *wary* of it. I know I shouldn't be; I know it's a cruel thing to feel. But it's too much of a change to trust immediately. A complete one-eighty makes me nervous.

Another chair scoots away from the table, so I practically roll down the stairs and bolt into my room. I hop onto the bed and nearly land straight on top of Ben.

"Hello," I mumble into a pillow.

"Hm." Ben sighs. "I take it the meal didn't go well?"

"Were you listening?"

He looks confused, as if it hadn't occurred to him to spy on us. "No. But you wouldn't be throwing yourself into the room if it went well."

"They started talking about me like I wasn't even there." I shift around to face him. "Nina called me spoiled and said I can't stay hung up on that night—on *you*—forever."

Ben places a hand on his chest, feigning offense. "So *I* was the problematic topic?"

I give a weak laugh. "Yes. And it all happened in front of my dad's new girlfriend, poor woman. She must be devastated to see what she'll be marrying in to."

"I'm sorry, back up." Ben looks appalled. "He has a girlfriend?"

I shrug. "Pretty sure. I wonder if I should warn her about Nina or just let her figure it out."

I don't mention the parts where my dad stuck up for me. It's a bratty thing to do, to leave out the niceties, but I haven't *seen* the niceties in years. I want to make sure they'll stay.

Ben runs his thumb over my wrist absentmindedly, and it's so nostalgic that I feel dizzy. I shiver, both at his touch and the coldness of his skin. "I'm so sorry, Cici."

"It's fine." I sigh. "Maybe she's right, in a way."

He shakes his head once. "No."

"No?"

"No." He flips my hand over, palm-up, and traces my fingers. "I'm going to say something, and you're going to think it's cheesy."

My lips turn up. "I won't laugh."

"You might." His tone is airy, unbothered. "But maybe…maybe I'm back because you guys didn't let go of me."

I tilt my head. I still haven't thought about the *why* of things, not deeper than a surface level. Part of me was just waiting for a logical answer to appear, but that won't happen. Logic doesn't exist in this situation. I've got to come to terms with that.

"A lovely starting theory," I tell Ben.

"I thought so, too."

A knock on my door follows his words, and suddenly, I remember that I forgot to close it. Luckily, *I've* stopped talking, so it doesn't look like I'm having a conversation with the wall. "Cici? Can we talk?"

My stomach churns at my dad's voice. I flop around on the bed for a second before sitting up. "Yeah."

Dad walks in hesitantly. He sits on the end of the mattress, looking at me as he does. He's probably waiting for me to tell him to leave. I don't.

Ben is already in the corner of the room, sitting on the rickety armchair. It's kind of comical having him around, listening so I don't have to recount the conversation later.

"I'm so, *so* sorry about Nina," Dad starts. The empathy in his voice is real and confusing. "That was…very uncalled for. I don't know what possessed her to do that, but it won't be brought up again. I promise you."

*Nothing possessed her, she's just an old hag,* I want to say, but I bite my tongue.

"It's fine." It's the furthest thing from fine.

Dad shakes his head. "It's not. You shouldn't have to talk about anything if you don't want to. It won't happen again, and I mean that."

Instead of giving him another response, I press my lips together. I've only been here for a few hours, and already, he's acting like a new person. Nothing like the dad I knew.

Nothing like the dad that left me.

I don't remember a lot from my childhood. Most of it was pushed out of my mind one way or another, but a few things stuck like glue. Dad and I's last real conversation was probably our most memorable.

I was young. So young, I thought I could waltz into the living room and fix whatever was making Mom cry and Dad yell.

*"Where are you going? Why do you have a suitcase? Why is Mommy mad?"* I had asked him, tears and snot running down my face.

My dad's answer was simple. *"Mommy is mad because Daddy doesn't love her anymore."*

I shake my head, pushing the words out of my mind. That's in the past. It happened years ago.

"Can I go to town tonight?" I ask suddenly. Good subject change; Ben looks proud. "Just to have a look around."

Dad nods before I even finish the question. "Sure, yeah. No problem at all. Would you like me to come? Just to show you around."

I start to say no. I shouldn't, but I do.

"Sure," comes out instead. "I've got no sense of direction anyways."

Dad smiles, either not reading my hesitation or completely ignoring it. "Okay, awesome. I can either drive us, or we can walk."

"Walk, please. I was on the train for hours."

"That sounds good." He stands from the bed. "I'm going to change. I'll be ready whenever you are."

"Same," I tell him as he walks out.

Groaning, I roll over to the edge of the bed. Standing up seems like a chore, but I haul myself to the closet anyway.

"You didn't tell me he got a personality transplant," Ben muses.

I open my suitcase and dig through the unpacked mess of clothes. "Well, I don't know how long it's going to last."

"Surely he would have made the transplant permanent."

"I'm serious, Ben." A sweater snags on my suitcase zipper, and I yank it away, only making it worse. "You know what he said about my mom. I don't want the same words directed at me."

His face sobers up at that. "I know, Cici. I know."

He does. He knows more than most. But he doesn't know of the hollow pit in my stomach, the one that's filled with a mix of hope and dread. The one that shouldn't even be there in the first place.

Regardless, I grab a jacket out of my bag and shove all the other things back in. I don't think I'll even need one, but I run cold, and the basement itself is freezing.

Just as I go to close the suitcase, I notice a big lump in one of my pajama tops. I yank it out and unfold it, only to find one of my fresh notebooks from home wrapped in the fabric.

"Marcus," Ben says from behind me. "He stuck that in there while you were gone."

I frown, flicking the bookmark attached to the top. "He's determined."

"He thinks you need it."

He may be right, but I'm not going to find out. Not here.

I zip the suitcase and set the notebook on my nightstand. I won't use it, but it's pretty. A green-blue color.

It was my favorite unused notebook I had. Marcus knows me well enough to know that.

"Feel free to scare Nina while I'm gone," I say, pulling my jacket on. "Rattle some silverware or something."

Ben untucks my hair from my collar. "You're not serious."

"I would literally swear under oath that I'm serious."

He grins, looking out the door. "We should wait at least a week to drive the woman mad."

I tip my head. "Three days."

"Five."

"Deal."

# CHAPTER TWELVE

The walk into town is not what I'd call fun.

Truthfully, it's just tense. I think of any possible conversation topic to start with, but everything that pops into my head is kind of snarky. I'm in a mood because of the crick in my neck, and taking it out on someone will ruin what little positivity I possess.

"Well…" Dad finally says, but he doesn't follow it up with anything.

"How long has this been here?" I blurt, pointing to a statue a few yards away.

Dad stares at the thing with a furrowed brow. It's a bronze-colored dog, placed randomly in the middle of town. "I'd say five years. I don't remember exactly, but it's pretty new."

"Is it like…significant? A specific dog?"

"I also don't know the answer to that." He laughs. "Sorry."

"It's okay. Just curious." *Just trying to make conversation.*

I chew my lip out of habit. Small talk is something I deeply hate, and that's basically what this is. I walk ahead of my dad just to get away from it. He doesn't bother catching up.

"Is there anywhere you want to go?" He asks from behind me. "Some places may be closed since it's later in the evening. We can come back tomorrow."

"Not really," I answer. "Just thought I'd see what my options are for the next month."

"Well, all the shops are in this part of town. Downtown is empty. There isn't much to do there." He pauses and waits for my response. I don't say anything, so he continues. "See anything you like? Anywhere you might want to go?"

I take another look at the places off the sidewalk. There's a small bakery, a thrift shop, and a few antique stores on the further end. I see a record shop and a library on the opposite side, so I walk in that direction.

"Jones's Records?" I ask, pointing to the door. "Can we check it out?"

Dad follows without question. "Fine with me. This place is old; they'll have some nice vintage."

"Or just trash."

He laughs. "Or that."

We step through the store's dirty glass door. It's definitely the first of what Dad described—old and vintage. There's a magazine rack on one wall, and another is fully lined with records. It smells like coffee and paper and window cleaner.

I walk up to a crate of old records and flip through a stack of them, only recognizing a few of the names. Some of the covers are old and yellowed, but the actual vinyl inside is undamaged. I feel eyes on me and look up to find dad right beside me, watching.

"Is there any reason to buy one?" I gesture to the crates. "Does Nina have a record player?"

He nods. "There should be one in the basement with you. I'll find it when we get back if you buy something. Do you recognize any of those?"

I dig through the front of the crate, picking up one to show him. He laughs when I hand it over, and I don't miss the way his eyes brighten. As if he's proud of something so silly. "Bon Jovi? Seriously?"

"Of course. This is my homage to Marcus." He and Don are the reason I still listen to this stuff. I can't say I'm mad about it.

Dad wanders off while I'm flicking through another box of records. I find nothing, so I tuck the Bon Jovi album under my arm and go to the counter.

No one is at the register. I see no employees anywhere, so I scour the displays as I wait. A bunch of CDs and cassettes are propped up on wire racks.

A certain one catches my eye. At least twenty CDs, all from the same band.

Ironically, it's the one I've been avoiding since last year. *The Adolescent: Headlights!*

My stomach roils and my eyes prick with tears. I pick at my nail until it bleeds, desperate for the bite of pain to distract myself. Crying over a CD in public would be sort of strange, and it's much too early in this trip for tears.

"UGH!"

I jump and look up from the display rack. A girl with bright red hair is behind the counter, dumping one of those coin rolls into the register. Her face is all scrunched up like she's annoyed. I don't ask if she's alright, only because she won't hear me. Her headphones are playing so loudly that I can hear *Just A Girl* word for word.

She throws the paper casing away when it's empty. I take a miniscule step forward, ready to hand her my record, but she grabs another roll and repeats the task. And then another. One more. She never looks my way, not once.

I glance over my shoulder, curious if I'm at the right place to check out. There's not another counter or register anywhere, nor another worker. Maybe she simply hasn't noticed me.

That, or Ben's ghostiness is rubbing off on me.

I start to wonder if I should say something, but the girl grabs the record and flips it over to find the price. "This all?"

"That's all," I say.

She looks at the cover, then at me, then back and forth a few times. "How old are you? I haven't sold one of these to someone under thirty in a long time."

I laugh. "Some of us have it melted into our brains from how we were raised."

"Gosh, you don't have to tell me. I had this memorized before I could talk." She punches a few keys on the register. "Are you from around here? Asking because I rarely see a new face, and I've never seen you before. So *you* are the new face."

I shake my head. "No. I'm visiting my grandma and dad for a month. I just decided to take a quick walk through the town."

"Ahh. Well, if you return, I highly recommend the tea shop on this block. I had to sell a kidney for a cup, but it's good."

"Might be off the table. This record is the most overpriced thing I can afford."

The girl looks offended for a second, and I panic. Surely I can't have annoyed her already. It's only been two minutes since I opened my mouth, and that was on my *nice* spectrum of jokes.

I'm safe, I realize, because she laughs and opens the register. "Fair. Your total is $19.89."

I hand her a wrinkled twenty-dollar bill. While she gets the change, my dad rounds the corner, looking stunned that I've already paid.

"I would have bought that for you, Cici," he says.

I shrug. "It's no big deal."

The girl gives me my change and hands me a brown paper bag. When I turn to leave, she stops me.

"Hey," she says. "What's your name?"

I raise an eyebrow on reflex. "Celia?"

A nod. "M'kay. Just curious. Like I said, there are no new customers here. When we get one, I make note of it."

"Understandable. And your name?"

"Michelle, Mickey, I don't care. Call me whatever." She puts her headphones back on and starts dumping more coins in the register. I recognize it as a dismissal and leave the store, Dad right behind me.

✳✳✳

When we get back to the house and part ways, I do my very best to sneak around Nina. It's hard, considering I don't know the house *or* her schedule well enough to avoid her.

Of course, since I'm me and have my luck, I walk into one of the living rooms and meet her eyes. They still look as devilish as they did at dinner, only now, they aren't lined with makeup.

"Cici. Sit, please." Her voice is soft and I don't trust it. I'm giving my dad *way* more of a chance right now, and it's shocking, but it feels right. Especially after this evening.

"What is it?" I ask cautiously, taking a seat across from her.

"I am so sorry for everything at dinner. I didn't realize how badly you were still hurting."

The tips of my ears burn as I remember her words.

*Carlos, she's acting so spoiled.*

"Thank you," I say numbly. "I'd just appreciate if we didn't bring it up anymore."

"Of course," Nina says. "And who knows, honey. Maybe we can find you a darling boy by the end of this trip! Speaking of which, you'll need to start dress shopping soon."

I blink, completely stunned by the instant switch-up.

*She thought that was an apology.*

"Thanks, Nina." I keep a tight smile on my face because I'm an A-list actress in this house. I have to be. "I will next time I'm in town."

"Great! You might even find something fun to look into at the banquet—a future job or something!"

"What's the dress code?" I ask, ignoring her comment.

She gives a lazy shrug. "Somewhere between business attire and cocktail dresses."

I don't have a single clue what that means, but asking is not on the table. Nina must read my confusion, though. She laughs and waves a hand through the air. "Just wear a nice dress that covers mostly everything."

Simple enough.

"Last thing." I wring my hands together in my lap, hating what I'm about to ask. Nina thinks so little of me and my family already—this won't help that case. "I don't really have the money for a formal dress. If I'm going to be the one paying for it, I'll just have to skip out."

Nina laughs again, and the sound is grating. "Oh, Celia. You aren't paying for it. I'm not a monster! Tell the owner to stick it on my tab. If there's a problem, I'll take care of it later."

I exhale. "Okay. Perfect. Thank you."

"Not a problem! I want you to enjoy your trip here, Cici. Besides, I didn't figure you had enough money for it."

I can't be offended by that because she's right.

"Thank you," I say again. "That's very kind."

She nods, and I leave.

# CHAPTER THIRTEEN

The next few days, I do that thing where I hole myself up in my room and only come out for food and water. I've quite mastered the routine, and I even upgraded from my previous run. Now, I've got a DVD player and a ghost to keep me company.

Also, that notebook Marcus shoved in my bag. The thing hasn't stopped glaring at me.

It's in my lap right now, opened to the first blank page. I've got a dried-out glitter pen I found on the floor and jumbled thoughts.

But I'm going to write something. Even if it's a singular word. I will.

Exhaling, I uncap the pen and scribble until it writes. I zone out for a second and end up covering half the space with blue sparkly ink, but I don't bother turning the page.

I just start writing.

\-

*A heart. One that had a gaping hole.*

*The girl wondered what could possibly be so much as to fill it. Words?
Actions? They mattered. Of course they did. But she wondered if they
were enough.*
*Things could not be taken back. Wounds could not be healed with
kind smiles and gentle touches.*
*"But I'll accept it anyways," she thinks. Her heart is still cracked,
held together with weak threads of memories.*
*Little more could hurt.*
*Damage is an inconsequential thing.*

-

No, no, no, no, no.

I slam the cover down, not caring that the pen is still inside. That is *not* what I need to be focusing on right now. I've kept emotions buried for a good while—a little longer won't hurt anybody.

Shaking my head, I set the notebook back on the nightstand. It's fine. I wrote, and that was my only goal. Those words were enough. And anyways, I've got other things to focus on. Writing is extremely secondary in priority.

"Hey," Ben says from the doorway, reminding me *exactly* what I have to focus on.

"Hi," I say, and my tone makes it sound like I'm hiding something. I guess I *am*, really: the notebook, and the singular paragraph inside. But it isn't that big of a deal—certainly not worth acting like I've committed a crime.

Ben raises a brow, clearly decoding whatever is on my face. His eyes go to the book, but he doesn't address it. "Everything okay?"

"Yeah, totally." I sit a little straighter. "What's up?"

He tilts his head. "Well, Cici, it's been three days since you left this room."

"Incorrect. I've gone upstairs for food."

"Cheese cannot sustain life."

"Yes it *can*."

Ben chuckles. "Come on. You have to go upstairs and get outside. Fresh air and sunlight are good. Healthy, even."

"I don't take orders from Casper-esque boys."

He gapes, but the corners of his mouth are fighting a smile. "That isn't funny."

"You're trying not to laugh. And for your information, I'm going to do it." I take a deep breath, close my eyes. "I'm going to go upstairs."

"Mm-hmm. Alright."

"I am."

"I believe you."

He shouldn't. When I reach the second to last step, my feet stop moving. He has to coax me to even look over the railing.

"See?" Ben says, gesturing to the empty living room. "It's fine."

I step back and knock into his chest, ignoring the fact that one more step would have us tumbling down the stairs. "There isn't even anyone here. I should just go back down." I fully turn toward him. He looks mildly disappointed in me. "To the room I go!"

Ben puts his hands on my arms, presumably to hold me in place. "Cici."

"*What?*" I frown. "I like it down there. I have a bathroom and blankets and *How to Lose a Guy in 10 Days* on DVD. That's all a girl needs."

"Save for food, water, air that isn't dusty…"

"It's fine."

"You can't hide down there forever." He squeezes my shoulder. "It's creepy."

"Says the ghost," I mumble. "But wha—"

"Cici, you okay?"

I jolt so hard that Ben grabs my elbow to steady me.

My dad appears in the doorway, looking a little confused as to what I'm doing. It's understandable; from his perspective, I'm standing on the stairs, talking to a banister.

"Yeah, fine," I say quickly. "You scared me. What's up?"

"I'm sorry. I've just—I've got some news, I guess."

"Is everything okay?"

His face implies that he isn't sure. I look around the room, still empty except for us and a suitcase.

One that wasn't there a moment ago.

"Are you leaving?" '*Again?*' my brain adds onto the end. I'm thankful it doesn't slip out of my mouth.

Dad shakes his head. "Quite the opposite, actually."

"Ohhhkaayyy," I say, waiting for an elaboration. He already lives here; it's not like he's moving *in*. The other option isn't presenting itself to me right now. "That doesn't really tell me anythi—"

"SURPRISE!"

The sound comes from the kitchen, followed by another, more blood curdling scream. The latter, from Nina. The first, from an all-too familiar voice.

"*Marcus?*" I ask, running into the kitchen.

He's standing in front of the oven, arms wide, looking like he's just struck gold. His clothes are wrinkled, like he fell asleep on the way here, which makes me wonder *how* he got here.

Nina is the one that catches my full attention, though. She's standing against the fridge, a hand pressed to her forehead like she just had a stroke.

"HE SCARED ME!" She cries. "HE'S SO LOUD!"

"Surprise," Marcus whispers, making Nina roll her eyes.

I bite my lip to stifle my laughter. It's only been a week, and he couldn't live without me. Braving a stay with Nina is probably the nicest thing he's ever done for me.

"I was just about to leave for work," Nina says, shuffling to the sink for a glass of water. She fills it to the brim, swallows one gulp, then pours the rest down the drain. I watch as she straightens her collar and stiffens up, looking among the three of us. "I'll be back around nine. I've got meetings on top of meetings, and the *paperwork,* and I *hate* my client this week and…"

Nina lists about ten other things she hates before leaving. The three of us stay pin-straight and silent until we hear the garage door close.

"SURPRISE!" Marcus says again, at full volume and through a massive smile.

I laugh as he envelops me in a big bear hug, squeezing at least half the air out of me. I cough dramatically but he doesn't let go. "I'm absolutely sick of staying in my run-down apartment, and your siblings beat me with lightsabers yesterday, so I'm here! Miraculously! Be thankful."

"How long are you staying?" I ask when he releases me.

He scoffs. "So. You're already trying to get rid of me."

"Eh."

"Hm." He smooths out his *Shrek* t-shirt. "Maybe a week. A few days. I just wanted to visit. Apparently, we talk a lot, and—oh, I can't even say it."

"You missed me," I say, grinning.

"Never!"

"You did, and it's okay. I carry this…this constant weight—"

"Oh good grief."

"—of being the coolest, hottest, funniest cousin. I get it. Everybody wants my company."

He rolls his eyes, probably second guessing his decision to visit.

I put my hands on my hips. Only now do I remember that I'm still in pajamas and hardly look presentable. Not that anyone here cares. Nina might have, but Marcus scared the daylights out of her before she could speak on it. I'll have to thank him for that.

Ignoring that, though. I look like a slob.

"I'm going to change," I announce.

"Show Marcus to the guest room," Dad says. "There's another one right next to yours. If Nina is using it to store things, he can take the one up here."

"How many guest rooms does one person *need?*" Marcus says, gaping.

Dad laughs under his breath. I can tell he's thought the exact same thing before.

Marcus and I go downstairs, Ben on our heels. We have much to discuss and so little time before Nina returns.

"Well, personally," Marcus starts, "I think that my presence warranted a much warmer welcome."

"That *was* warm," I say.

Ben shrugs. "Yours was warmer."

"Mine was fake."

"A fluke," Marcus adds.

"No, not that. I'm extremely lovable."

He snorts.

The other guest room is down the same hall as mine, just like Dad said. It's adjacent to the room I'm occupying, which is nice. I can knock on the walls and annoy Marcus while he tries to sleep.

He gets his suitcase semi-unpacked in no time. It reminds me that mine is still *fully* packed, unzipped and strewn out on my floor. I've got no plans of changing that. That's sort of the point; I'm living out of my suitcase because I'm not staying. It's the principle of the thing.

When Marcus is done, we go back to my room. I slip into my closet and change into a *different* set of loungewear, then take a seat on the end of my bed. Ben sits beside me and Marcus lays on the floor.

"You can sit up here," I tell him. "It's a full bed. There's room for three people."

He shakes his head. "Nope. Good down here. Now, start from the beginning. You found out that only *we* can see Bennet?"

I forgot that was the last thing we talked about. "Yeah. But first…" I reach into my nightstand and grab the record I bought a few days ago. Attempting to keep it a surprise, I put it behind my back, but Marcus sees and snatches it from me. Basically throws me aside to get the thing.

His eyes are falling out of his head when he examines the cover. "You went into town and bought this all for me."

"Not exactly. Enjoy."

"I will," he says in awe. "But I'm just shocked you left the house."

*"Ha. Ha."*

"No, he has a point." Ben leans forward, elbows propped on his knees. "She didn't want to, but I told her that staying here for long periods of time is unhealthy."

Marcus looks around. "This is a nice basement, though. It has a window."

"And a fridge," I say.

Ben sighs. "Still."

Marcus grins and turns his attention back to the vinyl. He goes to the record player in the corner, the one Dad found and dragged into my room. It takes him a second to figure out how to use the particular model, but when he does, *Let It Rock* blasts through the room.

He hugs the cover to his chest and closes his eyes, a hypnotized smile on his face. "I love you, C."

"Gag. Never say that to me again."

He laughs, and Ben laughs, and I try to laugh, but something twists in my chest. This is so reminiscent of old times. It's *exactly* like it used to be.

The three of us were always 'alone', but together. We didn't go out, didn't make friends. We spent what time we could with each other. Some would call it codependence or obligation, but it wasn't like that. Everything we did was by our own volition. It's the only way we really knew, and I still haven't found another. I don't *want* another.

And for some reason, seeing it happen again is absolutely gutting. Probably because it's illusive. Misleading. There's going to be an end somewhere because there already was one.

*You can try to change the ending, but it's already over.*
*This is not real.*

The song ends while I'm still in my daze. Marcus turns the record player off, snapping me out of it with a heavy sigh. "Okay. *Now* tell me everything. Last thing I heard is that Ben can't be seen."

Right. "Well, we found that out on the train ride here. I tried to pay for two tickets, and the conductor was like, 'Uh, miss, there's only one of you', so we realized something was off."

"We have no real way to test the *why*," Ben says. "Therefore, we have no new information for you."

"A damper, really." Marcus sighs. "What lie did you tell Nina and your dad? Is Ben a felon or a BFF?"

"They can't see him, which makes me think we're right about the whole *ghosts only haunt acquaintances* thing. They left before I met him."

Marcus looks at Ben. "You know you can do great things with this, right? Like tie Nina's hair in knots while she's asleep or something."

I clap. "That's what I said!"

Ben chuckles. "I'm not evil."

"What is deserved, even if disgraceful, is not evil," Marcus says wistfully. He seems to think on his words for a breath, then jabs his pointer finger at me. "You should write that down, C. I like that line. We could use it."

"For what?"

"When we co-write a bestselling novel." He leans forward like he's going to tell me a secret. "That's why I'm trying to get you back on your writing groove."

"Oh, joy. When were you going to tell me about these plans?"

"Today. I had it in my calendar."

Ben snorts. "The fact that you possess a calendar is more shocking than the get-rich-quick plan."

Marcus eyes him. "I can see why you're bitter. Really, I can. But you could try to hide it."

Smiling to myself, I lay my head back on my pillow. The ceiling fan is on its fastest setting, so I pick a blade and watch it spin while Ben and Marcus argue.

"There's something wrong with you," Ben says, laying down beside me.

"That may be." Marcus sighs. I'm expecting a further statement, but he doesn't say another word. He just stands and leaves the room, not bothering to close the door.

Ben hums. "Well. That was simple enough."

"It's always simple with him." I grab the quilt and tug it over my waist. The sun is setting, and the room is cold from the air conditioning, so I don't feel bad about getting cozy.

My eyes meet Ben's, and a line forms between his eyebrows. I know the look—it's a silent question, one asking if I'm okay. Seeing it now, even though I've seen it so many times before, is a whole new experience.

"Don't judge," I tell him. "I know all I've done is *laze*. I'm just…"

"Drained?"

I shrug. *Drained* is a weird way to put it, but it's the truth. Physically, I'm fine. Mentally, it's a different story. We haven't done anything these past days—Nina is busy, Dad is busy, and I refuse to put jeans on. It's given me too much time to be present with my thoughts.

But instead of explaining all that, I just say, "Kind of."

"Take a nap."

I peek over my shoulder, out the window. It's only seven. If I go to sleep, I won't wake up until morning. I could eat or watch a movie or something, but the extra blanket on the end of my bed is *extremely* tempting.

"Take a nap," Ben repeats, grabbing the blanket in my eyeline. He unfolds it and sets it over me. I'm shocked when he presses a kiss to my scalp, not meeting my eyes.

# CHAPTER FOURTEEN

The clock beside my head is buzzing. When I open my eyes, it feels like there's a glaze over them, but I manage to read the clock.

It's 8 AM.

"We slept for thirteen hours," I mumble, propping myself up on my elbows.

Ben's eyes flutter open at my voice, and he looks confused. He's on top of the blankets, still wearing his clothes from yesterday. I guess he fell asleep when I did. "We slept for *thirteen hours?*"

"Apparently. That's a new personal best." I throw the blankets off my body and walk to the bathroom, feeling oddly rested for once in my life. I squeeze out the last of my travel toothpaste and start to brush my teeth.

Ben walks in and stands behind me, and I notice his hair is completely messed up from sleeping. "How do you still look tired?" I ask, laughing around a mouthful of toothpaste.

"I'm not tired, I just haven't woken up. There's a difference."

I spit into the sink and rinse, then turn to face him. His hair is covering his closed eyes, so I brush it away from his face. "Ghosts are sleepy, hm?"

He lets out a tired laugh and smiles down at me. "That makes sense, I guess."

"Ugh. *EW!* Nasty." Marcus stumbles down the last three stairs, gagging with his hands around his throat. "Stop this cutesy crap, please. It's odd with the circumstances."

I gape. "I told him he looks tired."

"I'm sure there was *something* there."

"I literally don't see—"

"Leave it." Ben rubs his eyes. "It's useless."

"Fine," I say, knowing he's right. "Good morning to you too, Marcus. You didn't consider waking us last night?"

"Do I look like an alarm clock?"

"You've got the IQ of one," Ben says.

Marcus scoffs. "Go back to sleep."

Laughing, I turn back to the sink and wash my face. "So. What are our plans today?"

"Well," Marcus starts, "I think Nina may have a whole *family fun* type of thing planned, except it's only us and your dad."

"Oh, gosh." I groan. "Board games?"

"Board games," he says flatly. "I'm so sorry. I tried to get us out of it. Played the *irritable bowel* card, if you know what I mean. Nina gave me a bottle of Pepto Bismol and told me to shut up."

Ben breathes a sigh of relief. "I've never been so thankful to be a ghost."

I elbow him, and he only laughs. "I guess we'll go to town tomorrow," I say. "Maybe even later today. Surely, she'll be done with us by afternoon. Why is this starting so early, anyways?"

"Don't even try to understand the workings of Nina's mind." Marcus crosses his arms. "But it's fine. We can be annoying if needed, and maybe she'll let us out of it."

"Oh, absolutely. That's our strong suit."

✳✳✳

Surprisingly, we aren't annoying enough, so half an hour later, I'm plotting a murder.

Games are a very serious matter to me. In fact, the term *'game'* just takes away from the importance of it. I've never understood people who aren't competitive. It isn't a game, it's war.

"So, Cici," Dad says while Nina takes her turn. "Why aren't you in school right now?"

I really don't see how this is the time for questions. Clue is a win or die affair, and it is to be taken seriously. But I answer anyway.

"I finished a semester early because I did school from home," I say, eyeing Marcus. If anyone is close to winning, it's him. His last few guesses have been suspiciously calculated and I don't like it. "It was easier after everything happened."

"Plum, dining room, rope," Nina interjects, looking to us for an answer. "Celia?"

Shaking my head, I slide her my rope card. She rolls her eyes and gives it back, furiously marking her piece of paper. I almost laugh at how odd it is, seeing Nina do something so mundane as playing a board game.

"Why did you do school from home?" She asks, as if I didn't just explain why.

"To keep my mind off things. It kept me busy."

"Ah," she says. "And what about college?"

Apparently, the game is on pause now. It's my turn, but I'm not taking it mid-conversation. Marcus could beat me if I'm preoccupied.

"No college," I answer. "For now, at least. I'm only seventeen. There's plenty of time for me to worry about that."

Nina's expression is judging, but she stays silent long enough for me to take my turn.

I've had the answer for three rounds. I'm just being cocky.

"Plum, observatory, candlestick."

Marcus groans after checking his cards, and Nina frowns. Dad looks proud as I check the stack in the middle of the table.

"Are you right?"

I hold them up. "As always."

"Figured." Dad sets his cards and pen aside. "Another round?"

Marcus leans forward. "Actually, C and I were—"

Before he can finish, Nina's phone rings, making us all jump. She stands immediately and leaves to answer it, then returns within the minute. A pink tote bag has appeared on her left shoulder, as well as a scowl on her face.

"I'm out," she says. "I've got to host a quick meeting this afternoon, and I can't afford the company. My assistant needs a swift kick to the—*Oh! Celia!*"

Her eyes pin me, and I freeze. "What?"

"Go to Belle's today."

"Pardon?"

"Belle's. It's a little dress shop in town. I need you to get your dress for the banquet. Remember—a modest one. Nothing hanging out, nothing we have to alter. We've got no time for that, and we're proper women."

I scrunch my nose up. Marcus does the same.

"I'll get a good one. Promise."

"Good," she says. "I'll see you all at…some point." She waves a hand at us and runs off to the next room, quickly swapping Family Nina for Work Nina.

And just like that, we're free.

Dad tells us that he has plans as well, and that this game day thing was *not* his idea. Apparently, he's working slow, infrequent shifts at some restaurant in the next town over. I get the urge to ask where, to ask if that's his everyday job and if he enjoys it, but I don't. That can all wait.

Marcus and I go to our rooms to change. The door to mine is wide open, and Ben has taken it upon himself to look busy—he's making the bed, currently trying to flatten the quilt. There's a big lump in the middle of it. It's probably a stuffed animal or a balled-up shirt, but he doesn't seem to care.

"We're leaving," I tell him.

He looks up, completely abandoning the bed. "Thank God."

I chuckle and walk to my suitcase. Clothes are still thrown across the rug, so I halfheartedly stuff them back inside, no doubt mixing the dirty with the clean.

I grab a green sweater and a white skirt and change in the closet. My boots are old and don't really match the outfit, but I pull on a pair of socks and wear them anyways.

Once I'm ready, I go down the hall and pound on Marcus's door.

"Let's get out of here before Nina comes back," I say, talking loudly enough that he can hear me through the plywood.

The door swings open and Marcus steps into the hall. His outfit is the most random thing I've ever seen—black jeans, band t-shirt, and what *looks* like a fur-lined parka. I'm going to assume that it isn't, but with him, I seriously cannot be sure.

"It's not that cold outside," Ben says.

Marcus huffs. "I was cold when I packed at home, so I accidentally packed winter clothes."

"So just…go without the coat?"

"But my arms will get cold."

I sigh. "I'll carry your coat if you get hot."

He beams. "Thank you, C. You're a godsend. Truly."

"Truly," I repeat.

I grab my backpack, and we leave out the garage door.

✳ ✳ ✳

We keep our mouths shut until we're in town.

It's windy today, and leaves are swirling around us like little tornadoes. They're dead and brown, but it's still a nice contrast of color.

"What have you done here so far?" Marcus asks, nearly running into a lamppost. Ben and I ignore it.

"I met my dad's new girlfriend—*alleged* girlfriend, rather. She's really nice, but the meeting was awful."

"I can guess who to fault for that. Continue."

"Uhm, I went to a bakery and a record store. There was a girl there that I talked to, but I haven't seen her since. That's the only other dose of interaction I've had besides Ben."

"Is that *all?*" He sounds shocked. "You've been here for over a week!"

Those words sound less like a jab and more like a countdown.

"I'm just waiting for the banquet," I say honestly. "I sort of thought I'd get more acquainted with Nina, but we kind of botched that on the first day."

"At least things are better with your dad, though," Ben says.

I nod and kick a rock. "That's true."

"He's really trying," Marcus says. "Even with me. He's trying."

It's crazy to me, to really see it. How involved Dad has tried to be, just over the span of a few days. He's asked me about things I haven't spoken of—or even *thought* of, for that matter—in years.

I've given him the most basic, evasive answers, but that's my own problem.

"I know he is," I say instead. "And if all goes well, there's a chance we'll talk regularly."

Even at that, the wishful tone in my words scares me.

I spent a lot of my life learning how to hate him. It's weird to teach myself the opposite.

Thankfully, conversation tapers off. We window shop for a while, deciding that it's not the wisest to spend all our money in a remote town.

Well, *I* decide that. Marcus, on the other hand, drags us into a video game store and runs laps around the place.

"You guys don't understand—this is like, the coolest thing right now. And it's only *thirteen bucks*?!" He runs from shelf to shelf, completely overwhelmed.

"I don't even think he has a gaming console," I say to Ben. He's watching the whole ordeal over my shoulder, laughing quietly in my ear.

"He either bought one while you were gone, or he's in deep, deep denial."

Marcus runs back up to us, arms full of game boxes. This is oddly reminiscent of the twins running up to my parents and begging for a new toy.

"I need all of these," he says, nearly out of breath.

"You have enough money for…" I count the number of boxes he's holding. "*Seven* video games? Did Don give you a raise?"

"Did you rob a bank?" Ben asks simultaneously.

Marcus snorts. "I'm living off of instant noodles and the meals I eat with your family. Draw your own conclusions." He shifts the boxes in his arms and takes a few off the top. "I'm only going to get two, because I'm learning to be *responsible*. If you guys want to pitch in on one or four, however…" He waves a bright yellow box in my face.

I grab it from him and place it on a shelf. "Sorry, no. Get what you want and let's go. I want a croissant before I play dress up."

He sighs and sets a few boxes down. It takes him a good ten minutes to decide which games he wants, and even then, he walks around the store to make sure they're *really* the right ones. Add five minutes for him to check out the cashier display, another three for him to contemplate buying a headset, and you have the reason I'm getting cranky.

"Let him live," Ben says quietly. "He's never seen so many games before."

"I know. But I want a cupcake."

"I thought it was a croissant."

"It's a cupcake now."

"Ah." He puts a hand on my shoulder, guiding us toward the door. "Let's just leave him here and get your cupcake. We can find your dress and wander around town until he's calm enough to leave."

I cross my arms. "Okay."

"Okay," Ben says, and we leave the shop.

The bakery is across the street and completely empty. I get a cupcake for myself and two scones for Marcus, knowing what a big deal he'd make if I didn't. Ben watches in utter horror as I eat my cupcake in two bites. I stuff Marcus's scones in my backpack, and we begin looking for Belle's.

The location of the boutique is a mystery. We walk around lazily while keeping an eye out for it. It's mostly a chance for me to look at mannequins through windows and talk to Ben. Despite being with him every day for the past week, it hasn't seemed like enough time.

"I think…" I bite my lip, because that was it. That was the extent of my conversation—I have nothing else to say. Maybe that's for the best, considering it *looks* like I'm talking to myself.

Ben clicks his tongue. "Why are you even going to the banquet? Like, seriously."

"I don't think I have much of an option," I admit. The wording gets under my skin—it makes me feel weak, like I can't stand up to Nina, but that isn't the case. "I know there's a right answer, and it wasn't to refuse. I still want to be on her good side, at least for the length of the trip. Plus,

I want a fancy dress. It'll make me happy to spend her money."

"Okay. But you hate fancy dresses."

"And I *love* spending money."

"That, you do." Ben chuckles. "And we have…no idea where this store is?"

"Not a clue," I say. "This way is more fun."

"Is it really?"

"It's like a scavenger hunt." I cross my arms and tug my sweater tighter around me. The barely-there breeze is enough to make me shiver. "Plus, it's a small town. It can't be hard to find."

At my words, Ben's face lights up. "There." He points across the road to a run-down strip mall. A big purple sign reads *Belle's* above one of the doors.

"Good eye."

"Thank you. Now, let's buy you a dress. *Fun.*"

Laughing, I grab his sleeve and drag him to the shop.

# CHAPTER FIFTEEN

I lied.

I think I do like fancy dresses. Belle's is like a candy store with ribbons and glitter.

*"DO YOU SEE THIS?"* I scream-whisper, holding up a puffy pink dress. It's got tulle going every which way, so much that I'm almost sure I'd get tangled in it. The sleeves look like they'll only cover my shoulders, and the neckline is low, but not so drastic that my Nina would throw me out of her event.

Ben crosses his arms and grins. "You liar. You do like dresses."

"I do, and I'm finally okay with admitting it. This realization has changed my life." I'm flicking through another rack of dresses when I notice the lady behind the counter, watching me with an odd look. She's glaring over her red glasses like I'm about to shoplift or something.

*Have you never seen someone look at dresses before?* Is what initially runs through my head. But then I remember that she can't see *Ben,* and I was just having a conversation with him. Perhaps her reaction is valid.

"Sorry," I say to her, adding a smile. She jolts a little when she knows I've caught her staring, but I continue. "Gotta consult with all the voices in my head, you know. It makes the choice easier."

The woman looks at me, agape and absolutely horrified. I smile again, aware that she'll probably leave me alone for the rest of my shopping trip. Until she has to ring me up, anyways.

A few seconds later, she goes to a room behind the counter and closes the door. The lock clicks sharply, and I can't contain my laughter.

"Smooth," Ben muses. "So very smooth. Also lowkey."

"Indeed."

Over a matter of minutes, I've collected three hangers on my wrist: the pink dress that sent me into a spiral, a strapless, deep blue one with little gold sparkles, and a plain black one as a backup.

Ben and I—along with the woman hiding from me—are the only ones in this store, so I go behind the changing curtain and try the pink dress on.

I frown when I see myself in the mirror. It's hideously unflattering and *much* lower cut than I first thought. The fabric bunches up around my waist, and the weird bow in the center makes me look like a Christmas gift. A bad one. The box everyone avoids in White Elephant.

Hesitantly, I go back out to ask Ben's opinion. I'm not getting it regardless, but it's still nice to have someone verify my hatred.

"I hate it," I state. "I look like a half-wrapped Christmas gift that ends up being underwear or socks."

"*Never* knock the gift of socks," Ben says solemnly. "But you're partially right. On the half-wrapped part, at least. Nina will burst into flames."

"That's a tempting offer." I sigh dramatically and go back to the dressing corner. Tugging the zipper loose proves to be a difficult task, but eventually, I'm out of the pink and into the blue.

*This* dress sends me into cardiac arrest.

It fits me perfectly. The fabric hugs my waist but flares out enough to give me a balanced look. The sleeves fall just off the shoulder, and it somehow pulls everything together.

Plus, it makes my boobs look really good. That's all a girl can ask for.

I yank back the curtain with full confidence, spinning around before I even start talking. "This one. It's perfect. Look at it. *Look.*"

Ben does. He sits quietly for a few seconds, arms crossed over his chest. I keep waiting for a response, but one never comes.

"Well?" I ask shrilly, suddenly conscious about what I'm wearing. Maybe it's too much. Too revealing or something. Nina might scalp me for this one as well as the last. "Speak!"

"Calm down. You look great," he says softly, tipping his head to the side. "I like that one."

I fluff the skirt out. "Okay, good. I was getting it anyway."

He lifts his brows. "So we can leave?"

"Yes, we can leave." I snap the curtain shut and unzip the dress. "There are worse things to do than shop, you know."

"Oh, I know." He sounds like he's holding back a laugh. "But the store owner is staring at this sofa like there's a ghost on it—and there is, mind you. I think we should leave before she gets more suspicious. What if she tells the entire town that you talk to yourself, and then everyone thinks you're bonkers? Where would you go for cupcakes?"

I poke my head between the curtains, ignoring the fact that I've already unzipped my dress. Sure enough, the woman has cracked the door open. One eye is visible and staring directly at the sofa Ben occupies. When she sees me, she slams the door and locks it all over again.

"The poor lady," I mutter, closing the curtain. "I hate to scare innocents."

Ben only laughs.

When I'm back in my normal clothes, I take the dress up to the counter. The woman is still in the back room, now smoking a cigarette. I *do* feel bad for stressing her out, but to be fair, I didn't realize she was watching me. It couldn't be helped.

"Excuse me?" I talk loudly enough that she can hear me. "Uhm, I'm ready to check out."

Awkwardly, I stand in front of the counter, tapping my nails against the glass until I hear a lock click. The woman emerges from the break room, watching me from the corner of her eye with a revolted glare. She puts out her cigarette before speaking to me.

"No need to yell," she rasps. "I'm old, not deaf."

I shake my head. "Oh, no, I just thought—"

"What does it say on your tag?"

"What?"

"The price," she says. "What is the price of that dress?"

"Oh." The tag is twisted in the strap, so it takes me longer than it should to find it. "It says $199.90."

"Mm-hmm," she hums. "Cash or card?"

Suddenly, I'm panicked. If this woman thinks I'm crazy, what are the chances of her letting me use Nina's tab? My pockets contain exactly seventy-three cents and a tube of ChapStick. If she turns me down, I'm screwed. "See, I'm not sure. My grandmother said to put it on her account. Is that something you can do?"

The woman peers at me over her glasses. "Who is your grandmother?"

"Nina Lor—"

"Oh!" She cuts me off, her entire demeanor changing in seconds. My Nina must be the only Nina in this town or something. "The designer? Then yes, of course. She's got a tab here. Credit. We buy from her sometimes."

If I just bought one of Nina's dresses, I'll combust.

Discreetly, I peek at the tag, and I'm relieved to find *Belle's* stamped in pretty writing. It must be an original dress.

"Great," I say tightly. "Thank you so much."

"Of course!" The woman is absolutely beaming now. "Have a nice day."

"You too."

The woman is back in the break room, smoking a fresh cigarette before we even leave the shop.

Amused, I throw the dress bag over my arm. Ben and I step outside, and the chill in the air causes goosebumps to erupt over my skin.

"All right, Cici." Ben puts his hands in his pockets. "Where to now?"

I look around. There's still no sign of Marcus, but that's to be expected. Anytime he gets off his self-inflicted leash, he will run rampant. It's just in his genes.

"Jones's." I look up at Ben to find him already staring, studying me like always. "I went with my dad, remember? The record store. It was really cool. You'll like it."

"I have zero objections," he says. "Lead the way."

I grin and practically skip down the sidewalk. I've missed the silly little shop, odd as it is. The environment reminds me of home. Not that I'm exactly itching to go back right now, but still. That familiarity is something I've begun to crave.

Ben is enthralled upon entering the store. My chest warms, seeing him rifle through crates of vinyls like I did that first day. I knew he would like it.

Between the two of us, he's the music nerd. I love music and I always have. It makes up a good portion of what I was raised on. But for Ben, that was his lifeline. He *felt* music, so much deeper than I did. That was something he taught me, a piece of his heart that he shared.

*Write that down.* Marcus's grating voice fills my brain. *I like that line.*

I like it, too, because it's the truth.

I don't write it down, but I do file it away in the depths of my brain.

"This is really cool," Ben tells me. He picks up a few albums and looks at the covers, then sets them all back down. "Sort of shocked that you didn't buy the store out."

"That seems like more of a *you* thing."

He looks straight ahead. "I've got no need."

I blink, confused, right before his words hit me. He's right—he has no need. It's a harsh reminder.

"I also have no money." He nudges me with his elbow. "I'll guess that my finances were drained."

"I'll spot you a twenty," I tease, nodding to one of the CD stands. "If you find a gem, that is."

He smiles, but it falls quickly. I frown, wondering what could have happened in the span of a literal second. It isn't until I follow his gaze that I realize what he's seeing.

The very stand of CD cases I saw a few days ago.

"Wow," Ben says quietly.

I swallow. "Yeah."

He flexes his fist at his side, but it isn't out of anger. It's out of something deeper, I think. Something more like regret.

"Have you listened to them since?"

"I can't," I breathe, my voice cracking on the last word. It makes my face heat, my eyes sting. I don't know why I feel insecure about it—there's no need. But something about seeing it here, now, *together*, makes me feel tense.

"I wouldn't either," Ben says. He takes my hand, an unspoken comfort. "So, you got Marcus his Bon Jovi record here?"

My shoulders relax at his attempt to distract me. "It's the only thing I had to buy, and I felt the need to spend money."

He grins. "A good purchase."

"I thought so."

"Hey!" A voice calls from across the room. "You're back!"

I glance up to see Mickey waving. She looks shocked to see me again, but she's smiling when I walk over. "I didn't expect you to actually come back."

"I didn't either," I admit. "Not so soon, anyways."

"Well, there isn't really anywhere else to go."

"I've learned that quickly."

I thumb through a crate of records. Ben is at my side, still holding onto my fingers. I hand him a beat-up Jeff Buckley album, trying to be discreet since Mickey is watching. He examines the thing and wrinkles his nose. I grin and put it back, tucking it behind the others.

"So, who's your friend?" Mickey asks.

I have never so vividly felt my stomach drop through the floor.

She raises a brow, waiting for a response, but I'm unable to speak. It can't be Ben that she sees, but who else? The store is empty, save for a seven-year-old licking the VHS cases.

*Marcus.*

Marcus was on the sidewalk. The game store is only across the street. Maybe she saw us outside earlier.

I blow out a breath, making my bangs fly away from my forehead. "Oh, Marcus? The one I met across the street? He's my cousin."

Mickey frowns and looks right beside me. Ben tenses, his hand tightening around mine.

"No," she says. "I didn't mean him. I meant *him*."

She motions to Bennet.

*She motions to Bennet.*

"What?" I ask stupidly.

Ben drops my hand like it's on fire.

Mickey looks worried that she just ruined something. And she has, in a way. My semblance of peace, what little thread I was holding onto like a life raft. It's gone.

"I didn't..." Mickey stammers. "I was only asking—"

"No, it isn't that. I just...you can see him?"

*Smooth, Celia. So smooth.*

Mickey laughs as if I'm kidding. "Of course I can. I saw him when you guys walked in, and I watched him judge that record. By the way, do you have a problem with Jeff Buckley? That's a lovely album. It deserves its respect."

Ben's face is entirely blank. "No?"

"Good, good," she mumbles, looking seriously comforted by this. "So who are you?"

I bite my lip. Ben is still frozen, still used to going unnoticed. To keeping silent.

"Uh, we…I'm…" He starts multiple sentences. Not a single one finds an end.

"That's Bennet," I finally manage. "He's my boyfriend."

The word is foreign on my tongue.

Mickey nods slowly, clearly taken aback by our behavior. I can't even blame her. "Okay, then." She holds her hand out. "Nice to meet you."

Ben stares at her arm like it's the first time he's seen one. From Mickey's perspective, it probably looks like he's nervous about a handshake. *I* am nervous about this handshake, but still.

I hold my breath as Ben raises his hand to hers.

Their palms touch.

And nothing out of the ordinary happens. Not a single thing.

"Well, you guys are weird." Mickey forces a laugh, oblivious as she steps away. "I'm gonna stop that kid from licking the VHS cases. Bye!"

I open my mouth to respond, but no words come out. It's useless anyways—by the time I'm registering things again, Mickey is back behind the counter, headphones over her ears.

Ben and I race out of Jones's, and we keep on in the direction of the game store. I'm not even watching where I'm going—Ben literally has to stop me from walking onto a K-Mart parking lot, grabbing me by my hood and tugging me backward. I nearly drop my dress bag in a puddle.

"Cici," Ben says, trying to grab my attention when we reach the sidewalk. I'm completely out of it—my eyes are trained on a postal box while I try to sort out what just happened.

"*Cici*," Ben repeats, firmly this time. "Hey."

"I think I might be sick," I say, scratching my throat.

He shakes his head. "I don't know her."

"I know. I know, I just…what's going *on*?"

He shakes his head again, and that's our answer.

I take a breath, chew on my thumbnail. I'm trying to rationalize a situation that *isn't* rational, and it's not working.

We have one fact, one question, and no answers.

Mickey can see him.

*Why can she see him?*

# OCTOBER 10, 2008

When our clothes are dried, we go back to my house. I refuse to wear this outfit to a concert, and my hair is frizzy from the rain. It must be dealt with.

I tell Ben to play with my siblings while I get ready. It makes them ridiculously happy; they like to do a lot of talking and little else.

I have no idea what to wear to something like this. Semi-casual, I'd assume, but not *too* casual. The only things I even have washed right now are a red plaid skirt and a black shirt, which seems like a decent choice. I stole Ben's denim jacket from the dryer without his knowledge, so I put it over my shoulders whether it matches or not.

Ben is sitting on the couch when I go back to the living room. The twins are on either side of him, small bowls of popcorn in each of their laps. They're extremely occupied with an episode of Looney Tunes on TV.

"Hel—"

"SHH!" All three of them urge.

I blink, stunned. Ben looks at me from the corner of his eye and grins at my shock. *We're invested,* he mouths.

Amused, I step in front of the TV, only to gain a chorus of scoffs. Ben included.

"Cici!" Jace whines. "MOVE!"

I hold out a hand. "I'm going to borrow Ben for the evening. Do I have you guys' permission?"

Maisie giggles. "No! He's staying here with us."

Ben sighs. "I'm sorry, guys. I've got previous arrangements. But don't worry. We can watch Looney Tunes tomorrow, okay? I'll be back. Promise."

Jace gives a shrug. "It won't matter. The doggie gets crushed always."

Ben puts a hand to his chest and gasps. "Spoiler!"

The twins burst into a fit of laughter, spilling popcorn on the carpet. It gives us enough time to slip away and leave the apartment. Right before I close the door behind us, Mom appears from the laundry room with a basket on her hip. Her expression is stern. "Be home by eleven."

"We will," I call back. "Probably."

I close the door before she can respond.

Ben and I run to the sidewalk and cross the street, beginning our walk downtown. Clouds roll in above us, and I notice how dark the sky has gotten.

"Is this a good idea?" I ask, tightening Ben's jacket around me.

He knocks his shoulder into mine, and I grin against my will. "If it gets too bad, we'll call a cab."

"Okay," I tell him.

We keep walking, even as thunder cracks.

# CHAPTER SIXTEEN

I don't know what to do.

This wasn't supposed to be a problem.

Ben and I haven't moved from our spots on the sidewalk, right outside the game store. I sit down on the concrete and lean my back against the building. Press my hands against my eyes and try to think.

"You don't know her." I say it like a question, but I know it's true.

"No," he says. "I don't."

I lift my head. "Do you? Like, are we forgetting?"

He shakes his head, certain. "No. I don't think so. Unless it's from a very long time ago. But *why* would she remember me?"

"That's the thing. She didn't remember you. Not your name or face, at least."

Ben exhales, and I feel halfway between exhaustion and hysteria. I can't imagine the looks I'm getting right now; I'm sitting on the concrete, head in my hands, talking to absolutely nothing.

Another thing Mickey doesn't understand. She was referencing nothing. Talking to *nothing*.

"Why are we worried?" I ask, attempting to reason with myself. Ben looks down at me, sort of like he thinks *I've* lost it, but I keep going. "Think about it. I didn't panic when I could see you, and neither did Marcus. Well, okay. He did, but not in the worst way possible. I know I'm not the best example, but what if we just…explain it to her?"

As soon as it leaves my mouth, I know how ridiculous it is.

She doesn't know him. She doesn't know the past, or his story, or *anything*. And I can't explain this to anyone else. Especially someone whose reality isn't tethered to a hazy memory.

Ben chews on his lip. "I don't think we can do that. What if she like…calls the police for harassment? Or something?"

"Worst-case scenario is, she doesn't believe us."

"That isn't the worst-case. Not by a long shot. That might be the *best*-case." He swallows. "We need to think through it a whole lot more before we just 'explain' it to her."

I take a breath. "Okay. That's fair. We'll deal with it after Nina's whole dress banquet thing. That's my worry for the week."

Ben nods and offers me his hand. He pulls me off the ground and I steady myself on my feet. There's a pressure building behind my eyes, but I do my best to ignore it.

"We can maybe tell Marcus," I offer.

"We'll see," Ben says.

But we don't. I don't think we even consider it, not past that moment. We go silent the second Marcus steps onto the sidewalk. He starts telling us about the game he bought, so it doesn't matter.

It shouldn't seem so difficult. I've never kept anything from Marcus before; never even considered it. But for some reason, telling him that somebody else can see Ben is the strangest thing I can imagine. It feels like something I shouldn't voice.

When we make it back to the house, we still haven't mentioned it. The good thing is, we don't have to—Nina has turned the entire front room into something that looks like a baby shower.

Helium balloons are tied to every flat surface, and the tables are covered with champagne glasses, all filled with a fizzy drink. The dresses and suits thrown around are the only clues that this isn't a baby shower. Also the fact that none of these women are pregnant.

Ben and Marcus take the liberty of sneaking down to the basement. According to Marcus, this is not a party they want to attend.

"Hi." I clear my throat and knock on the door frame. Six women look up at me, all tearing their eyes away from the clipboards in their laps. I notice Kat sitting on the sofa, giving me the same smile she wore that night at dinner.

"Oh, Celia!" Nina exclaims, rising from the sofa. Standing for me is suspicious enough, but the fact that she walks across the room to usher me inside is even more concerning.

"What's going on?" I ask, tossing my dress over a chair.

All the women give me a once-over, which Nina quickly dismisses. "Ladies, this is my granddaughter, Celia. She'll be accompanying me at the banquet this weekend. I'm hoping she'll meet some people, maybe even someone to sign with!"

My face must twist with confusion, because one of the women begins explaining. "Nina has been looking for models for weeks, but it was getting late, and we're still one short. It was so kind of you to volunteer! We're hoping this could be an opportunity for you—she's told us how interested you are. We're so happy you decided to come!"

You have got to be kidding me.

Modeling.

That's it. That's the whole reason she asked me here.

*So she can save money on models.*

I'm not a model. Never wanted to be one. I'm comfortable enough in my own skin, but still not a fan of people blatantly judging me.

I fist my hands at my sides to keep from smacking Nina, who is definitely within arm's length. It would be *so* easy, and yet…

"Can I have a quick word with you in the hall?" I ask calmly.

Nina puts on the fakest smile I've ever seen. "Of course, honey."

"Great." I might chip a tooth from clenching my jaw.

Nina is on my heels as I leave the room. She follows willingly, only because she wants me to go through with this. I have no qualms about backing out. I'll return the dress. Burn it if I have to, I don't care.

When I'm sure we're out of earshot, I drop the act. "What is wrong with you?"

She has a challenging look on her face, and it doesn't waver. Nina has never backed down. Clearly, she sees no need to do so right now.

"Look," she starts, her tone cold. "I'm not playing this nice act any longer."

"*This* is your nice act?"

"I'm letting you stay here for free. For a month. You've eaten my food and you've stayed in my house. You can do one thing for me."

"It isn't about that!" I sigh. "I wasn't aware any of that was *leverage!* I thought you wanted to get back in my life for the right reasons. I thought that was why you invited me—to see you and Dad, and to clear things up. But you brought me here to *model.* Because—let me guess—modeling equals collaborations, equals more money for you. Right?"

She looks deflated. It's the first time her face has ever shown emotion. "Yes."

My face heats. Somehow, her confirming what I already knew makes me feel worse. I thought maybe Ben was right, that I could trust her at some point. But I don't see that happening anytime soon.

It's money. It is *always* money.

I take a deep breath, still contemplating the right thing to do. Do I leave without another word, or do I suck it up and help her out? She's family, yes, but she's never treated me as such. I don't see why I should have to be any better.

Then again, there's a difference between her and I. Nina may think I'm a spoiled brat, but I know there are two sides to every coin. That somewhere down the line, something had to break inside of her, too. Something had to make her this way, just like things changed me for the worse.

I don't have to be generous. But I don't have to be as selfish as her.

"Fine," I whisper. "I'll go to the event, and I'll talk to people."

Her face lights up, but I'm not done.

"But," I start, and a sour frown forms on her face. "I'm not going to act genuine about this…this modeling career you seem to have made for me. Did you really think I'd consider it?"

"It isn't permanent. It's just a brand deal."

I shake my head and continue on my tangent. "You can either tell them that I never wanted this in the first place, or you can get the deals through your own work. If you can't get me off that hook, then find someone else. I'm sure lots of girls would be your personal mannequin."

Nina's face is such a complex mix of emotions that I'm not sure what she'll say next. It seems like years before she lowers her head. "Okay. You win. That's it. I can't argue; that's all it was."

I swallow. Stay quiet.

"Just stay for the banquet. Be good for the banquet, Cici," she says.

"I will. I'll do what I need to do for the evening. But after, you will not hear from me again. After I leave this house, I'm gone. You've lost me."

Nina blinks as if I've shocked her. Maybe I have. She's clearly never been put in her place, and it's bittersweet being the one to do so.

Without another word, we walk back to the living room, and I put on that fake smile. All the ladies are occupied with their wine glasses and stacks of papers, so I assume they didn't hear anything.

That, or they're trying to look busy so we don't know.

"I'm thinking we could get a lot of offers at this event," Kat says before addressing me. She looks me up and down again, and I am instantly regretting my decision to help with this. "How tall are you?"

I shrug. "I've got no clue. Probably like, five foot six?"

She nods and writes something down. "Can you walk in heels?"

"Not at all."

"Can you learn?"

"It's not likely."

"Hmm, okay." She nods again, like this is groundbreaking information. Suddenly I feel like some experiment, and it makes my stomach feel heavy.

Nina still looks a little defeated.

I hope I embarrassed her.

"That's all for now," Kat says, flashing me a perfectly straight smile. "Do we have any more questions?"

The other women shake their heads.

"Then you can go," Nina says, before anyone else can speak. "Thank you, honey."

"No problem," I say quietly.

I go back downstairs, where Marcus and Ben are hiding from the *party*.

My cousin is sprawled out on the floor, no shock, and Ben is on the end of my bed. He meets my eyes with a false look of peace, one that I'm starting to recognize very well.

Marcus is oblivious. I can't fault him, obviously—we haven't said a word about anything.

"I'm a model now," I state plainly.

Ben sits a little straighter. "Expound."

"I've got it," Marcus says. "Nina tricked you. Or threatened you. Or put a spell on you. Am I right?"

"Yes. Option one."

"One out of three is good."

I take a seat beside Ben, wondering if we should mention the Mickey thing. Is it even worth bringing up right now?

"Marcus," I start, dragging his name out so I have time to think. "Let me give you a hypothetical."

"My favorite. Go."

"What if…what would you think if I said, somebody else can see Ben?"

Marcus doesn't pick up on the tension in my voice. He's preoccupied with a roly-poly on the floor. "I'd say, that's extremely weird and perhaps nothing is even real anymore."

"A lovely perspective," Ben says.

"Would you tell them?" I continue. "Or would you let it go?"

Marcus shrugs. "I guess it depends. Is it out of curiosity? Worry?"

"Let's say a mix of both."

He breaks his attention away from the bug to stare at me. "Is this really a hypothetical?"

"Yes," I lie. Ben looks over at me, his face blank, but he doesn't correct me. "Just in case it happens or something, I don't know."

Marcus sighs. "Well, I think I'd tell. Just because I like to talk. You know how I am."

"We do," Ben says.

"Thank you, Marcus." I lean forward to untie my shoes. "This was all very insightful."

"I'm just smart like that. You know, I've been thinking I could be a motivational speaker. Or start a podcast."

"The latter," Ben tells him. "I recommend the latter."

# CHAPTER SEVENTEEN

Days pass. Ben and I still don't tell Marcus the truth.

I feel kind of terrible about it.

We discuss it constantly, any time we're alone, and something about it is consuming my mind. I'm so tired of thinking. Of *worrying*. Ben and I have been in such a tense state since Mickey spoke about him, and I want it to go away. I want it to go back to…well, not normal, but whatever we had going on.

The problem is, telling Mickey feels like an option. Something we don't *have* to do. And that's not a great mindset to have.

We could definitely get away with it. It's not like we're staying in this town forever—we aren't even staying much longer. She'd never know if we just left it alone.

But it seems wrong.

I don't sleep well the rest of the week. I've basically given up on it. Being groggy turns into my default setting. Watching movies through the night turns into something I despise.

By Friday, Ben forces me to sleep. He says that I have to be alive to model, and if I die, Nina wins.

I change into pajamas and lay face down on my bed. Ben lays beside me and mimics what I'm doing, then sits up a few moments later. "I don't get how you breathe like that."

I prop myself up on my elbows and take a deep breath. "You don't. You just hold your breath."

"That sounds awful."

"It's not the most comfortable, but having your face buried in a pillow is."

He laughs, presumably at my random habits, then shifts around until he's lying normally: on his back, hands crossed over his stomach. "This is so weird," he says quietly. "All of it."

"I know." I turn my head and look at him. *Really* look at him. His eyes are a little darker, and his usual subtle smile isn't on his lips anymore. He seems…almost fainter, but that's ridiculous. It's probably the awful fluorescent light-bulbs Nina has.

Maybe he's looked like this the whole time, and I've been too wrapped up in his presence to notice.

It doesn't change that I'm grateful for him being back. But it does remind me that I don't know the rules of this whole ghost thing, and Ben doesn't either.

"Sometimes, I wish none of this had ever happened," he whispers.

My breath hangs in my chest.

*What?*

"I don't know what to say to that," I say. "Isn't…isn't this good?"

"Is it?"

"Of course it is," I respond shakily. Part of me wonders if he even hears it—my voice is hardly audible.

"I just don't get it," he says. "Like, the whole Mickey thing makes no sense. I don't know her, Cici. Why can she see me? Isn't any of this weighing on you? Don't you won-der?"

*Yes, I think. Of course I wonder, but the details stopped mattering to me. It's worth it. All of this is worth it to me.*

Instead of saying any of that, I just say, "It's worth you."

Ben rolls his head toward me. His mouth is pulled into a frown, and that worried crease between his eyebrows appears. I'm almost certain my expression mirrors his.

"Maybe," he says, not looking away, "we should consider the alternative to this being a positive."

"Which is?" I ask dumbly.

"Don't you realize what's going on, Cici? You aren't sleeping. You aren't doing well. You're stressed, anxious out of your mind. And it's all because we have no idea what to do about *anything*."

I finally turn away, locking my gaze onto the ceiling fan. "I don't know what you're implying."

"I'm just a burden. To you, and Marcus, and—"

"Stop." I shake my head. "Stop that. You aren't."

"All we've done is worry, Cici. You're going to make yourself sick, and for what?"

"For this," I say firmly. *This*, whatever it may be, is all I have right now. I don't care how messed up and unconventional it is. I'll hold on until I can't anymore.

Ben chuckles, but it sounds wrong. "That's not a good enough answer."

"It's an answer nonetheless."

I wait for him to argue. I'm almost anticipating it. Instead, he looks at my face, at the exhaustion in my eyes, and he sits up. "You need to sleep. You have a busy day tomorrow."

"We need to talk."

"We need to shut up for a bit," he says, a hint of humor in his words. "Sleep. I'll be here when you wake up."

I open my mouth to say '*no, we don't need to shut up,*' but Ben pulls all the blankets over me. He runs his thumb under my eye, catching a tear I didn't know had fallen. "I'll be here when you wake up," he says again, quieter this time.

I turn the words over in my mind. That single sentence makes me feel ill. Makes me realize what's really bothering me.

It isn't Mickey, or Nina, or Dad.

It's because I've been so naïve lately, and I'm finally seeing it.

Ben may *not* be here when I wake up. He can't promise that he will.

This is fragile. It's all in vain.

We are nothing more than a house of cards, reality being the gust of wind that will ruin us again.

# CHAPTER EIGHTEEN

Nina wakes me up early to go over everything for the banquet. I haven't laid eyes on a clock, so I have no idea what time it is. I only know that I should *not* be awake.

"Okay!" Nina starts, sitting down on the sofa in front of me. There has to be some coffee in her veins, because she's extremely perky. "Let's go over the basics."

"What could I possibly need to know?" I ask. "I just have to talk, right?"

"I'm going to go over some simple things," she repeats. "I've only got three rules for the day, and I don't feel like I'm asking too much."

I will be the judge of that. "What are they?"

"One: please hold civil conversation with agents. This could be a big deal for me, even if you don't stick around to do anything. Two: try not to eat, at least until—"

"What?" I cut her off. "Nina, no. I'm going to eat."

She huffs. "If you *must*, please don't eat anything high in salt."

"Why?"

"Because salt makes you bloat!"

I blink. "I was probably bloated when I bought the dress. If you wanted a Barbie doll model, I'm going to fail you."

Nina waves me off. "Third and last: do not embarrass me. No spilling drinks or food. No stumbling over words, using vulgar language, or—"

"Breathing, speaking, existing…"

She sets her jaw. "Just don't. Please."

"I won't," I say, fully aware that I could be lying.

Nina leaves the room, so I close my eyes and lean back against the sofa cushion. Twenty seconds and I'll be out cold.

Unsurprisingly, I don't get that chance, because Nina returns with two girls behind her. They look just as awake as she does. I'm still in Snoopy pajamas, contemplating whether coffee is a good idea.

"We're hair and makeup," the girl with blue hair says, clearly sensing my general confusion. "We'll fix you right up, doll."

"Why so early?" I croak. It's only nine, and the event isn't until this evening.

The girl just laughs, and the tall one beside her joins. "It's a process."

"So I assumed."

A man enters the room with a salon chair in his hands. He places it in the middle of the room and leaves without a word. I wonder if that's his only job, or if he gets to do more interesting things than carrying a chair.

"Sit down," the blue-haired girl instructs. "I'm going to start on your hair."

"Do I get a say in how it looks?" I ask.

"No," she says, dragging a brush through my tangled curls. "Ms. Birdsong gave us a strict guideline to follow for your *glamor*."

I nearly roll my eyes at the word, but I'm too distracted by the fact that I forgot Nina's maiden name. She goes by Nina Lorena to the public and Just Nina to me.

"Hold still," the other girl says, leaning right in front of my face. A yelp of surprise escapes me when she brings a brush to my face. "I'm only putting eyeshadow on you!"

*Please, for the love of everything, don't make me look like Bozo the clown.*

"Can I have a mirror?"

"No," one of them says. I can't see which. "The final look is a surprise."

I fidget with my fingers. Sitting still isn't something that I'm especially skilled at, but the girls don't speak, so I don't either. I try to shut my brain off instead of thinking about what happened last night, but it doesn't work very well.

*I'm just a burden,* Ben had said.

What would possess him to think such a thing? Have I done something to make him think that?

I don't think so.

"Are you guys almost done?" I suddenly ask, because in my head, it's been hours since they started.

They both snort. It's more dehumanizing than a simple laugh. "Doll, how long do you think we've been working?"

I ignore my urge to shrink back into the salon chair. "I don't know. An hour, maybe?"

Another round of laughter. "It's been twenty minutes at most."

"Good grief," I mumble.

"You'll thank us when we're done," one of them says, and I shut my mouth again.

It really does take them a while to do my makeup. Once they're finished, I'm fully convinced I look ridiculous. How can makeup take three hours and *not* look like circus prep?

The blue-haired girl hands me a mirror, and I gasp at my reflection.

They've done an incredible job. The look is natural, even though it took *years* to do. Glitter shines on the corners of my eyes, and it's the only thing that actually looks like makeup.

One of them curled my hair and braided a few pieces on my scalp to look like roses. My bangs look nicer than they ever have, so I rightfully assume I have no idea how to style them.

"I love it, actually," I say, and the girls laugh quietly. "Thank you guys so much. Sorry for being cranky."

"It was our pleasure," the taller one tells me. They join hands and give me a dramatic bow, then walk out of the room.

Nina enters seconds later, gasping when she sees me. Per usual, she's in a three-piece suit, so I guess that's what she chose for the evening. I don't know why I assumed she'd be in a prom dress or something. Glitter is very *not* Nina.

"You look great, Celia!" She claps her hands once. "Now go change into your dress. It's almost time to leave."

Wordlessly, I hurry to my room. I assumed Ben would be talking to Marcus or something, but he's sitting on my bed, clearly waiting for me to walk in.

Maybe he's getting bored here. Maybe he thinks *I'm* bored here.

Maybe I should remove my brain for the evening and have a moment of peace.

Ben stands up as I grab the dress from my closet. "You look incredible," he says quietly. Cautiously.

"Thank you." I smile. It isn't a fake one, but it's more forced than usual.

*Why* did his words last night affect me so much? Why can't I think about anything else?

"I've got to change, then I'll be gone for the night."

He runs a hand through his tangled hair. "Are you sure you don't want me to go? It won't really matter that I didn't buy a suit."

I'm vaguely aware that he's making a joke, but I don't laugh. "That's okay. Unless you just *want* to go. But Marcus probably needs some company."

He frowns. It makes his entire face darken.

I take my dress and go to the bathroom to change. Putting it on without ruining my makeup proves to be extremely difficult, but possible. It takes me a good five minutes to make sure everything is in place and nothing is slipping out.

The instant I look at myself in the mirror, I feel as light and happy as I did at Belle's.

I'm not vain. But I look really good in this dress.

My only dilemma is, I can't zip it.

"Seriously?" I try to twist around so I can reach the back. It doesn't work—I'm practically spinning in circles, like a dog chasing its tail.

Sighing, I unlock the door. "Ben?"

"Hm?"

"Zip this, please," I say.

For some reason, I'm embarrassed to ask him for help. I shouldn't be; I know that. But in the past twenty-four hours, I've created this entire problem in my mind, and avoiding him until I can sort out my thoughts seems logical.

We both deserve for me to figure it out. Whatever *it* is. I'm not tangling things up anymore.

Ben zips the back of my dress without a word, his fingers cool on my spine. He meets my eyes when I turn around. I get the urge to look away.

"You look great," he says again, his voice weaker this time.

"Thank you," I breathe.

We just look at each other for a while. I don't know if this weird tension is coming from him or me, but it's here, and it's extremely real. Just looking at him feels wrong, and that's the *last* thing I want to be feeling.

*But it is wrong, isn't it? He's right. He shouldn't be here.*

I don't process anything else, because Ben scoops me up in his arm and squeezes me into a hug. I inhale quickly at the shock, a newfound mix of comfort and terror that he's able to do this. That he's still here.

And suddenly, I understand why I'm so upset. So drained.

My excitement has worn off. Now I'm back to reality, back to the truth. This can't last forever.

But still, I don't make any move to leave his arms. It hadn't even crossed my mind.

"We'll talk when you get back, okay?" Ben whispers. "We just have a lot of stuff to figure out right now. It's going to be okay." He runs his hand down my back. "It'll be okay."

I nod because I don't trust myself to speak.

He releases me, dropping his arms back to his sides. "I'm so sorry for anything I said—"

"No." I shake my head. "It's fine, Ben. It wasn't that."

He just nods.

"Cici!" Nina shouts from the top of the stairs. "The limo is here!"

I pinch the bridge of my nose, ignoring the makeup I'm probably rubbing off.

"I'll see you later," I tell Ben.

And I leave without waiting for a response.

# CHAPTER NINETEEN

Nina's limousine has a TV.

I was sort of unaware that was a thing. I've seen them in movies, but I thought it was just that: a movie prop. How does it even work? What's it connected to? There's not a satellite dish on top of the vehicle, and it isn't prerecorded. At least, I don't *think* it is. Nina is much too enthralled by this soap opera for her to have seen it before.

"Do you always get a limousine with a TV?" I ask.

Nina looks confused for a moment. She leans forward so the driver can hear her talk. "Randall. Do they make limousines without televisions?"

"Yes, ma'am, they do," Randall answers.

"Mmm," she hums, sitting back in her seat. "Then yes."

"And you enjoy these soap operas?"

She blinks. "What else is there to watch?"

I shrug, halfway amused. The correct answer would be *anything else,* but honestly, I can't argue. The woman on TV slaps the man she's talking to, then starts screaming at the top of her lungs. Tears are flowing down her face, yet it doesn't affect her makeup in the slightest.

I'm quite hooked now.

Nina and I sit in silence, both locked in on the show until we arrive. The driver stops us in front of a very fancy building. For a moment, I'm convinced we're in the wrong place. It looks like a palace—white marble with windows galore, a dome ceiling with a chandelier. The limousines parked near the water fountain only convince me further.

"I wasn't expecting this," I admit.

Nina scoffs. "It's a model walk. What else did you expect?"

I open my mouth to answer her, then stop short. "Wait. I'm walking?"

"What did you think 'modeling' meant?"

"I thought I was like…talking to people? Like you implied?" I sigh, hearing how ridiculous the words are. *That's* why Kat wanted my measurements and shoe size. I should've known, but a runway never crossed my mind. "I don't know. I just didn't think about it."

"Clearly not," she mumbles, and suddenly, I'm tempted to back out. It's such a petty thought, but I don't really care. I'm more worried about the upcoming runway thing, and the fact that I'm probably going to fall on my face.

Nina gently grabs my elbow, making me jolt. "Please, Cici," she says. "I just need this one thing, and I need it badly. I should've clarified, but you agreed so easily, and you're just so headstrong, and…it was wrong. I'm sorry. But I wasn't risking it." Her voice is extremely quiet now. "I need this so, so badly."

I study her expression for a heartbeat. The limousine driver has already parked, and the fact that Nina won't budge means something much more than her reputation.

It means money.

"Business isn't great right now, is it?"

She slumps back in her seat. "No, it isn't. I've hardly gotten any business in weeks. A decent turnout at this event will be a miracle."

I bite my thumbnail and look out the window. Yes, I'm headstrong. A little mean when it comes to this. To Nina. But I'm not a terrible person, and I won't purposefully throw something that means a lot to her. That's not what I want.

"I'm sorry things aren't going well," I say quietly. "I'll do this for you. Even though everything in me is saying to back out, I won't."

Nina lets out a breath, almost like she was terrified I'd get out and walk back home. "Thank you. Thank you so much, Celia. You have no idea what this means to me."

"Miss?" Randall stretches around to face us. "We've arrived."

Nina scowls at him, adding a *tsk* for good measure. "Thank you, young man. We can see that."

The young man and I both suppress an eye roll.

Nina opens the door and leaves the vehicle, waving her clutch purse around. I stay for a split second longer and lean forward. "I'm sorry about her," I tell Randall.

He gives me a knowing look in the rearview mirror. "I'm her usual driver. I'm used to it."

✳ ✳ ✳

The second we walk into the banquet hall/runway place, I bolt to the nearest bathroom and throw up.

Pure fear washed over me the second I walked in. I was expecting, what, eighty people at this event? But no. There are at least two hundred people in the main room, more in the hallway. It's all black out curtains and spotlights, and each chair is occupied with a person or placeholder.

I hide in the bathroom for as long as I can afford. Heels clack on the floor, and somebody knocks on my stall door, even though I'm still knelt on the floor.

"Hey, I'm gonna be a minute," I force out. "Can you maybe get someone to replace me? Or move the time I walk?"

"No!" The girl squeals. "We can't! You only have one outfit. One!"

"My head is in a toilet bowl right now. Is that not a valid excuse?"

She stomps one high-heeled foot before leaving. When I know she's gone, I focus on calming down.

I don't know what's wrong with me today. This isn't serious. If I botch this whole thing, it's not a big deal, and it doesn't affect me—I'll never see these people again.

My nerves, to put it simply, are shot.

When my stomach stops trying to kill me, I decide it's time to leave this bathroom. I wash my mouth out multiple times at the sink, ruining my lipstick in the process. Hopefully someone can fix it.

I wipe my mouth one final time when a blonde girl bursts through the door. She throws her hands in the air. "Finally! You're good. Let's go."

"I'm not—"

She grabs my arm and drags me from the bathroom before I can finish my statement. I feel sick again by the time she tosses me into a styling chair.

"Can you walk in heels?" The girl asks, rifling through a box of shoes.

"I previously established that I cannot."

"UGH!" She cries.

I have to hold back a laugh. Her dramatics are Nina-level, and that's saying something. But it isn't *my* fault I can't walk in heels. My mom doesn't even wear them. I was simply never taught.

The girl comes back and fluffs my hair up with her hands. She fixes my lipstick, then pulls a small rack of dresses across the room. "How do you feel about purple?"

"Like, as a general rule? Or—"

"Do you look *good* in purple?"

I shrug. "I don't know. I wear it."

"Good enough." She yanks a dark purple dress off the hanger and holds it up. It's kind of hideous in my opinion—a short cocktail dress with sequins across the bust. Maybe fancy people like these types of clothes. "You're walking in this."

I laugh, because that thing is about two sizes too small. "Funny."

"*FUNNY?*"

"Yes, funny. Why is it so tight? I don't think that will go over my hips. Or boobs. Or anything."

"It's going to fit," she says sharply. "Now stand up and put it on."

"I think you're crazy."

She doesn't argue. Instead, she pulls me out of the chair, unzips my dress, then yanks it off my body.

"Uhm, *excuse me*—"

"I'm not looking," she says, and she isn't lying. Her eyes are toward the ceiling, and my dress is draped over her outstretched arm. "Just put it on."

I snatch the dress and step into it quickly. I'm halfway naked, pointlessly fumbling around with the fabric, but she keeps talking.

"Don't break a thread. I'll help you with the zipper. And the straps. And the cross-back thing. Oh, did you—"

"Zip it," I snap, holding the dress to my chest. She huffs and zips it immediately. It's like a dang vacuum sealer. I absolutely won't be breathing tonight.

When I look in the mirror, I immediately want some sort of trench coat. A straight jacket, even. Anything will work.

"It's only fifteen seconds on a runway," the girl says, sensing my discomfort. "It's not so bad. If I could be out there instead of back here, I would. Count your blessings."

She looks annoyed, maybe even mad. The bitterness in her eyes and tone tell me not to address it.

"Okay," I say, unsure of what else there is. It's clear that I'm making an enemy, and I really don't want to. I can't afford anymore. "Uhm, how long have you been working in the modeling world?"

The girl sits back in one of the styling chairs. "About six years. I got on it right out of college. Wanted to model, got rejected a few hundred times, then settled for behind the scenes."

I wring my hands together, resisting the urge to bite my nails. "I'm sorry."

"No big deal," she says, even though it's clearly a big deal. It means a lot to her; that much is obvious. "I figured things out. And anyways, we gotta find you some shoes to walk in. Heels, flats, or sandals?"

"Flats, please."

She finds a pair to match the dress's color exactly. "Okay. Size?"

"Eight."

"Perfect."

She sets them on the ground, and I slip them on my feet. They're much more comfortable than they look, and they *look* like mouse traps.

"You look hot," the girl states plainly, crossing her arms.

I look over at her, mildly taken aback, but she's laughing. "What? The dress looks good on you. You have a decent pair of legs."

"I feel like a fish."

"Oh my gosh, take the compliment."

"Thank you," I say, shocked to hear the sincerity in my voice. "What's your name?"

She wrinkles her nose. "It's Cherry."

The fact that she's wearing a bright red dress makes this one hundred times better. "Cherry? Like the fruit?"

"Yes. I'll never forgive my mom for that."

I laugh quietly. A moment of silence follows, and I assume it's time for me to leave, but Cherry keeps talking. As she seems to enjoy.

"You aren't as aggressive as you initially seem. Your grandmother made you sound like a total witch."

I wince. "She does that sometimes, yeah."

"Celia Greene?" A guy sticks his head in the door. He's wearing one of those headsets with a microphone and holding a clipboard to his chest. Picture perfect, according only to my imagination. "We need you on the runway."

A sentence I never thought I'd hear in my life.

"Go get 'em," Cherry says, squeezing my hand.

I don't have a choice, so I follow the man out the door.

# CHAPTER TWENTY

The runway walk isn't half bad. I quickly learned that the trick is to zone out. Forget about everything but your feet. The camera shutters flashing every which way made that increasingly difficult, but it mostly worked.

When I get backstage, Cherry congratulates me.

"You were so good!" She says, dragging me back to the room we occupied earlier. She unzips my dress and hands me the one I bought at the boutique. In the three seconds that I'm undressed, I feel like a hairless cat. It's excruciating.

"What do you have to do now?" She asks, zipping up the Socializing Dress. "Did you even want to do this? Most people would be, like, giddy right now. Oh my gosh, also. Your legs looked *so* good under that light! You need to tell me what moisturizer you use. Now."

I give a tired laugh. "I don't know. Whatever bottle I find on my bathroom counter, I guess."

She frowns. "Lucky."

"As for this part of the banquet?" I go back to her first question. "I haven't got the slightest clue. I think Nina wants a brand deal or something."

"Your grandmother would do a lot of things for a collaboration," she says. "She's a well-known name in the fashion world, and she's made that seem like a negative thing."

Even after living in Nina's house for days on end, I know very little about her. I'm beginning to wonder what I've really missed out on.

"Do you need your makeup freshened or anything?" Cherry asks, her tone perky again.

"No, I think I'm good. I should probably get out there, though."

She nods and gives my hand another squeeze. "Have fun."

"Why don't you come with me?" I ask. "Nobody will know any different. Maybe you could weasel your way in with some agency."

Cherry smiles weakly. "I don't think that's a good idea."

"But why? Think about it. You have a unique name. That might get you noticed. What's your last name?"

She crosses her arms. "That is *so* extremely confidential."

"I was practically naked in front of you three minutes ago."

"Don't care. I cannot tell you my last name."

I squint at her. "It's something crazy, isn't it?"

"Stop."

"Cherry Blossom or something."

"*Stop*," she says again, this time through a laugh.

"Oh my gosh. I've got it."

She glares at me. It's not even remotely menacing.

"It's Cherry Pitt. Your name is Cherry Pitt."

I wait for confirmation, waving a hand to speed up the process.

Eventually, she gives in. "My mother hated me. But if you tell *anyone*—"

"Your secret is safe with me," I promise her. "But anyways, imagine seeing that name in magazines. *Cherry Pitt.*"

"I will have to think up a fake name."

"Probably smart."

Cherry rolls her eyes. "I suppose I *could* sneak out there. Steal an hors d'oeuvres or two."

"You should."

"And *you* should leave," she says. "Your makeup will start to smudge soon!"

I shrug. "I don't really mind."

Cherry practically tosses me out of the room for that.

Wandering aimlessly is something that seems to be a new habit. I've got no idea where I'm going, and I don't care to find out. Noise from some sort of party floods my ears, but I can't pinpoint the direction.

I crouch down behind a comically large plant when my phone rings from my dress pocket. The pockets were something that Cherry pointed out—I was unaware of them before she told me. If I'd known, I would've chosen this dress with no question.

My mom's name is blinking on my phone screen, so I answer.

"Cici!" She says, her voice joyful. "Hi, sweets."

"Hey, Mom." I plug one of my ears with a finger. The building's noise has only heightened, and I'm waiting for her to question it.

She releases a heavy breath. "I'm so sorry we haven't called. We haven't even *received* any—the phones have been down."

Guilt sinks like a rock in my stomach. Only now do I realize that I haven't tried to reach them. I haven't talked to them for *two weeks*. What if I've missed something important? What if something bad happened?

"What's all that noise?" Mom asks, interrupting my thoughts.

"Oh, uhm, I'm at an event with Nina. I walked on a runway. I don't think it was a real one, but still."

"Wow. That was the last thing I expected."

I laugh. "I'm sure."

"Did you have fun?"

"No."

She hums. "Well. *That* I expected."

Grinning, I peek over my shoulder. No one is in this hall, and I still haven't figured out where the music is coming from. There aren't any doors near me, but it sounds like a mariachi band rented out my ear canal.

"What's been going on?" I ask, squeezing my eyes shut. "Anything I've missed?"

Mom huffs. "No. Not really. Hey, has Marcus mentioned anything out of the ordinary? Acted off?"

"Uhm, not that I know of. Is everything okay?"

"Yes." Her voice is clipped. "Everything's fine. Just curious."

"Mom. You can tell me if it's not."

"No, Celia. There's nothing to tell." I can picture her firm, persuasive smile just from her tone. "I'll let you go, honey. It sounds…busy there."

I sigh. I'm reluctant to let that topic go so easily, but also, I'm ready to explore this place. There has to be some explanation for the noise pollution. "Yeah. It's a bit wild. There are like, forty blonde women that all look the same."

"That happens."

"Apparently."

Mom laughs quietly. I hear a door creak on her end of the phone—our laundry room, by the sound of it. She whispers something that I don't understand before responding to me. "I love you, sweets. I hope you're really doing okay."

"I'm doing great," I tell her. "I'll call later this week. Promise."

"The twins are dying to talk to you."

"I can't wait to catch up with them. I miss hearing about their second-grade woes." I smile to myself. "I love you guys."

"Love you, Cici," Mom says again, right before hanging up.

I shut my phone off and tuck it back in my pocket. Standing is an effort, given that I've lost all feeling from the thighs down. I shake my legs out for a few seconds before stepping into the hallway.

And then I scream bloody murder, because a boy is staring at me, and I thought I was alone.

"Here we have an odd specimen." The boy in front of me tips his head to the side. He's at least my age, maybe older. His voice is deep and quiet, and if I hadn't caught him empty-handed, I'd truly assume I was about to be axed. "Alone, female, eighteen—"

"You sound like a serial killer. And I'm seventeen." I've got no idea why I'm correcting him, save for the fact that I love being right.

He laughs, brightening his already boyish face. I think he attempted to style his brunet hair, but it's fallen now, barely staying put around his glasses. "I was sorely mistaken, then. My bad."

I gasp. "A man who can admit his mistakes? I'm shocked. Stunned silly, even."

"Have I rendered you speechless?"

"No. That's quite impossible."

The boy says nothing, so I start back down the hall.

He follows.

"And you are?" He asks, loosening his tie with one hand.

"I don't talk to boys who sound like serial killers."

"Well, that was an honest mistake."

Stifling a laugh, I look over at him. "I'm Julia," I say dramatically. "Julia Roberts."

"The movie star?" He places a hand over his shirt pocket. "I'm thrilled and honored and a bunch of other words that end in '*ed*' to meet you."

"Exhilarated?"

He snaps his fingers. "That's the one."

I grin. "And *you* are?"

"Oh, Bond. James Bond."

"I should've known. It's all in the fancy suit, right?"

It's definitely not. What he's wearing can't even be called a suit—only a button-down shirt and slacks. I'm guessing he had as much knowledge about the dress code as I did.

"It's certainly not in *this* suit," he says. "I think it's just my charisma."

"Ah."

We turn the corner. I realize that I'm following *him* now, not the other way around. He must be leading me to the correct place because the music keeps getting louder.

"So," I say, "assuming your name *isn't* James Bond—a hypothetical, mind you—what would I call you?"

He laughs quietly. "You would call me August. Though I feel that James Bond fits me better." August looks at me. "But since you definitely aren't lying about your name, I'll continue calling you Julia."

I look straight ahead. "My name is Celia."

"Celia," he repeats. "See, that fits you better than Julia Roberts."

"I'll let my parents know they chose correctly."

August takes a step away from me, just barely, and something in me is relieved. It's a subconscious thing, so much that I don't even know what *it* is. I just know that my shoulders relax at his distance.

"What are you doing at something like this?" I ask randomly.

He looks at me again. I continue looking at the wall. "I'm here for the business portion of things, unfortunately. My father told me I'd *never* make it as a model, and that—"

"AUGUST!"

That word is shouted by a plethora of voices. Just by the sound of shoes smacking on tile, I know that it's a gaggle of teenage boys. A very *loud* gaggle, at that.

"Oh," August says, tapping his head like he forgot something. "I'm also here to win a bet."

"What?"

He grabs my elbow. "Follow me."

"I don't—"

"SHH," he urges.

For reasons I don't know, I'm being dragged down a hallway, and the footsteps of the alleged boy band grow louder. Before I know it, August and I end up in the actual area of the banquet. Balloons and people and cameras are *everywhere*.

"Are we being like…hunted?" I ask, slightly out of breath.

"It's possible." August offers up his arm. I hesitantly loop mine through his. "I can't really explain."

"Try."

He scratches his jaw with his free hand. "Basically…I need you to be my date. Just pretend."

My mouth falls open. "You *what?*"

"Okay. Listen to me. It's a stupid bet with a bunch of stupid boys. Five minutes."

"No!"

"It's for a hundred bucks."

I blink. "Pardon?"

"Yeah. And all you have to do is be my date. *Pretend*," August emphasizes.

"What's the bet even for?"

"Well…" He sighs. "Whoever gets a date with one of the models gets the money."

I nearly laugh in his face. "August, I'm not a model."

"You walked."

"I didn't know what I was doing!"

"Could've fooled me."

I ignore him. "Is that really the only rule?"

He shrugs. "We're boys. We didn't set any specific ones."

Exhaling, I weigh my options. Honestly, what's the harm? I'd do the same if I found myself in a similar situation. It isn't likely, but it could happen.

And anyway, I can get money out of this.

"I'll do it for twenty percent."

"Deal," he says instantly. "Man, that was…way easier than I expected."

"Did none of your friends think to lie?"

August looks offended. "We are an *honest* and upstanding group of young men."

"So that excludes you."

"If that's what it takes for a hundred dollars, yes."

I laugh, just as footsteps come around the corner. I'm not shocked to see teenage boys, but I was expecting more than two.

"August," one of them says. "You were hiding from us."

"Gentlemen." August looks at his left wrist, which has no watch, and sighs. "Has our time come to an end?"

"Unfortunately." The one with curly red hair nods. "Theo managed to put down a whole tray of shrimp *and* scare six girls away."

"Four," the boy, who I'd guess to be Theo, corrects. "Only four girls. And also, you didn't do any better. August is the only one with any sort of game. She's an Audrey Hepburn reincarnate!"

I am not an Audrey Hepburn reincarnate.

August gestures toward me. "Clearly, I'm incredible. We get it. Pay up."

Theo grumbles as he pulls out a few crisp bills. He smacks them into August's palm, and the other boy does the same.

"How much did he pay you?" The red-haired boy asks me.

"Twenty percent."

Theo groans. "I knew it! Is that even allowed? Joshua, do something."

"It was never stated illegal," Joshua murmurs. A giggle escapes me by accident, and he shoots me a glare. "I'm sure *you're* enjoying this."

"Tons," I say, grinning as August slips me a twenty. "You guys really didn't think to do the same?"

"I thought we were playing fair," Theo says, running a hand through his hair.

August smirks. "All's fair in love and models."

"Not true or relevant. Anyways, we'll be leaving now. Dessert table is open."

"You can probably get more shrimp if you hurry," I tell Theo.

He attempts—and fails—to wink at me. "I like you. Optimistic."

That's the last thing I hear before he and Joshua race to the shrimp.

I choke when Theo nearly runs into the door frame. August snorts from beside me, his shoulders shaking with restrained laughter.

"Well," I start, swallowing down my own amusement. "This has been very entertaining. Thank you for the cash. But I should probably get back to mingling, or whatever I'm supposed to be doing right now."

"As should I." He holds out his hand and I shake it. "Julia."

"James."

He walks away. By the time I look over my shoulder to see where he's gone, the crowd of people has already made him disappear.

# OCTOBER 10, 2008

My house is close enough to the downtown area for us to walk. It's almost a little *too* close, given that you can normally hear the parties and drunks. Walking isn't the best idea, but it's pointless to get the car out just to drive a mile.

I wrap my hands around Ben's arm as we walk. "I'm a little nervous about this."

"Why?" He asks, and his voice soothes me, just a bit.

I shrug. "Don't know. Walking always worries me."

"We don't have to go if you don't want to." He stops and puts his hands on the backs of my arms, gazing at me so intently that I have to look away. "Really, Cici. I don't mind. We can stay home and watch movies or something."

His proposal is tempting, but I really do want to go. A local concert sounds like a good way to shake things up. Otherwise, I'll end up asleep on the couch while the twins draw on my arms.

"It's fine," I say. "Really, I'm excited. I say we go."

He smiles and kisses the top of my head. "Okay. Awesome. I promise you, it'll be fun."

I slip my hand into his. "It will."

"And we can always leave, anytime you want. If you get bored, or feel unsafe, or—"

"I know," I say, poking his side. He laughs and throws his arm over my shoulders.

The rain picks up as we walk.

"Well. This is inconvenient," Ben mumbles.

"Very." I look around for a store. At least *one* of them has to sell umbrellas. I think that's a drugstore requirement, along with crosswords, Ibuprofen, and reading glasses.

"There," Ben says suddenly, pointing across the street. A drugstore is right at the corner with hardly any customers inside. "Jackpot."

"Thank God," I mumble, dragging him by the hand toward the store.

We stumble through the door and dry our shoes, then start looking for the umbrellas. To our luck, they're right by the register, next to a rack of reading glasses and walking canes. I forgot all about the walking canes—another drugstore essential.

I dig through the umbrellas and find one with pigs all over it.

"This," I say, holding it up like a trophy. "I want this."

Ben reaches around me and grabs a plain black one. "This one is three dollars cheaper."

I fake a frown. "But the pigs."

"This is what the economy wants."

"Then let them have it."

He buys the umbrella.

# CHAPTER TWENTY-ONE

As is my right, I stay hidden for most of the evening.

Nina didn't give me any pointers or conversation topics, so I'm pretty much useless toward the work she wants done. I feel guilty about it for all of three seconds. It goes away after four different ladies show me photos of their dogs.

Overall, I'd call it a win.

It's been hours since I've seen Nina. People have started clearing out, and the sky is black through the arched windows. I have no idea what time it is. Despite everyone having a Rolex on their arm, I can't get a look at one.

"*Cici!*" Nina hisses.

I whip around and find her ducked behind a dessert table, covering her face with her bedazzled clutch purse.

This has to be a joke.

I stumble over to her. She catches my arm and roughly yanks me to the ground. My knees break my fall, which is extremely unfortunate. This dress does nothing to cover them.

"Okay, ouch," I snap. "What is going on?"

"We have to leave," she whispers. "My ex-fiancé is by the punch table."

The punch table is exactly twelve inches away. I'm not sure why she thought this was a good hiding spot. There is no doubt in my mind that that man can hear us.

"Which ex?" I ask, just to distract her.

It works well enough. Nina gives me the most threatening look she's mustered up all day. "Not the time, Celia."

"We can run for the door."

She shakes her head. "I can't run."

"I mean, you don't have to be an *Olympian* or anything, but we can—"

"I can't run," she repeats forcefully. "I messed up my knee last year. I'll faceplant if I even try."

I almost say that we *should* give it a try, but it's obvious that Nina is in no mood for jokes.

"Why don't we distract him?"

"*How?*" Nina asks. "He's got a Malibu Barbie in front of him!"

That is a great point. The only things around us are knives and fondue forks, and it seems like a bad idea to chuck one at the man.

"Okay, I've got it." I take a breath. "Give me your shoe."

She gasps. "My shoe? My *shoe?* My shoes cost more than your dress!"

"Well, that's plain ridiculous." I hold my hand out, and reluctantly, she removes her heels. "Now. Be ready to run."

"I told you, I can't—"

"Be. Ready. To. Run."

She rolls her eyes. I get up on my knees and peer over the edge of the table. I hardly even know what her ex-fiancé looks like, but there's only one man at the punch table, talking to a girl at least twenty years younger than him.

"The pretty young blonde? With fake-looking boobs?" I whisper.

Nina scoffs. "I cannot believe him."

I take this as a yes, and I throw the shoe at her thigh.

Obviously, I feel terrible about this. The feeling worsens when she screeches like a bat and clenches her leg. But it *does* work—the older man grabs her elbow and goes to her aid immediately.

"GO!" I urge, trying to get Nina on her feet.

She jumps up. Despite her not being able to run, we're out of there in seconds. The limousine is already pulled around front. I wonder if she called for it, or if they just guess when to arrive.

Either way, I don't get to ask. Nina practically flings us into the vehicle when we reach it.

"That was close," she breathes, closing the car door behind her. "And I'm down a shoe. A *Louis Vuitton*! I've never been more heartbroken!"

I look out the window. "Well, I'm not paying for another."

She laughs. Nina, *my* Nina, laughs. Tonight must have gone well for her, besides the whole affair from three minutes ago. Maybe she got the deal that she wanted. But I don't ask, because I don't really want to talk.

It's midnight when I finally check the time. My brain shut off three hours ago, and now I know why. I wasn't made to stay awake for this long; I was made to sleep.

When the limo pulls into Nina's drive, that anxious feeling settles deep in my stomach again. I don't know why it's so insistent on staying when I can't control anything.

Everything I've worried over is completely out of my hands. And still, I can't stop wanting to scream.

"Thank you, Cici," Nina says when we're inside the house. "For everything. I mean it."

"You're welcome," I tell her.

She gives me a slight nod and leaves the room, so I go downstairs.

Before I even consider going to my room, I stop by Marcus's. I tap on the door frame, not really worried about waking him. There's always a chance he's awake, so I'm not shocked when the door swings open.

"You're home," he says.

"You're observant."

"How'd it go?"

I shrug and walk into his room. "Fine. I had to do a model walk, which I wasn't aware of. Kind of my fault, but whatever. I also threw a shoe at Nina's ex-fiancé's girlfriend. She looked my age. So yeah."

He blinks at me like I'm insane. It certainly must sound that way.

"Did you retrieve the shoe?"

"No. And Nina acted like it costs more than our mortgage."

"It probably does."

I laugh under my breath. There's no doubt he's right.

"Hey…" Marcus starts, and his tone of voice scares me. "What's up with you and Ben?"

My stomach drops. "What do you mean?"

He pats the end of his bed. I finally sit down, tugging on the hem of my dress as a distraction. "I've picked up on it all day," he says. "For a few days, actually. Something is just off."

"Something is *off*?" I look at him. "He's a ghost, Marcus. Everything is off."

He just shakes his head. "What's up, C?"

"It's nothing," I lie. I don't want to tell him that I feel like a horrible person. That I feel like Ben is still here—with *me*—because of my own selfishness. That I want to talk to Dad, and even Nina on some level, but everything is weighing down on me and I think I'll break if I say a single word.

He presses his lips together, making them a thin line. It's his serious face. The one that tells me he's getting information out of me whether I want it or not. "You aren't telling me things anymore."

"I don't know what you're talking about."

"We used to tell each other all these things. Everything that came into our minds, everything that happened to us. I want to help you, C."

"This has nothing to do with you." My voice is harsh and my breathing quickens, and I want to stop talking but I know it's useless. I won't stop. Not right now. "I've got to deal with some things on my own. It's how the world works."

"Not for us." He shakes his head. "You don't have to deal with anything alone. Tell me what I can do to help you."

"I don't even know how to *ask* for help, Marcus. Okay? That's what's going on." I take a shuddering breath. "I don't know how to ask for help or say what's bothering me. I know how to be evasive and make jokes. Dad and I have barely discussed anything of importance because I won't let us. It's been idiotic small talk, because ever since I watched Ben die, I can't muster up a single feeling. And now that he's back, I have so many of them, and it's making me feel crazy. It all hit me at once this week—*today*—and I just…"

I let my voice trail off. Tears are stinging my eyes now, but still, I push them back.

Marcus swallows, looking stunned, but he waits for me to keep talking.

"I have no idea what I feel anymore," I whisper. "I haven't cried—*really* cried—since he died. I've teared up and whatever, but that's as far as I'll let it go. Because if I let it out, if I let *anything* out…" I shake my head. "Everything is going to come out, and it's going to be ugly."

The burning in my eyes worsens, and it's so pathetically unfamiliar. It makes me even more upset. Angry, even, at how foreign it is.

"C, I didn't know," Marcus whispers. "I mean, I knew, I just…I didn't know."

A sob escapes me, and tears roll down my face to accompany it. Marcus scoots to the end of the bed, stopping right beside me. He wraps a blanket over my shoulders and hugs me.

"Go ahead," he says quietly. "It's okay. Let it out."

So I do. I let go.

It isn't dramatic. It isn't some movie-montage meltdown, not at first. It takes a moment to feel anything past the tears drying on my face. But after a second of silence, of holding my breath, my chest hurts. And then I hear myself crying, and before I know it, I'm sobbing into my hands. I can't catch my breath, let alone hold it to keep quiet.

Marcus awkwardly pats my back, telling me that this is fine and healthy, and I know he's right. Granted, I can't breathe, but still. He's right.

I lay my face in my lap, ignoring the fact that I'm ruining my dress. My head is pounding and my eyes burn and my chest is so, *so* sore. A piece of tulle is the least of my worries.

For a moment, it feels like I'm never going to breathe again.

For a moment, I wonder if this overwhelming mix of pain and relief is better than nothing.

"It isn't fair," I choke out as soon as I can get a breath. "It isn't *fair.*"

"I know," Marcus says. "I'm sorry."

"He's going to leave again." My voice is muffled but I do nothing to fix it. "He's going to leave, and I'm going to shatter."

Marcus squeezes my shoulder and doesn't say a word. Just lets me cry until I have the hiccups.

It's a fair amount of time before my lungs feel back to normal. Until my eyes are mostly dried. When I take a deep breath and painfully hiccup once more, I realize that I do feel a little better.

I feel empty, but it's a much better feeling than what I started with.

Marcus wordlessly starts digging the pins out of my hair. I'm shocked to see at least twenty in his palm, and that doesn't even seem to be half. When he's found them all, he stands and puts them on his bathroom sink, then returns to the end of the bed.

"I'm ready to talk," I say, my voice thick and raspy.

He nods once. "Okay. Shoot."

I lick my lips. They're dry as sandpaper. "Ben thinks it would be better if he weren't here."

"And what do you think?" Marcus asks, unfazed by the words.

"I don't know," I say honestly. "I'm so incredibly far from reality right now."

"To be fair, me too."

I look at the cracked ceiling, chewing at my lip. "I kept telling myself not to see this as a second chance. Because it isn't. He isn't here. I'd be kidding myself to think otherwise.

"But…if I'm telling the truth, it's just…it's extremely hard not to think that way. It's what I let myself believe at first. And then, like, two days ago, the truth resurfaced again. And I haven't felt alright since."

I wonder if now is the time to tell him about Mickey. It doesn't seem like it.

"He also says he feels like a burden," I mumble.

"Why would he feel that way?"

"I don't know," I say again. "This is just…it's taking such a toll on us, Marcus, and I know why. It's finally clicking in my mind. The truth. The reason why I can't just shut the worry out and enjoy a single moment next to him."

He hesitates, but still asks, "Why?"

"Because we know the end, and it isn't this. It doesn't end with him here."

"I know," he says quietly. "You're right. It doesn't."

My head feels like a million pounds on my shoulders, so I lay back on the bed. "I just feel like an annoyance to bring these things up, you know? I already had something to deal with. My whole family had to process my boyfriend's death with me. That was my *thing*. I don't have a right to whine about my parental issues, or get upset that Nina made a snide remark. That isn't how it works."

Marcus stares at me as if I've committed a crime. "C, yes you do. You have just as much right as anyone else. What you've been through doesn't invalidate what you're going to go through. And if anyone claims otherwise, give me their name and address, okay? I'm being serious."

I laugh, though it sounds more like a cough.

"You're so strong," he continues. "And I know you hate hearing that. But I mean it with as much sincerity as it can hold. Anybody that truly knows you would wholeheartedly agree with me. You've been dragged through the mud multiple times, but it's never changed how you treat people. Not truly.

"You're giving people second chances. You're facing things that have hurt you, and you're facing them head-on. Just because someone is giving you crap for not healing fast enough doesn't mean it's the truth. You're still kicking, C. That's enough."

Even though my cheeks are sticky with tears, I smile. I feel like crying would be an appropriate response to his words, but I don't think I'm capable at the moment.

"Thank you, you mom-adjacent idiot," I say.

Marcus smacks me square in the face with a pillow. "Love you, too."

I sigh, debating whether to sleep at the foot of his bed for the night. That way, I won't risk waking Ben, and I won't have to talk to him until tomorrow. But Marcus coaxes me across the hall, probably because he'd rather not have me sprawled out on a twin bed.

I have to actively force myself to go to my room. It's only a few steps across the hall, but after tonight, it's an excruciating journey. I feel like my soul was sucked out through my eyeballs.

When I flick the light on, Ben stirs.

He isn't awake—or *wasn't*, rather. He sits up groggily and looks around. "Morning?"

"Midnight," I clarify. I mindlessly claw at the zipper of my dress, but Ben stands and unzips the top before I can. I walk to the closet and change, thankful for another moment to myself. A moment to think. Breathe.

"How did it go?" he asks.

"It was alright," I say. "Can we talk in the morning? I'm kind of tired."

"Yeah. Are you okay, though?"

"What do you mean?"

"Cici," he says, and his tone is obvious, even with the closet door between us. "Are you okay?"

I didn't think about the fact that he could probably hear me bawling. That isn't extremely convenient for my argument.

"No," I say honestly. "But I'd rather talk tomorrow."

He doesn't answer. I pull on a pair of old sweatpants and a tank top, then brush my teeth and scrub off what's left of my makeup. When I flop back on my bed, I turn away from Ben. He's looking at me and I do everything in my power to keep my eyes off him.

Unsurprisingly, I fail.

I turn toward him, and my tears fall.

"Cici," he says, frowning. He runs a finger under my eye, catching the one tear that managed to escape. I find his other hand and lace our fingers together. Just to touch him. Just to see if I can convince myself—again—that this is halfway real.

But it isn't.

And I can't. Not tonight.

"I hate this," I whisper. "So much."

"I know," he says, nodding. "I'm so sorry."

My breath catches, and I hold it there in my chest. I curl up on the pillows and tug the quilt tightly around my body.

Ben stands, only to turn the overhead lights off. A moment later he's back at my side. I can't see him, though—I'm facing the opposite way, and all the lights are out. The moon does little to illuminate the room tonight.

"You know I loved you more than life," I hear him say. "I hope you never forgot that. Not for a second."

It isn't a question. He knows he's right.
I don't think he can see me in the dark, but I nod.

# CHAPTER TWENTY-TWO

I'm so exhausted from the previous day that Ben actually has to wake me. He tries to be nice about it—he gently shakes my shoulders, says my name softly.

As a result, I accidentally kick him in the stomach.

"OH MY WORD—"

"I'M SORRY, I'M SORRY!" I say frantically, grabbing his wrist and pulling him off the ground. "You know how I am!"

"I'm *painfully* aware, yes." He sits on the end of the bed, letting out a breathy laugh.

I rub my eyes. "What time is it?"

"Ten or so." He shrugs. "Didn't think you'd want to sleep the day away."

A bold assumption, truly.

"How long have you been awake?" I ask, looking at myself in the mirror. My eyes are puffy and my lips are cracked, and I look about as good as I feel.

"Not long," Ben says. "Maybe ten minutes."

I nod in response and grab my hairbrush. It's nearly impossible to rake through my hair, given the gallons of hairspray sticking it all together.

Marcus knocks on the door frame and walks in without waiting for a response. He's fully dressed and has definitely been awake for a while. I wonder why until I see a donut in his hand.

"You went into town?" My voice brightens at the thought of sugar.

"*And* Nina's gone. Perfect morning. Eat now or starve." He takes a huge bite of the donut—literally half of it—and leaves, stomping his way to the kitchen.

I give up on brushing my hair and yank it back into a ponytail. "At least he brought some for the rest of us."

"Can we talk?" Ben asks quietly, almost shyly. "I don't...I don't want to dance around this anymore, Cici. Something is wrong."

I swallow when I look at him. "Ben..."

"Please. Let's just get it out in the open."

"Okay. You're not real," I say simply. His expression feels like a knife in my chest; it's a mix of disbelief and sadness. "And I'm anxious. I'm so anxious all the time, and I don't know how to fill in the blanks anymore. You're slipping away because you aren't really here, and I'm learning how to deal with it all over again."

He runs a hand down his face, stares at the ground. "Of course I am," he mumbles. "I can't do anything about it."

"I know," I whisper.

"*We* can't do anything about it. And we're both aware."

"So what does that leave us with?"

He shakes his head. "You're smart, Cici. You know that all this will do is hurt you again."

I chew on the inside of my cheek. "I know."

"It's going to be worse this time."

Instead of saying *I know* a third time, I stay quiet.

Ben frowns. "Why are you letting me?"

"Why am I letting you do what?"

"Hurt you again."

I blink, unsure of what to say. He's right, of course. It's just like I told Marcus last night.

*We know the end, and it isn't this.*

He's going to leave. He has to.

"C, I'M GONNA EAT ALL THE FOOD AND I'M NOT KIDDING," Marcus shouts, then loudly chokes on what I assume is another donut.

"GIVE ME A FEW MINUTES," I yell back.

Slowly, I move to Ben and stand in front of him. His eyes search over my face, and this is the first time in a while that I haven't wanted to look away. I stand still as he takes my hand and messes with my fingers. "You'd better go eat. I have no doubt in Marcus's ability to put away a dozen donuts by himself."

I laugh quietly and pull my hand away from him. Ben stands, and we go upstairs. I don't bother changing; Nina is gone, and I can wear whatever I want. Nobody else cares in the slightest.

Marcus, shockingly, didn't eat all the donuts. There are two boxes, one unopened, so I know I'm safe. He and Dad are sitting at the bar with a donut in each hand.

"Save some for me," I joke, grabbing a chocolate donut with powdered sugar.

"Mornin'," Dad says through a mouthful of food. "Are you busy today?"

I shake my head. "No, I don't think so. Why?"

"I wanted to take you to a diner on the other end of town. I'm pretty sure you haven't been there yet. We could go this afternoon and catch up, since you've been busy with Nina."

He's very right. I've hardly talked to him since my first day here.

"That sounds great," I say. "This afternoon?"

"Sure. Whatever time you want." He stands from the barstool and dusts the donut glaze off his shirt. "I've got some work to deal with before tomorrow. I'll be back around noon, and we can go from there."

"I'll be here," I say.

Dad leaves the room, and I listen closely for the sound of a car engine. The second it starts up, I look at Marcus. He's finally stopped eating and is now staring at a napkin.

"Alright," I start. "Remember that hypothetical I told you about the other day?"

He answers without hesitating. "The fake hypothetical? Yeah. Who is it?"

I blink. "*What?*"

"I'm not stupid. Who is it? Someone you met here?"

"A girl at Jones's Records," Ben answers, not at all thrown by Marcus's admission. "That day you were hiding in the game store? We were dealing with that."

Marcus takes a long drink from his mug. "Do you have like…potential reasoning? Or proof? Or even lock picks?"

"Why would we need lock picks?"

"Well, if you told her that Ben is a ghost, she's going to have you admitted."

I sigh. "We didn't *tell* her. That's why we're telling you now. And my word is proof enough! At least, it should be. I wouldn't tease about this."

"She wouldn't," Ben says pointedly.

"Yeah, yeah, your word is proof enough, I guess…" Marcus pinches the bridge of his nose. "But we still have to find a solution."

"Exactly. So help us."

He shrugs. "Just ask how she knows you."

"What if she has no idea?" Ben asks. "She didn't remember my name or face, and I have no memory of her. Where do we go from there?"

"Well, I'd recommend *not* saying you're a ghost. That could get you in trouble."

I huff. "Marcus, we are not going to an asylum. And if Mickey doesn't know him…we still have to tell her, don't we?"

Both their heads turn toward me.

"Excuse me?" They ask in unison.

"What else are we going to do? Isn't it bad to keep her in the dark?"

Marcus shakes his head. It's nearly hysterical. "Absolutely not, C. When you go back home, you'll most likely never see her again. Do *not* mention it."

"Okay, well, I'm also curious."

"Curiosity killed the teenage girl," Marcus muses, swirling his mug around. "This is a bad idea."

"Those are the fun ones."

A lie. This won't be fun, but if I don't convince myself otherwise, I'll back out.

"This could go really wrong, C," Marcus warns.

I shrug. "All things can."

He crosses his arms and sighs. "This has to wait until I've left. I want no part in this."

"You won't even *have* a part in it, but fine." Ben shrugs. "We probably won't even be in town for a few days."

"Good, good," Marcus says. "Just make sure to call and tell me what happens, okay? I doubt she can react any worse than I did."

"You told us to call 9-1-1. That was extremely reasonable."

"Yeah, but *you* didn't even react."

I shrug. "I'm delusional."

Marcus opens the fridge beside me and takes out a two liter of soda. Instead of going to the cabinet for a glass, he unscrews the cap and drinks it straight from the bottle. I'm staring at him, horrified, and before I know it, he's guzzled half the bottle. He replaces the cap and puts it back in the fridge without a word.

Ben looks at him, his nose wrinkled in disgust. "You're joking."

"That's the first time I've done that," Marcus says, eyes wide as he points to me. "Promise."

"No. I'm never drinking an open two-liter again."

He cackles, and then a painfully loud burp leaves his mouth. He coughs and falls to the ground in a less-than-theatrical manner.

"Time of death, 10:12 AM," Ben announces. "I don't think you can survive if you swallow that much carbonation."

"I am not dead," Marcus says heavily. He writhes around like a snake before sitting up. "I'm just broken. Temporarily. I think."

"In the head, maybe."

He groans and burps again.

"Bennet, please babysit him while I shower," I say, stepping over Marcus.

Ben nods. "If he kicks the bucket, I'm not to be blamed."

Marcus claws at his chest, presumably having a heart attack by now. "Yes, you are."

# CHAPTER TWENTY-THREE

Dad comes back around noon as promised.

I'm already showered and ready by that time, so we leave as soon as he arrives. We drive instead of walk, and the only downside is the silence that isn't broken by anything.

The diner we park in front of looks beaten down. It's got the whole classic vibe—white and black checkered floors, red barstools, a jukebox in the corner. The smell of grease is the first thing I notice when we walk in.

We slip into one of the red booths and wait for someone to take our order.

"I've loved this place since I moved here," Dad says, the first to talk. "It's good. Cheap."

"Is it actually old? Or is it meant to look like this?"

He shrugs. "Don't know. I'm assuming it's old because everything here is."

I just nod. Since my chat with Marcus—*chat*, as in, bawling my eyes out—I've decided it's time to talk with my dad. *Really* talk with him. No more surface level nonsense that doesn't matter. I have questions and things to say, and I'm sure he does too. There's no point in keeping them inside.

"Who's Kat?" I ask bluntly.

Dad's face answers the question for me. His eyes soften at her name, and he tries not to smile. It's *so* obvious, but I still find myself awaiting an answer.

"We're seeing each other," he says, letting himself grin fully.

Nostalgia floods me at seeing him like this. That smile is the same one he wore when I was younger. It would appear when he saw my mom after a long day at work, or when he'd hug me in the mornings. I honestly never thought I'd see it again.

My heart is so happy and so broken all at once.

"Did you meet her through Nina?" I ask, because his answer provided very little information.

Dad scratches his chin absentmindedly. "Kind of. It wasn't Nina's *doing*, per se, but I was at her office. The right place at the right time, I guess."

"That's really great," I say, and I mean it. "She seems so nice."

"She is. She's amazing."

I wrack my brain for the rest of my questions, but they seem to have left me. Now I just want to analyze all of Dad's answers.

He looks at me, a sort of frown on his face. "I can tell you aren't thrilled, Cici. You have more to say."

"No, it's not that." I shake my head. "I'm really happy for you. It's just…odd, you know? To hear all of this."

"Why?"

I shrug again, blinking back the tears that tease my eyes. Crying so early in the trip may have been a mistake—now that I've let myself bawl, I'm not sure I'll be able to stop myself so easily.

"I don't know," I say. "Maybe because of the divorce or something. I mean, it's a normal thing, divorce is. It happens a lot. It *shouldn't*, but it does. I just…I don't know. It's

not like I feel as though I was born out of a loveless marriage, if that's what you're implying."

I snap my mouth shut after registering what I just said.
Yes, I'm stunned that I said it. No, it wasn't entirely acci-
dental.

Dad is completely silent.

"I'm happy for you," I say again, because I want him to
know I mean it. "I didn't mean that how it sounded."

"I want you to know something, okay?" He says it
firmly, but his voice isn't mean. It's more like he's determined to explain himself. "It wasn't a loveless marriage. We
were not a loveless family. I did love your mom, and I loved
you. I *still* love you, Celia. I just made a lot of mistakes, and
eventually, they weren't fixable. I messed up. But it doesn't
mean I didn't care for you guys. It doesn't mean that I
wasn't ever happy."

A part of me—the one that always talks before my brain
can think—really wants to argue with him.

*If you loved us, you wouldn't have cheated.*

*If you were happy, you wouldn't have been drunk at every turn.*

*If you cared, you would have stayed for me. No matter what. You
would have been there, and I wouldn't have assumed that it was my
fault I couldn't glue our family back together.*

But I don't say any of that.

Dad must be able to see the gears turning in my mind,
because he takes a deep, shaky breath. "I'm trying, Cici. I'm
trying so hard."

"I know," I say, because I do. He's making more of an
effort than ever before. And while I can't immediately forgive him for the things he did, I also can't hold them against
him so harshly.

Not when I want this back so badly. This relationship
we used to have.

"I thought you'd come back," I start hesitantly. "When
Mom told you what happened. I thought you'd at least call
or come to the funeral."

"Cici, I didn't…" Dad shakes his head. "I didn't think it was my place. At all."

"You're my *dad*. Of course it was your place."

"You didn't consider me your dad at that point," he says. "Don was your dad then. He's still a better dad than I can ever hope to be."

I don't know what to say. Is there *anything* to say?

"I'm not excusing what I did, Cici. But I couldn't be there for you."

I wring my hands together in my lap.

"I can now, though," he tells me. "I want to be there for you now."

Another round of teaching myself differently. Of learning how to know him again. It's obvious that he's changed—I've known that from the beginning. But remembering how it felt, how it feels right now…

*Just one day without a mess of feelings. That is all I truly want.*

"Good afternoon, you guys." The waitress appears and sets two menus in front of us, along with two rolls of silverware and a napkin dispenser. "What can I get you to drink?"

I'm scanning the menu just to look busy when I recognize the voice.

*Mickey.*

She is everywhere.

The classic diner outfit she's wearing is a complete contrast from her normal attire. It's enough to make me second guess if it's really her, but then she says, "Oh, hi. Are you following me?"

I laugh, fully aware that Dad is confused. "I was going to ask you the same."

"Well, no. Two jobs never hurt anyone." She rests her hands on her hips. "Also, the store is at my disposal. Family owned."

"Ah."

Dad finally shoots me a strange look. It's valid; I've got no real reason to know this girl, and we're talking like we've known each other for a while.

"This is Mickey," I explain. "I met her at Jones's a few times."

"Oh," he says, giving her a small wave.

Mickey waves back, then looks at me. "Did you kick your friend to the curb?"

I'm about to answer, to turn the conversation elsewhere, but Dad takes the liberty of answering for me.

"You've met Marcus?" He asks, laughing. "He's back at home, doing God knows what."

Oh dear. Oh no.

Mickey furrows her brow. "Marcus? No, I never saw him. I meant Bennet."

Fabulous.

I start sweating like a pig. This is *not* helping the fact that I'm already on edge. Even though Dad wasn't 'there' for Ben, he *knows* him. Knows enough to connect the dots, to realize something is up.

*Another reason we can't keep Mickey in the dark.*

"Bennet?" Dad asks, his voice tight. "As in—"

"Mickey!" I shoot up from the booth, and she takes a step back for me to exit. "Can I talk to you for a second?"

"I guess?"

"Good!" I walk a little further away, and she follows. It's not like we'll have privacy anyways—this diner is no bigger than Nina's living room. To be fair, it's a big living room, but still. Dad can probably hear our every word.

I wring my hands together and spout off whatever comes to mind. "So, here's the thing. My dad gets names super confused, despite them not being similar whatsoever. He also…" I lower my voice and peek at Dad. He's looking at me inquisitively, and I have no idea how to get out of this. "He doesn't…really know about Bennet."

Mickey nods instantly, understanding flitting over her face. "Oh. Gotcha. I won't say anything."

"Thank you," I say numbly. "It's just sort of messy right now."

"Hey, no worries. I shouldn't have even said anything. Sometimes I talk too much." She gives me a nod, one that tells me to just shut up and listen. Reluctantly, I do.

We walk back to the booth, and Mickey takes the order. This time, she says nothing off script. Nothing other than *'Okay! Do you want fries with that, or onion rings?'*. But the second she's gone again, Dad leans forward, clearly ready for answers.

"What was that about?" He asks. "Bennet? How did she know?"

I shrug. I hope it looks nonchalant, but it probably doesn't, given how tense I am. "I've probably mentioned the name in passing. She must have gotten it mixed up."

Dad pauses to think, to turn the idea over in his mind. He must deem it a valid reason, because he says, "Hearing the name sort of caught me off guard."

"Me too," I lie. "I was really confused."

His eyes are heavy on me. I know he's got more questions—it's obvious by his face.

Answering them before he can say a word seems wise.

"Ben died six months ago," I start slowly. "You know that. But you don't know that I was there when it happened. It was awful, and I feel like no one will let me forget."

I won't even let myself forget. Not while he's still here.

"I'm so sorry," he says, and it's what everyone says, because there's nothing else to say.

"Thank you," I answer. It's what I always say, too.

Unlike the other times, though, I've got other things I want to say, none of which I can voice.

*I'm currently living with the ghost of him. I'm having to rip myself away from him again because the memory is so strong, I can't grasp that he isn't really here. It'll be bad when he's gone. Maybe worse than the first time. But I'm too distracted, too in awe of his presence to care. So I sit and wait for him to leave again, to take another piece of me with him.*

A tear slips down my cheek. I forcefully wipe it away before Dad notices.

"It will get easier," he tells me. "Loss, I mean. I won't pretend to know what you went through, but it gets better. It may take years, but it does."

"I hope so," I whisper.

He's seen the tears in my eyes now. Picked up on the hurt in my voice.

He doesn't talk again. Neither do I.

# CHAPTER TWENTY-FOUR

When Dad and I get home from lunch, I go find Ben. My interaction with Mickey sort of set me off; I'm not risking her finding out the truth through a conversation like today's.

Ben is in Marcus's room, playing a game of what looks like Blackjack.

"I think you're insane," Marcus says, amused. "I think you're ridiculous! Do *not* call it—"

"Guys, hello." I sit down and turn the arrangement into a triangle. "We've got to tell Mickey. Now."

They both blink at me like they've lost their words.

"I mean it. She works at the diner, and she asked where *you* were." I point to Ben. "By *name*."

"Ooh." Marcus winces. "Not good."

"Not at all," Ben murmurs. "So we've got to figure out how to tell her."

I nod. "Yeah. The name totally tipped off my dad. I doubt she'll be around him again, but I don't care. We've got to take care of it before I go crazy."

Marcus sighs. "Well, first off, has she even met me?"

"What does that matter?"

He scoffs. "I'm fun, Celia. *So* fun, and I think she should have a chance to meet a fun person while we're here."

"That is so unnecessarily creepy."

"You sound like a psychopath," Ben tells him.

Another sigh from Marcus. "Pish posh."

"No, actually, what is wrong with you."

"He took a Benadryl," Ben says. "Pet a cat outside and nearly died. Apparently he's allergic to them, but the medicine is making him…weird."

"I think there are more important things in the world than money," Marcus says. He abandons the card game in front of him and starts waving the King of Hearts around. "Like *fake* money, or—"

I tune him out and speak only to Ben. "Can we tell her tomorrow? Please?"

He nods. "Yeah. We'll go tomorrow."

"Okay," I say on a breath. "Okay, perfect."

"But we leave in a week," Ben reminds me. "What do we do after that?"

"What *is* there to do?" I ask. "I can't hide you in my room forever. You aren't like a stray cat I picked up off the street."

On cue, Marcus sneezes. "Don't say that word right now."

I ignore him and continue. "Short answer: I don't know. I have no idea what we'll do."

Ben chews on his lip, his brows drawn together in thought. "I just wish I could see my dad."

My breath catches tightly in my chest. "I know. I mean, you *can*, technically."

"No." He shakes his head. "Let's worry about that when we get back, alright?"

"Okay," I say, closing my eyes. It isn't going to be that simple, not in the slightest. Honestly, I think it may be more complicated than the whole lot of things. But we can make it happen. Surely.

I have to make it happen for him.

✳ ✳ ✳

We waste no time getting to town the next morning.

Ben and I wait a long time before entering Jones's. I figure that, if we stand on the sidewalk for much longer, we'll look suspicious. So I open the door and step inside. Ben walks a few paces behind.

Mickey sees us immediately. The cord of her head-phones is all tangled up in her hair, but she stops tugging at it when we get closer.

"Hey, you guys!" She greets, a smile on her face. Her eyes go to Ben first. "I saw Celia yesterday. I expected to see *you* yesterday, too."

"I was busy," he says flatly.

"Ah, I'm sure." She turns to me. "So, you're already back. How bored are you really? It's not cool here. I could probably close at noon and nobody would care."

"It's either that, or the used lingerie store down the street."

Mickey scrunches her face up in disgust. "I thought they closed that. There was an…incident a few years ago…" She shakes her head. "Anyway, do you guys want to look around?"

Ben and I glance at each other. Mickey must see the nerves on our faces, because she stands straight again. "You guys aren't here to hang out, are you?"

"We just need to talk about something," I start. "Something that we don't really understand."

Her dark eyes flick between Ben and me for a long time. "What?"

"Do you believe in ghosts?" Ben asks. I nearly choke at his bluntness.

"No," she says. "I guess not. I've never had reason to give it thought. You mean like, the ones in movies that walk through walls and stuff?"

Ben laughs. Actually *laughs* in this situation. "No, we can't walk through walls."

Mickey catches on immediately. Her face drops and her cheeks turn cherry red. "You think you're a ghost."

"It's been in question."

"Okay, well, this is a waste of my time." Mickey grabs her headphones and starts untangling them again. "This is so stupid. Are you serious?"

"Unfortunately, yes."

With a sigh, she sets the headphones back down, having made no progress at all. I notice that her hands are shaking; mine are too.

"I can *see* him," Mickey says.

"Okay, so you can. I see him, too, but not many people do. We want to know why *you* can."

"Do you think I'm a witch or something?" A hysterical laugh escapes her. "Quit messing with me."

"I'm not," Ben says. "We aren't. I swear."

"He died last year," I say, forcing her attention to me. "And he's back, and we thought only people that *knew* him could see him. But for some reason, you can too. We're only curious why."

Mickey studies my face hard, like she's waiting for me to break into laughter and slap my knee. I think it throws her for a loop when I stay silent. "You're lying."

I bite my cheek. Of course she thinks we're lying. Any rational person would. But there has to be some way to prove otherwise.

At that very moment, an older lady walks past the window.

"One second, please," I say, jogging outside. I fling the door open, making the bells above the frame ring loudly. It stuns the lady, I think—she looks at me with raised, pencil-drawn brows.

"Hi, excuse me." I smile. "Could you help me with something? It won't take long at all. I've just got a question."

She tips her head to the side. "What is it, dear? Are you okay?"

"I'm perfectly fine," I assure her. "I just need to double check something."

"I'm not very good with this new technology stuff," she warns. "CDs and all that."

"It isn't about CDs."

That's all it takes for her to agree.

We walk back toward the store, the lady's cane clacking on the ground with every step. Mickey and I make eye contact when I open the door. She looks like she wants me taken away.

"Ma'am," I say, gesturing to Ben, "do you see a young boy standing there?"

The lady's face shifts into confusion. She shakes her head while adjusting her pink pearl necklace. "No, dearest, there's no boy standing there. But my eyesight isn't what it used to be…"

"Thank you," I tell her, smiling. "That's all I needed to know."

She looks a bit dazed. Rightfully so. But without another word, she pats my shoulder and walks out the door.

Hesitantly, I turn back to Mickey.

She looks like she's seen a ghost.

Or, rather, she looks *aware* that she's seen a ghost.

"No," Mickey says, and I notice that her face is redder now. "No. I don't know him, but I can see him, so you're lying. Unless I can't see him, and *I'm* the crazy one. But that's not it. Obviously—obviously, it's…" She swallows hard. "I don't know. Just leave."

"You *can* see me," Ben says, his voice urgent. "That's the baseline here. We just want to know why. Like maybe, if—"

"It's a lie," she interrupts. "And I would know if we knew each other."

"Not exactly."

"Please leave," Mickey says, chewing her thumbnail. "I don't like this. I can't stand being lied to, okay? Leave."

I look at Ben, and he nods.

"Okay," I say, defeat bleeding into my voice. "I'm really sorry. We won't bother you anymore."

"Good," she mutters. "Thanks."

We leave with more questions and no answers.

# CHAPTER TWENTY-FIVE

I drag Ben down into my reclusive territory.

It isn't a *complete* negative—we take the opportunity to hang out with Marcus. He's leaving soon, anyway. It's the last thing I need, but I can't very well tie him to the dresser.

"I've got bills to pay, younglings," Marcus says, waggling a finger at us. "Bills to pay, TV to watch, ramen to eat."

"That should be a t-shirt," I say.

"Get it made for Christmas."

The three of us are laying on his bedroom floor now, and the concrete is freezing. Ben put the Bon Jovi record on a while ago. It feels *so much* like old times that I've managed to shove reality out of my mind. Again.

"When are you leaving again?" Ben asks Marcus, hooking his pinky onto mine. Knowing that Marcus can't see makes it funnier. It's like we're kids again, trying to get away with something.

*This isn't the past*, I say to myself. *This isn't real.*

Those words aren't sticking today, and I'm aware of how dangerous that is.

"Day after tomorrow," Marcus says sadly. "I don't have a single thing packed, but we'll cross that road when we find the chicken."

"That doesn't make a lick of sense."

"It *means*," he huffs, "that we'll deal with it when I find the will to do so. The energy. Right now, the floor is my best friend."

"I thought *we* were your best friends."

"One of you is dead, and the other is my cousin. Forgive me if I'd like to branch out a little."

I grin to myself, a way to ignore the somber feeling in my chest. Marcus leaving has made me realize that this whole thing is coming to a close soon. I'm really not okay with it.

"What are you two gonna do without me?" Marcus asks. "You'll be back within, what, a week? Ten days?"

"I think so," I say. "And I don't really know what we'll do. I guess we'll either deal with the Mickey thing or deal with Nina."

He sighs. "A lose-lose, then."

"Precisely."

The room is silent for a moment, until Marcus sits up and looks at me. "You thought she'd be better too, right? Does it make me naïve?"

I shake my head. "No, it doesn't. I thought the same."

He lays back down and doesn't respond.

Conversation tapers off. Our new activity is belting out every song that plays. We sound flat out drunk with the way we're mumbling and giggling through every line. I don't think any of us have even *been* drunk, but I'm guessing this is close.

I keep waiting for Nina to come downstairs and scold us, but she never does, so we stay there and sing until Marcus falls asleep.

Right on the concrete floor. With no pillow or blanket.

"Should we wake him?" I ask, looking around for a clock. There must not be one in this room, because I can't find it. The room is honestly empty in comparison to the rest of the house—it's got a bed and a puny dresser, but no closet like mine does. This must be the *guest* guest room. The one Nina gives to people she doesn't like.

Ben stands first. "Leave him be. He's got to be comfortable enough; he's snoring. The poor thing looks exhausted."

I grab a blanket off Marcus's bed and lay it over him. I also attempt to stick a pillow under his head, but it doesn't really work. Maybe he'll wake up and roll over on it.

"Goodnight, you strange, strange man," I say to him.

He coughs in response.

Ben and I walk across the hall to our room. We've both been in pajamas for hours, so we climb into bed without changing. He reaches across me and turns the lamp off, then leaves his arm draped over me.

When his eyes meet mine, that well of sadness inside me opens up again.

"Everything is changing," I say quietly.

Ben just looks at me. I never hear him say a word.

I wish I could just *ignore* everything. It would make this so much easier, so much more bearable to shut my emotions off and keep everything buried inside.

But all these small things, all these minor changes, they all point to one thing. The one thing I've been aware of this entire time.

I'm getting so used to him being here.

And he *isn't.*

"I'm so selfish," I say quietly, under my breath.

Ben is already asleep. He doesn't hear me, doesn't say a thing. He's still as a rock and his arm is heavy across me.

And so, without anything else to keep my mind busy, I let that thought go further. I let my mind work through what it really means.

*I am selfish.*

The truth.

*I'm the most selfish person he knows. The most selfish person I know.*

Probably still true.

*If he's back, even for a little while, it doesn't have to be with me. Maybe it shouldn't be with me.*

I blink, shocked that my brain has the audacity to think those words. That one was a little too far. No permission was given for something like that to be said.

Lifting my head slightly, I study the look on Ben's face. His features are content, soft, and it's the most gut-wrenching thing I've seen in ages.

*He would tell me if he thought differently,* I tell myself. *He would tell me if he wanted to leave.*

And then I realize what a lie that is.

Carefully, while holding my breath, I roll over and reach for the nightstand. I'm on my stomach and Ben's arm is still over my back, but I'm able to get in the drawer.

I have so many things running rampant in my mind, and I just want them sorted out. That doesn't seem likely to happen unless I can *see* them.

What is my biggest concern? Where do my fears actually lie, and why can't I just *fix everything?*

I don't turn on the lamp. The moon is bright enough tonight that I can see without it.

The glitter pen is still dried up, but I scribble until ink appears and the page rips. I draw circles until I can think of what words to use, where to start.

---

*The past. That's all she had of the boy. No matter how real he seemed, no matter that she could feel him underneath her fingertips.*
*New memories, while made, were little more than a dream.*
*A lie.*
*Conversation is of the past. There is no future. She knows this, and so does the boy.*
*So why does she pretend?*

*Why does she let it go?*
*She knows the answer, and she suspects that the boy does too.*
*Because to live is to feel, and to feel is to bleed.*
*The boy can do neither.*
*But she is a veteran at both.*
-


When I cap the pen, I've already forgotten my words.

I throw the pen on the armchair. Rip the sheet out of the notebook, then in half, and stick it in the back cover.

# OCTOBER 10, 2008

The bar isn't as packed as I expected it to be.

We show the bouncer our tickets when we arrive, then try to find a table. The band is already playing, and by the looks of it, they have been for a while.

"We're late," I say.

Ben sighs, putting a hand low on my waist. "Well, Cici, I can't control the weather."

"No?" I grin and nestle closer to him. "We had to buy a pig umbrella, anyway. It was a necessary purchase."

"Definitely worth the seven dollars," he adds.

We sit at a corner booth, Ben across from me. He looks at the band over his shoulder, and I look at him.

He's beautiful. He'd hate it if I said so, but it's the truth. His golden hair always falls right over his eyes, but it's kept up enough that it doesn't look messy. His eyes are so green that I've always been jealous—mine are just brown. He says that he loves them. I don't believe it.

"What are you looking at?" Ben asks, meeting my eyes with a grin. He knows what I'm looking at, he just wants me to say it.

I won't give him the satisfaction. "The poster behind you," I say, flicking at my jacket's zipper. He turns to look at the picture, and I have to hold my laughter in. "It's an interesting piece of art. The dimensions, the color theory…"

Ben stands suddenly, then appears beside me and grabs my hand. Within a second, I'm up and out of my seat and his mouth is by my ear.

"Liar," he says simply, sending shivers down my neck. "Come on."

"What?"

He drags me away from the table, out into the crowd, then spins me around. "We can't just sit. Dancing is another necessity."

I laugh as his hands go to my waist. "Two occasions in one day."

"And in public. What a shock."

It actually is a shock. I hate stuff like this in public, but I can't be bothered to care today. Everyone else is so occupied with themselves, and half of the couples are being way more handsy than we are. We're just fine like this.

We dance for a good while, in every style I can imagine. It ranges from slow dancing to the absolute worst disco I've ever seen, but it keeps us entertained the whole evening.

When it hits nine, Ben's dad calls him. He steps outside to take it, and I follow. Staying in a bar—*alone*—past 9 PM sounds like peak stupidity. I won't do it.

I'm expecting Ben to receive a normal call, but when he picks up the phone, his eyes turn heavy with worry.

"Okay, are you alright?"

A pause.

"No, n—Dad, we can leave."

Another.

"Okay. We'll be there soon. Cici's with me, is that fine?" He lets out a shaky breath. "About ten minutes. Yeah. Okay, bye."

When he puts his phone back in his pocket, I blurt, "Well?"

He throws an arm around me and guides us around the corner, explaining as our feet hit the sidewalk. "My dad broke his leg. Are you fine with going to the hospital with me? I'll take you home right after, I just need to go there first…"

"Of course I am," I say. "What happened? Is he alright?"

He nods. "Besides the obvious, yeah. He dropped a hammer on his calf. Shattered it mostly, I think."

"How did he get to the hospital?" I ask, my stomach churning.

"A neighbor heard him screaming and decided to check on him."

"Wow," I mutter.

We walk a little faster, but only for a second before Ben stops on the sidewalk. He exhales, frantically looking around us. "We won't get there quickly on foot."

I map out where we are for a second. "Yes, we can. Let's go through the north part of town, hm? Isn't the hospital there?"

He drags a hand through his hair. "Yeah. Okay, that'll work."

I take his hand and keep walking.

We make a couple of left turns, then a right.

We don't say anything. Our only focus is on reaching the hospital.

And then there's a light, so bright and sudden that I freeze and close my eyes.

Ben's hands are suddenly on my body, grabbing me roughly. He shoves me away, so forcefully that I fall on my elbows and knees a couple feet from where he's standing.

And then there's a loud crashing noise, one that sounds heavy.

There are screams and I can't tell who they're coming from.

My heart is pounding and the car's headlights turn off, and I see Ben on the ground and a car on the sidewalk, not the road. There's *so much blood* pooling around him and it's sticky and splattered on my skirt. I'm trying to get my phone out to call an ambulance, but I start crying and then I start screaming because Ben is bleeding on the ground and *my hands won't work.*

I call his name. I say it over and over and over but he isn't saying mine back to me. He isn't saying a word.

The person in the vehicle runs away from the car, covering their face with their sleeve. The side of the building starts spinning and I think I'm hyperventilating but I have to call an ambulance before I pass out.

My head hits the sidewalk.

I barely hear the sirens when they decide to arrive.

# CHAPTER TWENTY-SIX

The next morning, I down mugs of coffee like it's essential for life.

Nina is in this house somewhere, and my senses are acute to the fact. I'm sitting at the bar, pouring my third mug of coffee in the past hour when she comes into the kitchen.

"Celia," she says, then pauses to look at me. "How much coffee have you had?"

I eye the half-empty pot. It was not half-empty before I arrived. "Next question."

"Hm. Have you by chance seen a pair of red shoes around this house? I thought they were in your closet."

It's comical to me that this is our most civil conversation yet, and it's over shoes.

"I don't think so," I say. "I mean, I haven't *looked*, but I don't recall seeing anything."

She sighs. "That's what I thought."

"Do you want me to go look—"

"I'm almost certain that girlfriend of your father's stole them."

My eyes go wide. "*Kat?* You think Kat stole something from you?"

"She was here the last time I saw them," she says, as if it's all the evidence she needs. "It wouldn't shock me. She isn't doing too great lately, Celia. That's why I'm helping her out. She needs a little extra work."

I blink. Apparently, my impression that Nina liked Kat was the wrong one.

"Let me check," I say, standing from the bar. "Before you get her booked for a crime she didn't commit."

"They're *red bottoms!*"

"I have no idea what that means."

Nina huffs but doesn't stop me from leaving.

I move quietly in my room, given that Ben is still passed out on the bed. I have no intention of waking him or Marcus this morning; that would open a door to conversations I'm not ready to have.

I open the closet and dig around the pile of shoe boxes on the floor. Nothing sticks out—I see a box of Nike's and a bag full of fabric scraps, but no shoes with red bottoms.

"Celia!" Nina calls from the top of the stairs.

I stand straight and turn to see if it woke Ben.

It didn't. Nina continues.

"Get changed," she says. "Someone is here to see you."

The idea of putting real clothes on is the most annoying thing I can imagine right now, but I'm in pajamas, so it needs to happen.

Semi-reluctantly, I change into shorts and an old Metallica shirt that Don gave me. I brush my teeth again and tug on a pair of socks so the visitor doesn't have to see my feet. I'd never subject my worst enemy to such a thing, let alone an innocent bystander.

When I look sort of presentable, I go back upstairs.

"Nina?" I call when I reach the living room. "I didn't see your..."

My voice trails off when I see the front door wide open, and the girl standing on the front step.

Nina hasn't even invited her in.

I clear my throat, unsure of where to look. Staring at the floor is definitely not my best option, but I do it anyway for lack of better.

"Hi, Mickey," I say quietly.

She pulls her bright-colored jacket tighter around her body. "Hey."

I motion for her to come inside. She hesitantly steps through the door, closing it behind her.

"Nice house," she says, looking up at the vaulted ceilings.

"It's ridiculous," I say flatly. "Two people live here."

"So a little extra."

"Very."

It's obvious that we have no clue what to say. We've never been this awkward—even the first time we spoke was smoother than this.

"Do I know why you're here?" I ask.

The wording of the question throws her for a second, but she nods eventually. "Yeah. Can we talk?"

"Let's go to my room," I say, leading her to the basement.

Nina is standing at the top of the stairs, watching, but she moves over to let us pass. I open the door to my room and find Ben awake, sitting at the end of the bed. He locks eyes with me the second I walk in, and then he notices Mickey.

I take a seat on the floor. She joins me.

"You're probably wondering how I got here," she says.

"A little," Ben responds.

She plays with the ends of her hair. "Well, I asked around until I figured out where you lived. It sounds creepy, but it wasn't like that. You mentioned a few things that gave me clues. Anyways, I'm here because I believe you."

I glance up at Ben to see if he heard that correctly, because I'm not sure *I* did.

"Really?" He asks in disbelief.

"Really," she says, almost unwillingly. "I've thought about it all night. It doesn't make sense for you to lie about it. And plus, the old lady. I can't see you bribing an old lady."

I shrug. "Not on a good day."

Mickey swallows before continuing. "I'm not apologizing for how I reacted, because that was totally valid."

"I don't blame you," I tell her. "I'm surprised you didn't call a psychiatrist or something."

She grins. Barely. "I considered it."

"My cousin told me to call 9-1-1."

"Also a valid response. I considered that, too." She pulls her knees up to her chin. "I considered everything but believing you. I'm still wondering whether this is the right decision."

Me too.

"Does the lady upstairs know about him?" Mickey asks me.

"Nina? No. She can't see him."

Mickey just nods. "Alright. Well, I've got to go—I have an opening shift at the store. But do you guys want to swing by today and explain everything? This little session wasn't enough."

I nod as she stands. She gives me her hand and tugs me up off the ground. "Yeah. We'll come by the store. Don't try to kick us out again."

She laughs. "I won't. Promise."

I walk Mickey up the stairs and to the door. When she's gone, and I see her steer the purple bike off the driveway, I sit down on the windowsill.

And I think, just for a moment, *What have I really gotten myself into?*

✳✳✳

That afternoon, Ben and I walk to the store. Mickey is excited enough—or, simply sick of working, I guess—to close the store for the time being.

"I'm using the *out to lunch* excuse," Mickey says, flipping the OPEN sign around and locking the door. "I'm also making my brother take my shift. He owes me; I took his this morning."

Instead of waiting for her brother to arrive, we walk to a small park just outside of town and sit at a splintered picnic table. I'm jittering an insane amount, and I can't figure out if it's from nerves or my caffeine intake.

"Alright. How does this whole ghost thing work?" Mickey asks immediately.

Ben clasps his hands together. "We have no idea. I just kind of…exist," he says. "We don't know how or why. It's not that bad, though. Nobody can see me, besides Cici and Marcus. And now you."

"Marcus?" She raises a brow and looks at me. "So that *is* a real person."

"My cousin," I confirm. "You almost had me caught a few days ago at the diner."

She scrunches her nose up. "Sorry about that. I was confused."

I open my mouth to talk, but she looks back at Ben. "So, what do you do now? Do you just like…do nothing all day? *Can* you do anything?"

He laughs under his breath. "All I've done is read and talk to Cici."

"What happens when you go back home?"

*That is the question of the hour.*

"We don't know." Ben answers before I can. "We don't know a lot of things."

Mickey sighs. "You guys should just stay here. I have no other friends, and this has been fun! Besides, how many people can say that they're friends with a ghost?"

"Hopefully none," I say. "But personally, I wouldn't mind staying. I just don't want to stay with my grandmother."

She tilts her head. "Bad blood?"

"More like actual mortal enemies," Ben says, mildly amused.

I shake my head. "It isn't *that* bad. I just kind of deemed her an awful person when she cut off my family over a divorce. She hasn't changed, but it's more bearable, I guess."

It isn't, and I have no idea why I'm defending Nina to a virtual stranger.

"I totally get that," Mickey says quietly. "That all happened with my family a few years back. It's ridiculous, and it feels like beating a dead horse when they make no effort."

"Exactly," I say, oddly comforted that she understands. It shouldn't be a shock, not really—we know nothing about the other. The main thing we've got in common is the ghost sitting beside me.

The rest of the conversation dulls in comparison to our first topic. We discuss everything from books to music to movies. Mickey judges me for saying my favorite show is Gilmore Girls. I judge her for not liking Fleetwood Mac. Ben judges the both of us for not having read Oliver Twist.

It's so different, this environment we're in. Ben's whole being is different. Mine is too. We're smiling a lot more than we have in recent times. I've heard his laugh more today than I have in the past weeks.

It tugs at my chest. I'm not oblivious as to why.

All Ben and I ever talk about is the end of things, and this feels like a beginning.

But it isn't.

I curl my knees to my chest and sit back, just observing. This is all surreal in a way, but there's a feeling inside of me that I can't identify. It's strange and uncomfortable; it feels almost sticky in my chest.

Maybe it's just the knowledge that this is fleeting, no matter what we say to the contrary. It's getting hard to pretend otherwise.

"Cici?" Mickey's voice pulls me out of whatever daze I'm in.

"Hm?"

"You alright?" Her brows are drawn together. "You look like you've just seen a gh—" She lowers her head. "Well."

I grin. "I'm good. Just tired."

"Do we need to go back?" Ben asks me.

I shrug and start tying my shoelaces together. "Up to you."

"Actually, I should get home." Mickey stands from the rotted bench. "I may have pinned my shift on my brother, but I've got chores."

"Can't you pin *those* on your brother?"

She snorts. "Uh, no. Paid work is one thing, free labor is another." She passes me her cell phone. "Put your number in there. We need to do this again before you guys leave town."

Silently, I take the phone and enter my number, handing it back to her without standing. She looks at the screen for a moment before waving. "See you guys."

"Bye," Ben and I say together.

When she's gone, far down the sidewalk, Ben looks at me with a heavy stare. "You okay, Cici?"

I nod. "I'm good."

"You look like you're in your own head."

"I'm always in my own head."

"I know," he says, and his voice is quiet. "But this isn't like always. I know you better than that."

He does.

And that's why I won't look at him, because despite my best efforts to hide everything, he can practically read my mind.

I don't want him to know what I'm thinking. Not right now.

*Maybe you should stay,* I think.

*Maybe we should leave now. Or never.*

*Maybe we should tell someone about you, I don't know.*

*I. Don't. Know.*

"Let's go home," I say, looking up at him. "Well, Nina's. You know."

Ben just stands, pulling me up off the bench by my wrists. He stays close to my side as we walk to the house.

# CHAPTER TWENTY-SEVEN

Marcus wakes me up at two in the morning by dropping an ice cube down my shirt.

"MARCUS," I screech, sitting up in bed and clawing at my back. Ben, unsurprisingly, sleeps through the entire thing. "What are you doing?"

"Come outside," he says, his voice flat.

This is suspicious and mildly horrifying, so I don't move. "I'm sorry?"

"Come outside," he repeats. "Nina has a pool."

"Nina has a *pool?*" How on earth did I miss a whole pool? Have I seriously been that reclusive?

"I want to go sit by it."

I rub my eyes. "But it's April."

"Okay. I still want to sit by the pool."

"So you want to catch a cold."

"There are worse things in life than a sneeze."

I huff, turning my head to see if Ben is awake yet. He isn't—he's out cold, hugging a pillow to his chest.

"Fine." I stand and grab a sweatshirt from my suitcase. I throw it over my pajamas, thankful that I slept in long pants and don't have to change.

Marcus and I go out the basement window, only because he doesn't want to walk up the stairs. It's extremely creaky and sharp on the edges, but we manage to exit without getting stuck or cut.

"This is ridiculous," I tell Marcus.

He doesn't speak. Just keeps his hands in his pockets as we walk.

This is odd, given that he never shuts up.

Nina's pool is in the ground, and despite it being forty degrees out here, there's no cover on it. The water is clear and cool when I dip my toes in. I sit at the edge, my legs crossed in my lap. Marcus sits beside me and does the same.

He's wearing jeans and a windbreaker at 2 AM. And actual shoes. Not slippers like what I grabbed.

"What's going on?" I ask quietly.

Marcus exhales and pulls a handful of pennies out of his pocket. He skips one on top of the water, and I watch it go all the way to the end of the pool before sinking to the bottom.

"I'm leaving," he says.

I blink and turn toward him. His eyes are trained forward, and he refuses to look at me for God knows what reason.

"What do you mean?"

"I mean that I'm leaving."

"Your ticket isn't for another two days," I say. "You can't leave."

He shrugs and flicks another penny at the water, not bothering to skip this one. "I have to. I'll get a cab."

"It's two in the morning."

"My mom called," he says, his voice firm, and I know enough not to speak after that.

Marcus's mom, my Aunt Lena, is about as present in his life as Nina is in mine. She's my dad's sister, and I've spoken to her two times in my seventeen years alive. Marcus moved out of her house the day he was legally allowed. It's why he's got the awful apartment, why he spends most days at my house.

If something is going on with her, something big enough for him to leave and *willingly* go back, then it isn't great.

He doesn't answer immediately. Instead, he holds out his palm and offers me a coin. I take one and toss it across the pool. We watch it with care, waiting until it sinks fully down to talk.

"She's sick again," he says. "Those were her exact words."

I bite my lip. "Sick, or…"

He laughs dryly. "Sick, drunk, it's all the same."

I knew that was the answer. I didn't want it to be, but I knew it was.

Suddenly, I remember my mom's phone call and her question about Marcus. She asked if he had mentioned anything out of the ordinary or acted strangely. I wonder if this has been going on longer than either of us know.

"I'm sorry," I say, aware that the words do nothing.

He shrugs. "She'll be okay. She didn't say more than that, I just…I don't know. I can tell it's bad right now. I need to go back. It's my fault. I haven't spoken to her in months. I shouldn't have just cut her off."

I frown. "It isn't your fault, Marcus."

He exhales shakily, chucking another penny into the water. This one hits the edge and lands on the concrete. "She needs money."

"No offense, but you don't *have* money."

"I also don't have a choice," he says. "But I'll figure it out."

Tears line his eyelashes, and I realize have no idea how to fix this. No idea how to make it easier for him.

"Do you want me to go back with you?"

He shakes his head before I even finish talking. "No. You stay here. Come back in a week, and I'll have everything fixed, and I'll tell you all about it while we watch *Legally Blonde*."

"You can't fix everything yourself," I tell him.

He looks at me knowingly. "Take your own advice, C."

My mouth falls open. How *dare* he address my problems when I'm trying to fix his?!

Marcus barks a laugh, clearly amused by my reaction. "Oh, c'mon. You can't act shocked. We both try to fix things out of our control."

"You don't have to *voice* it," I mumble.

He's still laughing, and I let myself do the same as he throws an arm over my shoulder. "Oh, we need a day off."

"A week."

"Month, even."

Sighing, I grab one last penny from Marcus's palm and throw it in the water. I'd love to see the look on Nina's face when she finds coins in the bottom of her pool. Maybe it will be a nice surprise when she cleans it for the summer.

Actually, no. She has people that clean her pool. No doubt about that.

"I should get going," Marcus says, pocketing the rest of the coins. "If I want to get a cab, anyway."

"You really think this town has a big cab service at night?"

He shrugs. "Big enough to get me one town over, at least."

"And you've got cash?"

"Enough," he repeats, and I leave it at that.

I know Marcus can take care of himself. He knows I can take care of myself. Sometimes, we just don't want the other to. And that's okay.

"We're gonna be alright, C," he says quietly.

I look over at him. "Yeah?"

"Yeah." He nods, looking sure of himself. "We will."

Somehow, that's the most comforting thing I've heard in weeks.

Marcus and I stay by the pool for a few more minutes before going back to the house. I go to his room and discover that he's already packed his things. His suitcase is by the door.

"Tell me everything when you get back, okay?" He says. "Like, keep the details straight."

"I will," I promise. "I'll even write them all down for you."

He grins. "I knew the notebook would come in handy."

I smack him in the shoulder. He gives me a suffocating bear hug before leaving.

I stand near the stairs until I hear the front door close. Part of me expects him to come back, to decide that he'll just wait and take the train tomorrow, but he never does.

Ben is still sound asleep in my room, still holding the same pillow. For a second, I consider waking him, just to tell him that Marcus left. To *talk*, at the very least.

Cautiously, I sit down on my side of the bed, about to reach out and touch his shoulder. He shifts and rolls a little further toward the edge.

I never wake him.

✱✱✱

Mickey texts the next afternoon and asks if we're free.

Of course we are, I tell her—Marcus has left. Dad is out at work and so is Nina. I forgot to ask Marcus if he said bye to them, but I sincerely doubt it.

Ben was shocked when he found out. He asked why I left him asleep, and I never found an answer. I didn't think it was necessary to wake him? I didn't want to discuss it? I thought he looked peaceful?

None. All. I don't know. I just didn't.

We're at the same park bench as yesterday, and this time, Mickey brought food. I take a bottle of some fruit flavored drink and a bag of chips. Ben doesn't take anything, obviously. I'm still not sure how that whole thing works.

"So, wait." Mickey takes a drink of her soda, playing off Ben's end of the conversation. "You just walked into a wall? I assumed ghosts could walk *through* walls."

"I did too," he says, laughing. "It was a shocker."

"Did you even get hurt?"

"Not really."

"Perks of being undead," I say.

She shrugs. "Sounds like it."

Ben tells Mickey everything from the past month, from our discoveries on the train to how alarmed we were in the record store. She asks nearly every question I can think of, besides the obvious.

How he died.

She doesn't dare voice that one. I mentally thank her for it.

Like the last time we were here, I take a moment to observe. To just watch. Ben is laughing at something Mickey said, and I watch his face brighten.

He's so happy. *I* feel happy.

It warms my heart. Kills it at the same time.

"I'm going to the bakery," I say suddenly, standing from the picnic table. My sleeve snags on a piece of wood, and I tug it free. "I'll be back soon."

"Do you want us to come with you?" Ben asks, looking up at me.

I shrug. "No, that's alright. Do you want anything, Mickey?"

She shakes her head. "No thanks. I've eaten there so much, I can hardly stand to look at it."

I take that as a dismissal and go.

I don't even want anything to eat. I just want to walk. To think.

The weather seems to drop a degree every day, even though it's supposed to be getting warmer. I pull my coat tighter around me the longer I walk, so much that I feel suffocated when I reach the edge of town.

The line to the bakery is wrapped halfway around the store. I'd normally leave, but this is prime people watching time. I can listen to the voices around me without having to register anything.

I stand behind a young mom and her son, watching him kick a pebble around on the sidewalk. I smile faintly, thinking of how I often do the same.

For some reason, I wish I had my notebook with me. Stepping out of my mind and changing my perspective seems possible with so much movement around me, and I sort of want to give it a shot.

So instead of letting that go to waste, I look around, and I think of how I'd write this if I chose to. How I'd word the emotions that are flitting around in my brain.

*The girl wonders what good it would do,* I'd start. *A change of people, change of scenery, change of heart. What good will it do when the heart no longer beats? When that breath—his breath—is gone?*

I swallow hard, but I keep thinking.

*She doesn't know. She worries constantly, all the time, that she will never find out. But some part of her knows that she must let the boy choose.*

*This time, it is up to him.*

*But she also knows that he will make the decision best for* her. *Not him. He has always chosen her, every time.*

*And how could that change?*

*It won't. She knows it won't.*

*He will bleed for her, and he will do it with a smile on his face.*

I open my eyes, letting the tears fall from them. There aren't many, and I'm not truly crying, but I let it happen regardless.

That's my fear, then.

That Ben will decide to stay with me, even if he doesn't want to.

*Even though it couldn't matter less.*

"Julia?" I hear a very distinct tone from behind me. "Julia *Roberts?*"

I stand pin straight, spinning around on my heel. "James Bond. It's nice to see you again."

August stands there with a goofy smile, though it's nearly covered by the ridiculous scarf around his neck.

"It's not that cold," I say. "Why do you have a scarf on?"

He shrugs. "I'm cold blooded."

"Like a snake?"

"Like a snake." He pockets his hands. "What are you doing out here in a *windbreaker?* Those don't even hold in heat."

"It matches the shoes."

August looks at my feet, clearly disappointed. "Oh, Julia. Those shoes are white."

"Exactly. Anything matches."

He grins. "You're a mess."

"It has been said before."

The line starts moving when I face forward again. It takes a few minutes to get inside the store, and when I do, I just order a chocolate croissant. If I don't eat it, I'll give it to Dad or save it for breakfast tomorrow. August comes up behind me and orders the same.

"Unoriginal," I mumble, adding a few *tsks* to aggravate.

"You're in an arguing mood."

"It's the normal," I say. "I was on debate team in high school. It's my *passion.*" I put an adequate amount of sarcasm in that last word, hoping he picks up on it.

Whether he does is lost on me, because he responds only to the first part. "You aren't in high school anymore?"

"Graduated early," I tell him. "Also, I got kicked off the debate team."

August gapes at me. "*How* do you get kicked off the debate team?"

"When you wail and cry during the argument so you can win the judges favor."

His jaw drops further. I raise my hands in an innocent gesture. "It was a bad day, okay? I'm not proud."

"You should be. Crying on cue is a talent."

"The school board didn't feel the same."

I check the time on my phone and realize it's been half an hour since I left the park. The walk didn't seem so long in my head, nor did standing in line.

"Hey," I mumble, shoving my phone in my pocket. "I've gotta go. Some friends of mine are waiting in the park."

"I'd expect nothing less," August says. "Julia Roberts is a known socialite."

I grin. "You don't give up, do you?"

"Never," he says, and I suddenly wonder if he means that in more ways than one. "I'll see you around?"

"Maybe," I say, trying to brush off my last thought. "I'm leaving to go back home in a few days."

He tilts his head. "Well, perhaps I'll see you before then."

"Perhaps you will."

August waves to me and walks away.

# CHAPTER TWENTY-EIGHT

Slowly, *very* slowly, I walk back to the park. My feet keep a dull pace, and every time I try to go quicker, I end up slowing back down. Maybe it's a subconscious thing.

When I finally sit down at the picnic table, it takes a second for the conversation to break. I stay quiet as Ben and Mickey laugh, the sound a result of some joke I didn't hear.

"Hey, Cici," Ben says brightly, turning toward me. "You were gone for a while."

"Were you?" Mickey's brows draw together. "Gosh. Time is getting away from me lately. I feel like my grandpa."

I clasp my hands in my lap, staring at a tree behind Mickey. A gust of wind hits me in the face, and I blame that for the stinging in my eyes. For the reason my vision is blurred with tears.

Mickey starts rambling on about something, and I'm relieved. I think I'm doing an okay job at hiding.

But I'm not.

Ben notices. He always does, and he knows it isn't the wind.

"Hey," he says under his breath. "Are you okay?"

I nod. "I'm great. What did I miss?"

Mickey fills me in. Apparently, they discussed *everything*, from her twenty-seven-pound cat to rumors about a man that lives three streets down. Ben never speaks; he just watches me with a concerned look on his face.

Mickey is talking about something I haven't registered when my phone rings.

"Hello?" I say sort of frantically, holding the device to my ear.

"Celia." It's Nina. "I've got your train ticket taken care of for the weekend."

I squint in confusion, even though she can't see me. "What?"

"I purchased it," she says. "I just wanted to let you know. I know you're in town, and I didn't want you at the station buying one."

"Oh, okay. Thank you so much."

She makes a humming noise before hanging up.

I pocket my phone and find two inquisitive faces watching me.

"Nina," I say, as if that explains it all.

Mickey just nods. Ben, however, is still looking at me with that worried expression, and I don't like it. Not one bit.

"We'd better get going," he says suddenly, standing from the bench.

I stare up at him with wide eyes. Does he know something I don't? Did something happen while I was gone?

*Is he about to make the decision for me?*

"Okay," I say, standing as well. I grab my croissant off the table and fold the bag until it fits in my coat pocket. "Bye, Mickey. See you before we leave?"

"If you can swing it."

"I'll try," I tell her.

Ben and I go before Mickey even stands. We start across the road, and neither of us say a word until we're back on the sidewalk.

"What's wrong?" I ask.

"Nothing's wrong with me," he says noncommittally. "But something is up with you. I can tell."

"No. I'm okay, Ben."

He looks down at me. Grabs my hand and weaves our fingers together. "You're lying."

Well, then.

"It's nothing," I say again. "And anyways, even if it were, I wouldn't want to discuss it here."

"Hence why we're going back to Nina's."

I nearly trip over a grate in the sidewalk. We don't talk again, not until we're at Nina's house, standing in the empty kitchen.

"Okay," Ben says, crossing his arms. "Let's talk about it."

"I don't know why you're so intent—"

"Because something is *wrong*," he says, and his voice is much firmer than I've heard before. "Something besides the obvious, and I don't know what. But I can feel it, and I *hate* it, Cici."

I lick my lips. How do I tell him? That I think he needs to stay, that I need to go? That there's no point in any of this, not really, when he'll be gone the next time I turn around?

"Ben," I say, deciding to just go for it. "I think…you should stay here."

His entire face falls. Immediately, I'm aware that was the wrong way to start this conversation.

"What?" His voice is so soft, so disbelieving. "What are you talking about, Cici?"

"You are not *here*, Ben. And we both keep forgetting it."

He swallows hard.

"It's selfish of me to want you to stay with me." I'm regretting my words as they form. "If we go back, if you go back to *my house* and *our town*, what can we do? It won't work."

"No," he says quietly. "No, that's not—no." Ben shakes his head, and his cheeks flush. "What are you talking about?"

"Maybe this will last," I say, aware that I'm lying through my teeth. "Maybe this is some insane second chance, but it isn't back home. And it's not that I don't *want* it." I exhale, my breath anything but steady now. "I want it so badly, Ben. But it won't work like that. It isn't possible."

A tear rolls down my cheek. I didn't even realize I was crying.

"Is this about her? Mickey?" He asks, and his voice cracks. "Or did you meet someone?"

And that's it.

That's my breaking point.

I don't know what to do. It's too late to back out of this, but even if I did, I don't see it ending differently.

"I didn't mean it like that," Ben adds, covering his face with his hands. "Obviously. I just…I didn't know—"

"No." The word is uncharacteristically numb. "No, I didn't meet anyone. This isn't about me. It's about logic and about *you*—"

"It isn't," he says. "This isn't."

"Yes, it is."

"You put your entire life on hold for me." Ben's eyes are red now, but he still isn't crying. I don't even know if he can. "You put everything on hold."

"Because I had no *choice*," I cry. "I didn't have a life anymore, Ben, because the one good thing I had was gone. But that doesn't mean I can like, keep you in my room until you just…just go *away* again."

I feel a sob slip out of me. Ben grabs my shoulders, but I don't look him in the eyes. I can't right now.

"Look at me," he whispers.

I shake my head, biting my lip so I don't cry more. My eyes are trained on his worn-out shoes.

"Cici, please," he begs, squeezing my shoulders. "Look at me."

I lift my head but keep my eyes closed for a few seconds. When I open them, everything is still blurry.

"You can't do this," he says, brushing my tears away with his cold fingers. "You can't."

"You're here for closure," I say, taking a breath. "I wanted you to come back and stay with me forever. I still *do*, Ben, but that isn't why you're here. You said it yourself! This isn't *real!* You have to stay while you've got some semblance of a chance. You need to take it, but I can't give you that. Not when I go back home."

He presses his fist to his mouth, closes his eyes.

And I see it.

I see a tear fall.

I see myself as the reason he's crying.

*I didn't know he could cry.*

"You're killing me," he breathes. "You are *killing* me, Cici."

"Ben, don't," I whisper.

"You blamed yourself for my death, and you were wrong." He takes a step to the side, leaving me here alone. Cold. Numb. "You were *so* wrong, but this…this is your fault."

That's the worst thing he could have said, and I deserve every word of it.

"I'm so sorry," I whisper.

When he doesn't respond, I ask, "Are you going to tell me you haven't considered it?"

He looks at me, and his eyes break my heart.

He isn't angry. He's never been angry, not at me.

But he's hurt. And I think that's worse.

"Considered *what?*" He asks.

"Staying here."

Ben instantly averts his eyes and stares at *my* shoes. It's all I need to see to know that I'm right.

"That's okay," I say softly. "It's fine for you to want that."

"But you're *right*," he says, frustrated. "It's not real. None of this is. I don't—" He covers his eyes and takes a deep breath. "I don't know. I don't understand."

He's worn down now. We both are. I think we're at some standstill, me leaned against the counter and him by the refrigerator. I hesitate for a second, but only that, before walking forward and pulling him closer. I wrap my arms around his neck and he hugs me back, so tightly that I nearly yelp.

"I didn't want to do it this way," he says, muffled by my shoulder.

"I know you didn't," I breathe. "I didn't either."

He doesn't step away. I can feel his shoulders shake against mine, and it threatens to break me. Threatens to crack this half-formed mask I'm wearing, one that will be useless after today.

So I just let myself cry. It is only a half-formed mask, after all. Ben knows me too well.

"I loved you, Celia," he says, and the past-tense along with my real name makes my head hurt. It makes this serious. "That never changed."

"I know that," I say.

"This means that you can move on, too. You got the closure you wanted." He takes a heaving breath. "You never needed me here for that, though."

"Yes I did," I say thickly, and he doesn't argue.

"We've got four days."

I blink. "That's it?"

"Yes. For now."

He says it like he has every intention of coming back. I let myself revel in the impossibility.

So we make a deal.

Ben agrees to stay here. We don't know what that entails, and I'll probably never find out.

I agree to go back home and live the life I forgot about over the last six months. It's a simple bargain, much more than his, but it's all I can do.

The garage door opens, so Ben and I walk downstairs. The second we're in my room, I find my backpack and take out two books and an ink pen. *Twilight* and *Wuthering Heights*.

I nearly laugh at the contrast.

I uncap the ink pen and bend the cover of *Wuthering Heights* back, then start writing in it.

*Dear Ben,*
*Ignore my choice of words—you know I'm a sucker for irony.*
*Just live. Please.*
*PS. I would write some joke pertaining to this book, but I never fin-ished it. Sorry. I lied to you when we were kids.*

I hand both things to Ben, telling him not to read the note until I'm gone. He nods and wordlessly does the same, taking my copy of *Twilight* and scribbling in the front cover.

We don't say much for the rest of the day. It isn't out of irritation or annoyance; we've simply said too much. Too many things that we did not want to say.

Silence is a lovely alternative.

# CHAPTER TWENTY-NINE

Ben isn't in the room when I wake up the next morning.

I lay still for a while, trying to go back to sleep. If I don't get up, my problems stay minimal. It's the whole *starting the day* thing that seems to be the problem.

Besides, I thought we'd talk this morning. But this is fine.

Emotions are swirling around inside my mind and chest. Yesterday evening is in my memory like a bad dream. It feels unreal. The only thing pointing toward it being the truth is Ben's absence.

Aware that my problems aren't going away, I sit up and grab my notebook off the nightstand. I uncap the pen, take a breath, and write.

-

*Sometimes, she felt as though she only had half a heart.*
*She thought that the boy took the other half with him.*

*Sharing her heart was something she didn't like, not at first. It was uncomfortable. Odd. Terrifying, she had said, when he asked why she was hesitant.*
*Because she was scared. Scared of how easy it felt to give it to him.*
*She had never been so eager and willing to share something before. So willing to let a part of herself go for someone.*
*But for him, she did. She would've given him the whole thing if he only asked her to. Every feeling, every emotion. Every thought that she knew no one should see.*
*He could have them all. He already did.*
*He knew her like the back of his hand. Better than she knew herself.*
*-*

I put the pen down and close the notebook, tucking it back into the drawer. Eventually, someone is going to find it. I just hope that day isn't today.

I watch the clock hit nine and roll out of bed—like, actually roll off the mattress and into the floor. I just stay there, because I have a headache and I'm too lazy to hike upstairs for Ibuprofen.

"Cici?" My dad's voice rings through the basement. I don't bother getting up, but he laughs when his feet stop outside my door. "You used to do that as a kid."

"Lay on the floor?"

"No, fall off the bed. I saw the whole thing when I was coming down the stairs."

Dehumanizing, but alright.

I stand and rub my eyes until I see spots. They feel like they're going to pop out of my skull and land on the rug. When I open them, I notice my dad is dressed for the day. He's wearing fancy clothes—a suit and tie—which is definitely not normal for him. The only time I've seen him wear something similar was to my granddad's funeral.

"Who died?" I ask, in perfect logic.

Dad chuckles and scratches his jaw. "Fortunately, nobody. But I've got a job interview today."

I raise my brows before considering that that might look rude. He never told me he was looking for work, but I'm not shocked. I can't imagine he wants to live with Nina forever.

"That's really great," I say. "Where are you interviewing?"

"At the bank in town." He looks in the mirror behind me to straighten his tie. I move to the left so he has a clearer view. "I haven't had good work in a while. Just a few jobs here and there, enough to pay rent to Nina." He pockets his hands. "I just hope this is something I can keep for a bit."

"That's great," I say again, hoping I sound more genuine than I often do. "I hope you'll get it."

Dad smiles. "Thank you. It's the first step in getting my life back to semi-normal, I think. Hopefully soon, I can move into my own house, *not* live with my mother…"

I let out a laugh. "I understand."

"I'm also looking at some apartments," he says quietly. His tone is almost nervous. "After the interview. Would you want to join? If you've got no other plans for the day."

The invite catches me off guard, but I'm not as surprised as I would've been three weeks ago. It's not a bad offer; Ben isn't here, Marcus is gone, and Nina will probably show up at some point. Leaving provides nothing but positives.

"Of course I will," I say. "What time?"

"I'm not sure, really. I'll check when I get back from the interview. Also." He squints at my face. "Are you sick?"

I balk, offended, but then I remember crying for an hour last night instead of sleeping. "Uhm. No. Just allergies."

"Ah."

With that, he checks his watch, mumbles something, and walks out of my room.

Dads are very gullible. Mom would never have believed that.

He isn't wrong about me looking sick, though—my eyes are swollen and my nose is still red. I go to my sink and splash some cold water on my face, then brush my teeth for far too long.

Getting dressed is a feat. I've worn my entire collection of jeans while I've been here (as in, three pairs), so I choose something a bit fancier. The only thing I have to fit that criterion is a brown corduroy skirt and a white sweater. It screams *autumn* instead of *the middle of April,* but it works.

The second I sit down to put my boots on, my phone rings from the nightstand. I flail around until I can reach it, then promptly knock it into the floor. There's a new chip on the corner when I pick it up.

"Hello?" I answer, not bothering to look at the caller ID.

"Hey, C."

"Marcus?" I sigh with relief. "What are you doing? How's Aunt Le—"

"Don't ask about that," he says, sounding drained. "I'll explain it all in person when you get back. That isn't why I called."

"Okay," I say slowly. "Why did you call, then?"

"I just need a distraction." I hear a car horn in the background, so I assume that he's walking outside. "How's everything going?"

I tug on the sleeve of my sweater. "I don't know how to answer that."

"Expound."

"I don't know," I say again. "Give me somewhere to start."

"Okay. What happened with Mickey?"

Oh lord.

"Well, *that* went well. Let's start there."

"That's good, then."

"Eh. She kicked us out of the store at first, then found us later and said she believed us. We've told her a lot since then."

I leave the details out for his sake, because I know he'd rather ask questions than be told all in one go. He prefers interactive story times.

"Makes sense," he says. In the background of the call, I hear a man yell at someone—presumably Marcus—for nearly running into him. Marcus seems to ignore this. "How's Ben?"

"Currently?" I say lightly, a giggle bubbling out of me. It isn't a genuine one. I'm feeling a bit delirious. "I've got no idea. He isn't even here."

"You ran him off?" He says it like a joke, probably because of my tone.

But I don't respond.

"C?" He says nervously. "You're supposed to laugh and argue, not shut up. What happened?"

"Honestly? I ran him off."

"Not funny."

"Not kidding."

"CELIA?!"

"I *am* kidding," I say, then pause. "Kind of. We just…I don't know. I told him what I've been thinking."

"Which is?"

I swallow. "That this can't go on, obviously. That I can't bring him back home. I told him he was given some insane, impractical semblance of a second chance, and he needs to do what he thinks he should. But I also know he'd make that decision for me over himself. And I won't let that happen."

*He chose me over himself last time, and it cost him his life.*

Marcus sighs. Keys jangle around, so I assume he's made it to his apartment. "You wanted him to stay, though."

"Of course I did."

"I thought you were going to lock him in your closet for the rest of his ghost-hood."

"I don't think it works like that," I say.

Marcus pauses. "I get it."

"Really?"

"Yeah. I mean, we don't know how long this will last. And no matter what we may have believed otherwise, Ben isn't here. Not how you want."

His last sentence is very quiet. I wonder if I was supposed to hear it.

"I forgot it too. For a little while." Marcus exhales. "When we were all laying in my room, being ridiculous? That was too real. It was weird to leave it."

I bite the inside of my cheek. "Really?"

"Really. No one's blaming you for being confused."

"Thank you," I say, exhaling. "I think I needed someone to validate everything."

"What did Ben say about it?"

I shrug even though he can't see me. "He thought it was about Mickey at first. By the end, I can't even remember. I was trying to stay out of my emotions and use logic."

"*Dang*," Marcus mutters, turning his sink on. "Didn't expect that."

"I know."

"Well. If you need to call me, I'm free. Anytime. Even if I'm working, I'll stop working. You best believe me on that one."

I grin. "Thanks, Marcus. And same."

"See you in a few days, C," he says.

"Don't break the store's coffee machine while I'm gone," I say, and we substitute that for *goodbye*.

✳ ✳ ✳

"The first apartment is pretty cheap rent. It's not in the absolute *best* condition, but I think I can fix it up enough."

Dad talks his way through the wrong turns we've made so far. I haven't been to this part of town yet, and I'm starting to think he hasn't either. Neither of us are good with directions *or* rules—I told him to turn right in a NO RIGHT TURN zone, and he took a left on a dead-end street. Our failed attempts at reading the battered street signs would be comical if they hadn't set us back.

We're ten minutes late when we make it to the complex. The building isn't dilapidated like Dad led me to believe—a little worn down, yes, but all good buildings are. It looks to be about twenty floors from the ground.

"I'm checking out an apartment on the fourteenth floor," Dad tells me, noting my gaze as I count the windows.

Eighteen. Eighteen windows, two with Spider-Man curtains. Not that it matters.

The automatic doors open as we step on the front rug. Immediately, a man approaches us, smiling and holding out a hand to be shaken. "Carlos Turner, I assume?"

"Yes," Dad responds, shaking the man's hand firmly. "Nice to meet you."

"We'll be viewing a place on the fourteenth floor, correct?"

Dad nods. "1406, I believe I was told."

The man pulls a clipboard out of thin air and reads over it. "Yes, exactly that. Follow me."

We do follow him. It's one of those stiff, awkward walks where someone should make small talk but nobody does. The elevator is the same level of quiet until I notice something weird about the buttons.

There's no floor thirteen. It goes *eleven, twelve, fourteen.*

"Why is that?" I ask, pointing right between the number twelve and fourteen. "Why isn't there a floor thirteen?"

The man sighs, sounding irritated but not rude. I'm assuming he gets this question quite often. Maybe that's why he doesn't talk first—he wants to see who's stupid enough to ask.

"The people who built this place were horribly superstitious," he says. "They thought it made more sense to skip it, rather than to have the cables snap on that floor."

"Interesting," I mumble, staring at the panel of numbers. "I can't agree with the bad luck, though. Thirteen's a cool number."

He raises an eyebrow now, seeming more intrigued. "Your birthday?"

"A friend's," I say.

Ben's.

The man gives a deep laugh. "Me too, actually. My wife's. How ironic."

I lean back against the wall, my hands bracing my lower back. This is a *very* slow elevator. Dad looks at me when the doors finally open, and I can tell he's nervous about this whole thing.

We follow the man to the door. He sticks a rusty key in the lock and twists it, opening the door to an empty apartment.

"Fairly nice space. Not huge, but not small. Two bedrooms, one bathroom, small kitchen and living area."

Dad doesn't speak for a few seconds. He simply observes the space, sweeping his eyes across the room a few times. The apartment guy and I wait as Dad walks through the rooms, basking in each one before coming back out.

"I like it. A lot." He looks at the man. "When would I be able to move in?"

"Beginning of next month."

Dad looks at me. "What do you think? You could have the big room if you wanted. I could put bookshelves in there for you."

I blink. A lump forms in my throat at his asking, at the fact that he cares. "Yeah. I love it. I think you could decorate it really nicely."

He smiles and turns back to the man. "Could we talk about rent?"

"The apartment is yours," the man says simply, walking out into the hall.

After way too long of talking about money and rent and down payments and a bunch of other things that go into getting an apartment, Dad and I celebrate with scones from the bakery. It's a good ten-minute walk from the apartment complex, I think—only a few minutes' drive, but I don't drive.

"You are way too obsessed with this place," Dad says, as if he didn't buy three scones for himself. "You know, I worked here back in the day."

"Really?" I ask. "I can't see you being a baker."

"Cashier," he corrects. "It used to be a bit more…hopping than it is now."

"Well, unlike everyone else, *I* appreciate the place. There are no good bakeries at home. One of them serves muffins cooked to ashes, and the other only has cardboard-adjacent cupcakes. Eating something that doesn't taste like Styrofoam is nice."

He grins as we sit at a small corner table. I'm smiling to myself, unfamiliar with this sense of joy I'm feeling, but when I look back at Dad, his face is straight. Completely solemn.

"What's wrong?" I ask before I can think the better of it.

He looks over my head. "I was bribing you with the bookshelves."

"What do you mean?"

"I'm sorry." He exhales. "Cici, if you don't want to visit me, just know I won't be mad. I completely understand, and I don't want you to feel obligated."

I pause. That wasn't what I expected to hear, and now that it's out in the open, waiting for a response, I've got no idea what to say.

For the first time, I wonder if that's why he wanted my input on the apartment, and the job, and his girlfriend. He wanted me to be okay with it all. Because he cares now, and he wants to be in my life as much as I'll let him.

"I want to visit you," I tell him. "As long as you don't make me talk to Nina."

He chokes on a laugh, his entire face brightening. "Why do you think I'm so eager to *leave?*"

The exact same laugh slips out of me. "Gosh."

Dad sits further back against the creaky chair. "I just want you to know that it won't be like last time."

*Last time,* as in, most of my childhood. The memories of what he did to my mom and me float to the forefront of my mind now, and I wonder if it's okay to tackle them. It feels worse to let them roam free.

"You'll be back in my life now," I say, more of a statement than a question. "On a normal basis. I'll be able to call you and you won't pick up drunk and angry, or out—"

"I won't," he says firmly. "And I know it's impossible to make it up to you, but I want to try. I want to be the dad you deserve. I've done such a screw-up job for seventeen years, but I can do better. I'll try to do better." He pauses and shakes his head, almost like he's carefully planning his next words. "No. I *will* do better, Cici. Period."

I twist the ring on my thumb. Bite the inside of my cheek. I didn't come here to reconcile things with my dad, not directly. Even today, I saw this as a distraction from Ben. An excuse to get out of the house.

But this is a positive. I'm finally seeing it as a good thing.

"Okay." I nod. "Yeah. I'd really like that."

He smiles. I see tears in his eyes, and I wonder if they're for joy or sorrow. Maybe both. "Thank you for giving me another chance. It means more than you could ever imagine."

I'm not sure what to say to that, so I nod and eat the other half of my scone.

# CHAPTER THIRTY

When we get back to Nina's, she's screeching about a rat.

"IT WENT UNDER THE COUCH!" She cries, hands in her hair, and I'm worried she'll rip it out from the roots. "CARLOS, YOU DIDN'T SEE IT! IT WAS THE SIZE OF A GOPHER."

"Correct, Mom. I did not see it, and I still can't." He's on his stomach on the ground, head angled to look under the couch. "I think it's gone now. Or, maybe—"

"Don't you dare say I imagined it!" She stomps. "I can't possibly have imagined something that ridiculous running through my house! I think he had bags! OH LORD—HE WAS MOVING IN."

"Mom, *please*," Dad says, standing from the ground. He does that grunting thing guys do when their backs hurt, then flops down on the couch. "I think we're fine. Put a few mouse traps out."

"I can't! What if I step on one?"

He looks at her, so appalled that I almost laugh. "As a person, you can't avoid a mousetrap?"

"I'm a busy woman, Carlos." She crosses her arms. "I don't have time to look where I walk."

Dad and I roll our eyes in sync.

"I saw that." Nina huffs and looks at me. "I've had a very rough day! Meetings were canceled, finances were run through—" She looks at the ceiling. "I'll be in my office until dinner."

I would respond, but she walks away before either of us has to.

Dad sighs and leans his head onto the back of the couch. His eyes close, and I count down *three, two, one*, before he starts snoring like a leaf blower.

Laughing to myself, I walk down the stairs to my room. I'm hyper-aware that a mouse could scurry across my foot at any time, so when I reach the bottom of the stairs, I basically sprint to my bed and jump onto the pillows.

In doing so, I almost crush the ghost laying there.

"Oh," I say, sitting up. "Ben."

"Cici." He says my name as if we're perfectly normal again. His voice is its usual tone—not angry, or hurt, or cold. I'm expecting any or all of those things, and not hearing a single one throws me.

He sounds…numb. Absolutely numb.

Me too.

"I didn't know you'd be gone," he says. "I would've left a note, or—"

"It's okay," I say. "I didn't plan on it either."

We stay quiet for a moment, shifting toward the other until we're face to face. Ben's eyes are so hollow, his face unreadable. I wonder what I look like from his perspective. I wonder if he can see the thoughts that I'm very poorly hiding.

"What are your worries?" Ben asks.

I frown. "My worries?"

He nods.

"I've got a lot," I say. "That isn't a fair question."

"Tell me just one."

I bite my cheek. 'Just one' is still too broad a category. I can't pinpoint my thoughts on a *normal* basis, but this? This is worse.

Regardless, I start thinking. The words will find their way out eventually, just like they always do.

"I am worried," I say, my tone cautious, "that when you're gone, nobody will ever know me again. No one can know me so wholly as you did. Especially not now.

"You—*this*—it's all a part of me. Something that will make me into another version of myself. And I cannot tell anybody."

He looks at me, his mouth pulled into a frown.

"Nobody will ever know me," I say again. "And all I wanted was to be known. I had that in you."

Ben reaches up and moves my bangs away from my eyes. "I'm sorry. I'm so sorry, Cici."

I shake my head as much as I can while laying down. "Don't apologize. How are you?"

"I'm okay," he says a second too quickly.

I wonder what we say now. What there is to talk about, now that we've accepted our ending.

"I was with my dad this morning," I say quietly, my way of testing the waters.

Ben's eyes brighten. "How did that go?"

"Good. He's getting a new job, hopefully. And an apartment."

"Really?" He asks, and I nod. "That's amazing. I'm happy for him."

"So am I."

Soon, our words turn to shaky breaths. There's so much I need to say, or at least *want* to say, but I don't know where to start. Is there a reason to say…anything? Do we bask in this silence, or do we talk and talk until we can't?

"I read your notebook," Ben whispers.

I whip my head toward him. "What?"

"The one in the nightstand. I found it." His throat bobs. "I'm sorry. I wasn't paying attention to what it actually was, and when I realized, I couldn't stop reading it."

I fold my hands across my stomach, unsure of what to say. No one was meant to read that, *especially* not Ben. But I can't be mad at him.

It's not like I tried that hard to hide the notebook, after all. It was shoved in a drawer.

"Well?" I prod. "What did you think of it?"

"I think that you're amazing," he says, and when I look at him again, he isn't looking at me. "You're so amazing."

"What do you mean?"

"Your heart is whole. I never took that from you."

It takes me an embarrassingly long time to remember what I wrote, but when I do, I shake my head. "You did. I didn't even know what I was capable of feeling until I met you."

Ben shakes his head in return. "You've still got your heart, Cici. It may be broken, but it's still yours. You are still capable of feeling, whether you want to be or not. That didn't change."

I feel a tear roll over the bridge of my nose.

"You feel—*so much*." His voice is so quiet. "You always saw it as a bad thing. And you thought that when I was gone, I took all those emotions with me. But I didn't. They're still with you. You're still sensitive; your heart is still soft. And it's beautiful."

I wipe my eyes again, keeping them on him. He's staring up at the ceiling fan, like he can't bear to look at me after what he just said.

"Are you mad at me?" I whisper.

Ben's face falls. "Mad at you?"

"About last night."

"No, I'm not mad at you."

"Okay," I say, suddenly embarrassed.

"I'd never be mad at you for something like this," Ben tells me. "I know you think I am, or that I'll resent you or something, but I wouldn't. And even if I did, that's my own problem. Not yours."

*Not yours.*

And yet, all of this is my fault.

All of it.

"What if that changes?" I ask.

He gives a quick shrug. "Then I'll be wrong, I guess."

I smile a little at that, because it's the most in-character thing he's said in a while.

Ben lifts his hand to my face, then drops it almost immediately, as if realizing what he's doing. I know why—it's all because of what I said, about our being too comfortable with this.

"So," I say. "What now?"

Another one-armed shrug. "We've got, what, three days?"

I nod casually, like that number isn't stuck in my mind as a countdown.

"Okay. So we do this for three more days."

"What is *this*, exactly?"

"I've got no idea," he says. "But it's good enough for me."

"Me too."

I mean it, but my words are weak.

❋ ❋ ❋

I pull the sick card after dinner.

Dad thinks I've got allergies anyways, so it doesn't prove to be difficult. I just have to fake sneeze once, and Nina banishes me to the basement.

Ben and I wait until it's dark to sneak outside. The window in the basement seems even creakier tonight, but it's still better than going upstairs.

Blankets, a pack of Twizzlers, a portable DVD player, and three comedy movies. That's what I've got stashed in my bag.

"This may be a bad idea," Ben says as he climbs out of the window. He narrowly misses a flowerpot, then manages to knock it over when both feet are on the ground.

"It might be," I mumble, shining the flashlight around.

Ben grabs my hand. It shocks me, given literally *everything* we've talked about in the past twenty-four hours, but I'm okay with it.

"It's terribly cold out here," he says. "Are you going to get sick?"

"Might help the authenticity. As far as Dad and Nina know, I'm already sick."

"Good point."

We walk in Nina's ridiculously large backyard, just past the pool and back fence, and lay blankets on the grass. I turn the old DVD player on and spread the movies out in front of Ben. "Pick."

He scrunches up his nose. There's a correct answer and he knows it.

"Choose wisely," I warn.

"I'm not watching *10 Things I Hate About You*—"

"Oh, come on!"

"You can quote the whole thing."

"I'm rusty," I protest. "I need a refresher."

He sighs and sits back. "Fine."

I grin and turn the movie on, even though I won't pay attention. I actually *can* quote it, so it's just white noise right now.

We look at the screen for a total of three minutes before we lay back on the blankets and stare at the sky.

"This is a much better idea," Ben says.

"What? We're laying on cold, wet blankets."

"No, we're stargazing."

"Stargazing," I repeat. "Okay. I like that."

"And we can just talk."

I look at him. "I think I've done too much of that in the past day or so."

Ben chuckles. "Maybe. But it's all valid. You're just…*so* persistent. I admire that about you, but I hate the outcome sometimes."

"I know you do," I say softly.

He exhales sharply, tracing his fingers over the inside of my wrist. His skin is like ice, even colder than the night around us. "Cici?"

"Hm?"

"I don't want to leave you again."

My stomach twists. "I don't want that either," I whisper. "I want this to last forever."

"I do, too."

"Do you think we could pretend?"

Ben turns toward me. "What do you mean?"

"Like, just for the evening." I shrug. "We could act like this is real. Tomorrow, we can face the truth."

"So…we lie to ourselves."

"Well, yeah. But only for one evening."

Ben grins, and it makes me do the same. "Okay."

"Yeah?"

"Yeah," he says, nodding. "We can do that."

And we do. We talk nonsense; we talk futures. We talk about the past and relive memories from years ago. It's pointless, perhaps more so than this whole thing, and it's going to make the outcome worse.

But still, we get lost in this lie, and we pretend.

Even while knowing what torture it'll be tomorrow.

# OCTOBER 10, 2008

*Ben was hurt.*

*Ben* is *hurt.*

*Ben is not here.*

I scream.

Cry.

Thrash around as someone tries to grab my arms.

Anything to ignore what just happened. What I just saw with my own eyes and what I'll never be able to erase from my mind.

Someone takes my arms and someone else has my legs, and they're sitting me up against the cool bricks of the courthouse behind me, but I'm choking on my own air and I don't know how to breathe.

"Inhale," a woman tells me, holding my face up. "Breathe. One, two—"

"What happened?" I croak.

"Inhale," she repeats, not answering my question.

If they don't answer, it must be bad. It's as simple as that.

"Where is he?" I cough.

The woman grabs my hand. I'm trying to breathe, I want to tell her, but I can only get out a few words at a time, and I'm not wasting my breath on such a thing.

"They're taking him to a hospital right now, honey. When you calm down and breathe, you can go too. We'll take you there. You can see him, and it'll be okay. Can you tell me if you were hurt?"

"This blood is his," I force out, showing the spattering of it on my skirt. "It's all his. It got on me."

"I know." She runs a hand over my hair. "It's okay. We'll clean your skirt."

There are still sirens and flashing lights and people running around me, and it's so loud and bright against the black sky. I squeeze my eyes shut.

I don't want to see anymore.

I don't want to *breathe*.

"He lost so much blood." I feel dizzy. "So much blood. He can't…he can't even be…"

"He's breathing, honey, but you have to breathe too. If you keep breathing, you can see him."

I cover my eyes with my fingers, letting hot tears slip through them. One breath in, one out. It seems like the most impossible thing to do. My chest is so tight that it hurts. My head is spinning. Every inch of my body is trembling.

But I breathe.

I make myself.

*If you keep breathing, you can see him.*

# CHAPTER THIRTY-ONE

I spend my last day with Nina and Dad. We play board games and eat strawberry cake, and I force one too many rom-coms on them. Nina and I perform a great balancing act; she doesn't ask about me, and I don't ask about her. Our conversation is superficial and I couldn't be happier.

Nina got my ticket for 9 AM tomorrow, so I use the quiet evening to pack my bags. I didn't bring too much to start with, but I've acquired a few things in my time here. I blame the record and book shops.

Ben is sitting on the end of my bed, watching me. The sound of the AC unit is the only noise in the room.

I fold up the last of my sweaters and end up sitting on my suitcase to make it zip. There's a gray sleeve sticking out one side and a red one sticking out the other, and it's nowhere close to being sealed.

"It all fit on the way here," I mumble, plopping down on it once more.

"Did you get anything new?" Ben asks.

I shake my head. "Not *clothes* wise." I pause. "Besides the dress. But that's in the closet."

The books and headphones are still on my nightstand. My pillow and blanket definitely aren't fitting anywhere, and my backpack is now being used to carry things I bought while here. So basically, I'll be carrying half my carry on.

I scoot toward my nightstand and take my book off the top, slipping it in my backpack. Before I realize it, Ben appears beside me, sitting on his heels like I am.

"What?" I ask, noticing his stare.

He presses his lips together in a thin line. Puts a hand on my shoulder. "You're an incredible person, Celia."

My body slumps on instinct. "Don't say things like that. It makes me feel bad."

"You need to hear it." His words are kind but his voice is serious. "And at some point, you're going to have to believe it."

It takes a lot of willpower not to cry. "I'm so glad I got to see you again," I say quietly. "*So* glad."

He smiles weakly, dropping his hand from my arm. "Cici, I can't be there when you leave."

I think my stomach falls through the concrete. "What? Why?"

"I can't," he says again.

"You have to. I need you there."

*Let me be selfish once more. Please.*

Ben frowns and scratches the back of his head. "You're making this worse for me," he says softly, no ill intent in his words.

"I'm sorry," I say. "But please."

He doesn't hesitate. "Okay. I'll be there."

"Thank you," I whisper. "Really."

Ben's eyes are dull. Something like guilt floods my body, but it's almost normal. It's all I feel around him anymore.

It's safe, somehow.

A baseline.

***

The morning seems to drag.

Nina and Dad see me off at the station. They both leave before the train arrives because they've got meetings for work. It gives me plenty of time to say my *other* goodbyes. I'm glad to do it by myself.

Mickey walks up to me first. Ben, obviously, came with me from Nina's house. We've kept to ourselves all morning, and I've been on the verge of crashing. Mentally, physically, emotionally, all of it. This is starting to take a toll.

I thought I'd at *least* make it home before it hit me, but when I woke up this morning, I felt like I'd been strapped to the top of a minivan and driven through a car wash. So no, I'm not looking forward to the ride home.

"I'm really gonna miss you, dude," Mickey says, clasping her hands. "I know I haven't known you for long, but could we keep in touch?"

"Sure we can," I say. "I can't just up and leave the girl who told me the lingerie store lore."

Mickey fake gags. Or maybe she actually gags. I don't think that was fake. "Don't. Please. I'm feeling queasy already."

I laugh. Mickey doesn't seem like the hugging type, which I'm very thankful for. I'm not either. She just waves to me, then says she has to go to her shift at the diner.

And then there were two.

Ben and I stand still for a few seconds before he grabs me, hugging me to his chest. It shatters the whole no-touching thing we've had going on all morning.

"I can't believe we're sticking to this," Ben murmurs. "We've established that we make poor decisions, but it's never been this bad."

I laugh dryly. "I know."

"We don't have to, you know."

"We do," I mumble, my voice muffled by his jacket.

Ben steps back and brushes my bangs away from my eyes. "Read the note when you get home."

"I will," I tell him. "Where will you go?"

"I don't know. Surely it won't be hard to sneak into a hotel room or something. It's not like anyone will see."

He's frowning. He's trying to smile but it isn't working.

"Hey. Don't look sad," I whisper. "Please."

He tips his head to the side. "Your train is leaving."

I laugh and ignore the tears welling in my eyes. "Are you trying to get rid of me?"

"Not at all," he says solemnly.

I don't move. I'm trying my hardest not to say *'screw all of this'*. Not to tell him to live with me in delusion. It wouldn't be the worst, though. Marcus could join us and we'll all be in solitude forever.

"I'll see you again," Ben says.

"You really think?"

He nods, but I don't miss the hesitation. "I'll make sure of it."

It's a promise.

One he'll break.

"Bye, Bennet." I force myself to say the words as I grab my suitcase and step away from him.

"I'll see you later," he says.

I take a seat on the train and close my eyes until it starts moving.

When I finally peek out the window, Ben is already gone.

# CHAPTER THIRTY-TWO

I don't let myself sleep on the train ride home—I know I won't wake up. Ever. I'll miss my stop and they'll have to drag me back home in a body bag because I got murdered.

So, rather than testing that chain of events, I put my headphones on and recount the events of the past month.

My first love came back to me as a ghost. I found a new bakery that I would both kill and die for. I made a few new friends. Marcus chugged a two-liter of soda. I was a runway model for one night *and* a pretend girlfriend for money.

Actually, that one sounds mildly concerning. May have to word that one a little differently.

But other than that? I slept a lot. Cried. Learned some things about myself and others.

I take out my notebook to write these things down. That way, I can look back on them in a week when my optimism is gone. It's only a matter of time before I forget every single positive. Before the negative pulls me so far down that I can't think straight.

My whole family is waiting for me when my train arrives. Jace and Maisie are squealing like pigs when I walk up to them, and they hug me so tightly that I'm convinced I'll suffocate at the hands of children. Marcus stands back, giving me a knowing nod.

"How are you?" Mom asks as soon as she releases me from a hug. "Did you have fun? How was your dad? How was Nina? Did everything go well?"

"Good, yes, good, kind of rude, and yes," I say.

She laughs, but all I see is how tired she looks. The darkness under her usually bright eyes is a dead giveaway. I'm wondering if it has to do with Aunt Lena. "Good, I'm glad. Now let's get you home."

I toss all my bags in the trunk of our car and hop in. The twins interrogate me for a while, but they get distracted by a bird a few minutes in, so Marcus goes next.

"Hey." He stops talking when mom turns to us, then continues when she puts her eyes back on the road. "What happened?"

"You first," I say.

Marcus shakes his head. He catches Mom's eyes in the rearview again and says, "Fine. Later."

I'm assuming Mom doesn't need to hear what he's got to say. Plus, if she hears anything about *my* topic, she'll think I had some week-long fling with a random boy and cried when I left. So I'm happy to leave it.

We move to safer subjects and include Mom, discussing what happened with Nina and Dad. She's glad that he and I are talking again, and she isn't shocked about Nina. I knew she wouldn't be.

When we're home, the day goes on normally. The twins and I play for a while; I talk with Mom and Don for an even longer while. Marcus hangs around the entire day. By evening, we're in my room, and I make him stay the night so we can actually talk. He agrees with no argument.

Apparently, his apartment is infested with bugs or something.

"You don't understand, C. They came out of the air vents." He shivers and swats at the air. He's lying on my floor right now, so I'm wondering if he's scared of bugs everywhere or just at his apartment.

"What kind of bugs?" I ask halfheartedly. Instantly, I regret it, just in case he makes me go across the street to see. He seems unbothered in my house, though.

"Ladybugs," he says.

I gape. "Marcus. That's normal. It's spring."

"I don't care. My math teacher in high school had a method to get them out of there, but I don't know it and I'm not about to act scared of ladybugs. Even though they're of the devil."

A laugh slips out of me, and he looks disgusted. "I'm serious, C!" He sighs. "They're horrifying. They look innocent, but they're tiny and they live in air vents! *And,* they make me think of this show I saw once—"

"They can't hurt you."

"One bit me before," Marcus says, horror in his eyes. "I swear. I'd swear on my life. I'd swear under *oath*! I held it and it bit me."

"I definitely believe you."

He waves a hand through the air. "You know what? Never mind. Just tell me what happened with you and Ben."

I swallow. "Can you tell me what happened with Aunt Lena first? Mom never brought it up."

Marcus's expression flattens. "Yeah. She's in rehab again."

I blink. "Oh, Marcus. I'm so sorry."

"It's alright." His voice is tight. "It was bound to happen. We'll get through it."

"How long?"

He shrugs. "Don't know yet."

I huff, burrowing deeper into the blankets. "Okay. You want your mind off things now?"

"*Please.*" He shifts around until he's sitting up. "Talk. I'm begging."

"Well, Ben stayed. I feel stupid for asking him to do so. That's all I've got for you."

Marcus groans. "Well, you are stupid."

"I know."

"But you did the right thing."

I sit up, sure I've heard him wrong. Yes, we discussed this on the phone, but it's weird to hear him back me up twice in a row. "Say that again. I need to record it."

That gets a laugh out of him. "I mean it. You did. For your own sanity, at the very least."

"What do you mean?"

"He's not here, C. Never really was." He turns until he's looking right at me. "And you know that."

My stomach sinks upon hearing the truth *again*.

"You think he wanted to stay there?" I whisper.

Marcus laughs. "No. He did that for you. But Ben also knows that this isn't real; he knows that this ends in due time." He shrugs. "He just would've dealt with it differently."

"What do you mean?"

"I *mean*, he would have stayed with you until he couldn't anymore. But that isn't what you need."

My right eye literally twitches. I think it wants to cry, but I can't right now. I've cried too much in the past days.

*I wanted Ben to make a choice for himself. In doing that, I pushed him toward the one best for* me.

"He didn't have to stay there," I mumble. "He wanted to, clearly—"

"This will hurt *you*." Marcus points at my forehead. "You aren't getting that. Ben won't be dealing with another loss after all this. Not in the same way you will."

He's right. Of course he is.

"How will I know if he's gone now?" I whisper. "How will I know if he leaves again? Is that why he agreed? So I wouldn't have to watch?"

Marcus frowns. "I can't answer that, C."

I translate his response to *yes*.

"I'm going to watch something now," I say quietly, desperate for something to distract me.

Marcus nods and hands me a few DVD cases from the stack by his blanket-cot on the ground. I take the disk player out of my bag and pop a random one in, turning it more toward Marcus so we can both see.

I don't pay attention to the movie; I only know it's *Legally Blonde* because I can hear Marcus humming the opening song. He eventually stops and pokes my shoulder, forcing me to sober up and listen.

"What are you doing for your birthday?" He asks.

I blink. "Huh?"

"Your birthday is in, like, a week."

I blink again, as if that'll do anything.

"CELIA LOUISE!" He props himself up on his elbows. "You forgot your birthday, didn't you?"

"I didn't *forget*," I lie. "I just don't care."

"But it's your birthday!"

"I literally couldn't care less," I say, pulling my blanket up to my chin. "It's just another day."

"But you're going to be eighteen! You've got to soak in your final Dancing Queen days!"

He sings the last few words. Instant reason to panic.

"Marcus, do not—"

He jumps to his feet. "YOU ARE THE DANCING QUEEN! YOUNG AND SWEET—"

I frantically grab some sort of weapon, which happens to be a plastic lightsaber Jace left in here. "THERE ARE CHILDREN SLEEPING!"

"ONLY SEVENTEEN!" He finishes with a bow. "There, see? That wasn't so bad."

I toss the lightsaber near the beanbag and flop back onto my bed. A smile involuntarily takes over my face. Marcus, above anyone else here, gets me. He really and truly knows me, and he knows that I don't want to mope. I want a distraction.

Granted, the moping is inevitable, but he won't be here for that.

"Sleep," I tell Marcus.

"Gladly. Turn *Legally Blonde* off."

"But you like this movie."

"Not while I'm trying to sleep! I can't sleep through a cinematic masterpiece."

"Understandable," I mumble, shutting the DVD player off. The room is quiet when the screen goes dark, and I turn off my bedside lamp, making the room pitch black.

I already know that it's going to be hard to fall asleep.

There's one thing on the forefront of my mind, and I can't shake it—Ben's wish to talk to his dad. That's the one thing he wanted from this, and the one thing he didn't get.

I shift uncomfortably onto my side. I haven't even *spoken* to Mr. March since October of last year. I've avoided him in every grocery store, every restaurant, all because I thought I was the reason Ben was taken from us. But now, after Ben being here and telling me what he wants, I want to see Mr. March.

Within three seconds, my mind is made up.

Tomorrow, I will see Mr. March, and I will get my things from his house, because if I don't at least *try* to heal, this was all for nothing. Everything will have been void.

It could go really well. Or it could be an absolute train-wreck. If the latter, I have no Plan B.

But I suppose that's the fun of it.

# CHAPTER THIRTY-THREE

Marcus, in true Marcus-fashion, has drooled over every inch of the pillow I let him borrow.

He's still passed out on my floor, one blanket twisted around his ankles and the other around his left arm. I step over him and go straight to my closet, fully focused on my goal for the day.

I'm going to visit Mr. March. I have to.

It can't hurt. It should be good for me. And anyways, this impulse will go away soon. If I have any hope doing it, it has to be now.

My closet is basically empty after my trip. None of my clothes got washed yesterday, considering I dumped my suitcase out onto the ground and called it good. In my closet, I find a pair of jeans that are torn in the leg and a red sweater that I haven't worn since high school. It works— it's not like Mr. March is a fashionista.

I yank on a pair of dirty sneakers and pretend it's an outfit. Halfway through tying the left one, Marcus makes my soul jump out of my body. He gasps and chokes in his sleep, and I'm sure he's having an aneurysm or something, but he's just waking up.

"Good morning," I say, moving to my right shoe.

"You scared me! *Where* in tarnation are you going?"

"I'm going to visit Mr. March."

He yawns, then coughs again. It genuinely sounds like a cat with a hairball. "Why?"

"I don't know. It's about time."

"Ah," he says. "So impulse."

"Yes, but still."

The house is dead quiet, so I tiptoe to the bathroom. I brush my hair and decide against makeup. Marcus steps into the hallway, still half asleep, and leans against the wall opposite of me. "You aren't going to tell him, are you?"

I scoff. "Do you want the man to have a heart attack?"

"No. That would be rude and vile, and I'm neither. I'm just thinking that there's more to this than an impulse."

I crack my knuckles. "No."

"Then what is it?"

"I just want to see him again. And..." I huff. "I think I want to see Ben's room."

"The boxes?"

I nod.

Marcus whistles, like, *Oh, you're screwed.*

He may be right.

The day of Ben's funeral, Mr. March *did* attempt to talk to me, but I was too busy crying and vomiting in the bathroom to speak. He told Don that I could get my things from Ben's room at any time, but he wouldn't bring them without request. I'd guess he didn't want to trigger more of a reaction than I was already having.

Of course, me being me, I still haven't gone. But that can change.

I braid my hair at the base of my neck and poorly fix my bangs before I walk to the kitchen. There's a legal pad and a Sharpie on the table, so I scribble out a note saying where I'll be for a while.

Mr. March's house is only a five-minute walk from mine. I consider turning around the second I see the blue door and the scuffed frame and the broken silver handle, but I don't. I lift my shaking hand and knock twice. As soon as I hear footsteps, I freeze in wait.

It feels like hours, but I'm pretty sure it only takes a few seconds for Mr. March to open the door. He's clearly shocked to see me—his face is blank for a moment before his expression softens, and he smiles, his eyes crinkling at the corners.

"Sweetheart," is all he says.

"Hi, Mr. March." My voice is embarrassingly quiet. I probably should have rehearsed this or something, but I didn't have time.

"Come in, please," he says, stepping aside so I can enter. As soon as he closes the door behind me, I wipe my shoes on the mat. I take a few deep breaths before I let myself glance around the house.

It looks the exact same.

The old kitchen table is still chipped on the corner, and there are drawings on the cabinets from when Ben was young. Shoeboxes full of baseball cards are set on a chair in the corner. A thick blue comforter is tossed over the back of the sofa, the one I used to steal when I'd come visit. I remember fighting Ben for it, telling him that I deserved it more as the house guest.

I don't know if I can do this.

"Do you want coffee? Tea? Anything?" Mr. March asks me.

I clear my throat. Swallow. "No, thank you."

He nods and sits in his recliner. *That* hasn't changed either—it's never moved from its spot in the corner. The thing is worn down around the bottom, and there are two marks where his shoes have rubbed the color off.

I sit on the sofa across from him and attempt to gather my nerve. "I just…I want to say that I'm so, so sorry."

"Cici, you don't have to—"

"I do, though," I say. "I'm sorry that I haven't visited Ben's grave, that I haven't even checked up on *you*. I'm so sorry that you couldn't be beside him when he died and that I took your place. If it makes it sound any better, I've blamed myself every day since, and I don't think I'll ever truly stop. Not deep down.

"Sometimes I forget that it wasn't just me. That he wasn't just *mine*. I understand how selfish that is; I've realized it more recently. But I'm so sorry, Mr. March. I'm sorry that you lost him too, and I showed no support. No return for what you gave to my family. To *me*. Ben loved you so much and so did I. I still do. I just…"

I wipe my cheeks furiously, hating the lump in my throat.

"Cici," Mr. March says quietly. "I hate that you blame yourself."

When I meet his eyes, I see that he's fighting tears, too.

"*I* blame myself. Every day of my life. Think about it— if I hadn't dropped that hammer on my leg…" He shakes his head and forces a dry laugh. It makes me feel sick. "He loved you too, honey. So much that it made him a little crazy."

I stay silent. He isn't waiting for an answer.

"I had to tell you that," Mr. March continues, keeping his voice at its usual soothing tone. "Just to make sure you know he wouldn't blame you, not in a million years. Ben was always a fair person, you know that. He would always correct you when you were wrong, but sometimes, he couldn't make himself."

He takes a breath, looks up at the ceiling fan. "You were his weakness, honey. I think, if you had burned this house to the ground, he would've blamed the match itself. Not you."

My mouth falls open.

I have absolutely no idea what to say.

Mr. March catches the look on my face, of me running that sentence through my head, simultaneously trying to remember and forget. He hands me a box of tissues. "I'm sorry, sweetheart. I didn't mean to make you cry."

I didn't even realize I was. "You didn't do anything. I needed to hear that."

He takes a breath. "Honestly, I thought you blamed me all this time."

My head snaps up. "*What?*"

"I thought that's why you never visited," he says. "I mean, not that it was expected or anything. I'm just the old man, after all." He laughs, the same dry one as earlier, and it gets a sob from me.

"No," I say. "I wanted to see you, but I thought you wouldn't want to see *me*. It was never about you. I loved you like a father, Mr. March, and I still consider you one to this day. I just figured you wouldn't want to be around me."

He frowns, but his eyes are still bright somehow. "We were both mistaken."

"Sorely," I add softly.

Mr. March sighs and shifts in his recliner. "Well, do want your stuff back? It's collecting dust. Has been for a while."

I bite down my lip. "Yeah. I'd like that."

"Do you need me to…?" He gestures to the stairs.

"No," I say instantly. It'll be ten times harder if he's there, watching. "I know where it is."

He nods and grabs the TV remote. "Alright. Take all the time you want, sweetheart. I'm here if you need anything."

I thank him and bolt up the stairs before I lose my nerve.

# CHAPTER THIRTY-FOUR

I stand in the doorway to Ben's room with now-dry eyes and absolutely no clue what to do next.

The bed is made, and the desk drawers and closet doors are all closed and it's so blatantly obvious that this room hasn't been touched in months. A thin layer of dust coats the dresser. All Ben's CD cases are still open and tossed on his shelf. The last time I saw this room is burned perfectly into my mind, and seeing it again feels strange.

I sit on the edge of the bed, my nerves on fire. I don't want to touch anything. It feels wrong; like everything in here is something sacred.

From where I'm seated, I see a pile of my stuff on a stool in the corner: random jackets, a purse that I thought was lost, and a few stuffed animals that Ben took from me. I'm guessing it's all been there since the funeral.

I stand and reach for the stuffed animals. The one I grab is a frog, and I so clearly remember the day Ben took it from me.

*I need it,* he had said.

*And why?* I asked.

*It matches my room decor.*

It didn't, and that was clear. Ben's room is the epitome of what I imagine all boy's rooms look like. Nothing matches, and nothing is actual decor.

Hesitantly, I set the frog down and move toward Ben's desk. There's nothing on top besides a cup of pens, a single piece of wrapped bubblegum, and one of those office desk calendars.

It's still on October of last year.

I ignore the urge to tear it to shreds.

The top drawer of the desk is slightly open, so I pull it the rest of the way. The first thing I lay eyes on is an envelope, and I'm surprised to see my name on the back. I grab it cautiously, like it's gonna shock me or something, and I squint.

*Celia Greene*

*August 3rd*

I start to breathe a little quicker. My only two options are to leave it here or open it, and I'm not sure which is better.

I dig a little further and find two more envelopes, both with my name and date on the back. They're all from different months.

Before I even realize what I'm doing, I've ripped the flap off the earliest one and fished the paper out of the envelope.

My heart sinks when I see Ben's handwriting.

*(August 3rd)*

*Dear Celia Louise Greene,*

*Hi, Cici. I'm planning to give you these letters for my birthday. I know that probably doesn't make much sense, but bear with me. I've never had a well-planned idea.*

*I know how happy gifts like these make you. That's what I wanted to get for my birthday—a smile on your face that I caused.*

*There isn't much to this letter. Nothing has happened since we last spoke, which was only a few hours ago. I bought you something at a pawn shop after I left your house. It's a necklace, and the charm is a cat.*

*If you don't get the joke, I may just be devastated.*

*I think you'll get it, though. If you haven't forgotten all my terrible (read: hilarious) jokes by now, then you'll remember this one. If you do happen to hate it, then spare my feelings, please. I'm only human.*

*I think I'll stop writing this letter. It isn't much of one, but it's a good introduction. Perhaps I'll have more to say next month.*

*We'll see if I actually remember to write these. Forgetfulness is my strong suit, you know that.*

*Love,*
*Your kind, handsome, incredibly intellectual (your words, not mine), best friend, Bennet*

The letter is now complete with a couple of tear stains.

I find myself clutching at my neck, wishing now more than ever that I hadn't taken that necklace off. Much like everything revolving around him, I left it behind the day of the funeral. I felt like I was choking every time I remembered the chain around my neck.

Really, I should savor these letters. There's only two left, and then I have nothing. Nothing new to learn about him, nothing else to keep me grounded.

And yet, I rip into the second envelope.

*(September 5th)*

*Dear Celia Louise Greene,*

*Hi, Cici. I haven't seen you since last week. Isn't that wild? I feel like we normally spend a few days a week together, either with your family or my dad. But no—this week, you were too busy. You were working, and I was working, and now I'm simply bored.*

*I spent the day pulling splinters out of Dad's hands. He was fixing the back deck all day, a task he did <u>not</u> need to handle alone. But he did, and now his fingers are bandaged up.*

*I'm starting to think these letters might be a bit shorter than I'd originally planned. I tell you everything in person, and nothing has happened. My life is boring, plain and simple. No need to document such a thing.*

*I think it's because you're with me for the good parts. Like, three weeks ago, we went to this awful movie premiere. The one with the aliens, remember? Gosh, that was so bad. We almost got kicked out for laughing when the blue alien died, and then cheering when the purple one did, too. I don't even remember the movie's name.*

*I remember something you said after, though. I think I'll remember it forever.*

*We were walking out, and you had your arms wrapped around one of mine, and you said, "You've got the most obnoxious laugh."*

*I only laughed harder, even as I tried not to, and said, "I know. It's a trait that builds character."*

*And then you looked up at me and said, "I love it. Even if it gets us kicked out of theaters."*

*Did you know that I hated my laugh before that?*

I suck in a breath, flipping the page back and forth, looking for more. I even try to peel the sheet of paper apart in case there's another.

But that's the end. That's where he left off; there isn't even a signature. I wonder if it was supposed to end like that, or if he got busy and meant to finish it later, but never got the chance.

I take a shuddered breath as I stare at the last letter. I have to save it.

The desk drawer is empty otherwise. I open a different one, and to my surprise, I find a stack of photos. Mr. March had mentioned a photo box at the funeral, but maybe he meant a photo *drawer*. This is more Ben, anyways.

I pick them up and start flicking through them. They're fairly recent—there's a few of us at random times throughout the years, at school functions and competitions before we were even friends. They progress backwards. I see him playing soccer with a bunch of boys, and then him at a go-kart track with his dad, and then one of him hugging a young girl at summer camp.

I flip the photo over to find a year.

I have never gasped so hard in my life.

*Summer camp, 1999*

*Bennet and Michelle*

Michelle.

*Mickey.*

We know why she could see him, then.

I tuck the photo in my jeans pocket and ignore the way my throat tightens. I continue to flip through the photos, wondering if there's more, or if this is what I'm left with.

I find nothing else of informational value, so I take the ones of him and me and put the rest back in the drawer.

All but the one of him and Mickey.

It's her. It has to be. That's the only way any of this makes sense. If she knew him back when they were kids, then Ben wasn't just some familiar stranger to her. He never was.

I take a shaky breath. I grab my things and the letters, and I leave Ben's room.

# CHAPTER THIRTY-FIVE

Mr. March is still seated when I walk back to the living room. He's turned on an episode of *Seinfeld* in my absence, so I sit down on the sofa across from him. He mutes the show and turns his attention to me.

"You found everything?" He asks quietly.

"Yeah."

"The letters?"

"Yeah," I say again. "Did you read them?"

After I ask, I realize what a stupid question it is. The envelopes were sealed, so he couldn't have.

Mr. March shakes his head, probably not even thinking that far into it. His eyes fall to the stuffed frog on the cushion beside me, and his face breaks into a smile. "That thing was yours?"

"Yeah," I say, laughing. "He took it from my room."

"I always wondered where it came from. I asked, and he said 'I stole it' and left it at that. I assumed it was yours, but I never knew. It was either that or my son was a kleptomaniac."

"He claimed it would match his room decor."

"His room is a train wreck."

"I know," I say. It makes me uncomfortable to find that the smile on my face is genuine. It doesn't last all that long, what with the nagging in my head that Ben is somewhere out there, but it's not like I can *tell* Mr. March. If Ben wants to, that's up to him. I'm not putting his dad in the hospital with a heart attack.

Mr. March unmutes the TV, sinking back into his recliner. "You like *Seinfeld*?"

"Never go a day without it," I say, standing. "Popcorn?"

"Buttered."

I grin and go right to the kitchen. Mr. March is a creature of habit, and I know where everything is. The popcorn has always been to the left of the oven, hidden under the cake pans from Ben. It will probably stay there forever.

I make the popcorn and return to the living room right as the episode ends. We start another, and we don't move for two hours, because the channel is running a marathon all day.

✳ ✳ ✳

Marcus is in my kitchen when I get home. During my month long trip, I forgot that he practically lives here, despite having his own apartment.

Mom and Don are standing over the stove, making pancakes in their pajamas. It's nearly eleven, which is an *extremely* late breakfast for them. They're always up and eating by nine.

I close the front door quietly in case the twins are still asleep, but it's not so quiet that Mom doesn't hear. Her eyes widen when she sees me. She drops the spatula onto the counter and crosses the room. I'm expecting to get in trouble or something, but she just hugs me. I relax slightly as Don puts a hand on my shoulder.

"How was he?" Mom asks, her voice muffled.

"Good. He was good."

She releases me, and the letters crinkle in my pocket when I drop my hands. It takes about two seconds for her to realize I've got something hidden away.

"What…" Mom spins me around by the waist, and I laugh as she takes the letter from my back pocket. Part of me wants to stop her. I don't want her to read them; I don't want anyone to.

"What is this?" She asks, unfolding the letter she grabbed. It's one that I opened, but I'm not sure which.

Her eyes scan the whole thing, but I know she isn't truly reading it. She's just looking for an answer. "Letters that Ben wrote to me."

Mom looks up. "Plural?"

"Yeah."

"Oh, Cici." She hands the note back to me. "I'm sorry. I didn't actually read it, I promise."

"It's alright," I say, shoving the thing in my pocket. "It isn't even that, I just…"

I don't finish my sentence, but she nods anyway. "Donald," she says to my stepdad. "Invite Neil over this week."

It's been so long since I've heard him called *Neil* that I forget we're talking about Ben's dad.

"Got it," Don says, walking toward the phone on the wall.

And yes, we still have a rotary phone. Everyone in this town still has a rotary phone.

Mom runs a thumb under her eyes, staring at the ceiling for a second before looking at me. "Have you thought about your birthday?"

I shake my head. That question is just as random as last night when Marcus brought it up, and just like then, I have no answer.

"Not really," I tell her. "I didn't think about it at Nina's—"

"That's okay," she says. I can tell that, somehow, the mere mention of Ben and his family has shaken her up, too. "We'll figure it out. We've got some time."

I give her a tight smile. "Yeah."

Marcus waves a hand through the air, reminding me that he's here. "I can't take this depressing energy. I'm going home."

"Please do."

"Oh, I am," he assures me. "I'd rather brave the lady-bugs than listen to this."

"That's normal at this time of year, son," Don calls from the kitchen.

"Yeah." Mom drags the word out. "That's actually…inevitable, I think."

He scoffs. "Well, you guys don't have them!"

"We do," I say, "but Maisie flushes them down the toilet."

Marcus grabs a half-empty soda bottle off the counter and opens the door. "Send her to my place, then," he says, right before leaving.

I don't shout anything through the door like I normally would. I'm almost sure it would end in a petty argument.

Instead, I go upstairs to my room, taking my new trinkets with me. I fall onto my bed, and my back does that weird, painful-but-soothing crack thing. I roll over on my side when I remember the photos in my back pocket. I don't want them to get crushed or bent up.

Also, the last letter. That's there too.

I can't open it. Not yet. The second my eyes hit the last word, I'll regret it more than anything else.

Regardless, I take the things out of my pocket and lay them out in front of me. The photos are a little wrinkled, but that's fine. I don't care about the condition of anything; I'm just happy to have them.

I drag my fingertips down my face.

I feel like a shell of a human, and I have no idea what to do about it.

Ben gave me closure. Mr. March gave me even more, and I'll forever be thankful to both of them for it. I needed it more than I knew.

But the pit in my chest? The one that filled with hope over the past month, then instantly ran dry? I did that to myself. I *let* it happen.

I know that it's only a matter of time before I go back to where I was last year. Marcus was right—I'll be the one dealing with this loss again. I'll take the brunt of it. And that's fine in theory; it won't be as bad. But it will be there, and despite what I've done to try to fend it off, it isn't enough.

A tear runs over the bridge of my nose. I tuck the frog under my arm and stare at my empty beanbag chair in the corner.

# OCTOBER 11, 2008

The ice pack against my skull does nothing for my headache.

Ben's been in surgery for hours. I don't know how many, but it's too many because I haven't seen him in what feels like centuries and I'm worried.

All I know is that it's past midnight, and his dad is in the back with a shattered leg so he can't do anything. Whatever they gave him for the pain reacted weirdly in his system or something, so he's out cold. My parents aren't here because the twins are asleep and they can't leave them.

So I'm just waiting.

It was a hit and run by a drunk driver, I'm sure. How else do you hit a person on the sidewalk?

Broken ribs. Internal bleeding. No limbs broken, miraculously. *Just all the vital stuff.*

A doctor walks into the waiting room. I don't pay him any mind, not until he says, "Is there a Celia Greene here?"

I ignore the dizzying pain behind my eyes as I stand. "Is he awake?"

The doctor nods, but it's hesitant. "He's been awake for a while. We've been letting his anesthesia wear off a bit, but…he wants you."

I set the ice pack down on a random table and follow him. He leads me to Ben's room but stays outside and closes the door.

It's a matter of seconds before I break down into a mess of sobs.

Ben is awake, and he's looking at me but he looks awful. His face is bruised and bloodied on one side; I'm guessing it's where he fell onto the ground. His arms look fine, somehow, but he *isn't*.

His blood is still on me. They never cleaned my skirt.

"Cici," he says, his voice strained. "I'm so sorry."

"Don't even say that." I try to get my voice under control as I walk toward him. "It was my fault."

He looks up at me and smiles. He *smiles* at me through all of this.

"We should've just gone the way you wanted," I say. "None of this would've happened. We'd be home by now, and—"

"Celia."

That word—those three syllables—stops me immediately. He never says my full name, ever. I don't like that he chose to right now.

"They let you come straight back, didn't they?"

"Yes," I say slowly.

He swallows and shakes his head, and my chest starts heaving again. "They don't…I don't think they let everyone do that. Not after a surgery."

It takes me no time at all to realize what he's saying.

"Bennet—"

"They can't do anything."

"No."

"I'm so—"

"Ben, *no*." I'm practically screaming, causing a scene and begging for absolutely nothing. "I'll…I'll tell them to try something else. There has to be something else. They can't just let you *die*—"

"Cici, please." His voice is breaking, and he chokes on the last word but I don't stop.

"No. *Please*, Ben, you can't do this! What am I going to do? What will I do?"

Ben's shaky hand takes mine. I try to cry quieter so the doctors don't think I'm having another panic attack, even though I think I might be, because everything hurts when I talk or move and I can't catch a breath.

This is pain. This is the most pain I've ever felt, and I'm not even the one in the hospital bed.

"Please," Ben says once more, and I finally let him talk while I try to breathe. He's crying too, but he's calm. Tired. A tear runs right over the bruise on his cheek and soaks into the bandage on his jaw.

"I love you," he breathes. "So incredibly much, you don't understand. I wish that I hadn't asked you to go out tonight. I wish I could take it back, because if this is hurting *me* so badly, I can't even fathom what it's doing to you."

I cough into the bend of my elbow. "Ben—"

"Let me finish," he says, and I do. I stay quiet. "I had so much fun with you today. We danced, hm? Twice." He puts on a smile. It's one of the most heart-wrenching things I've seen in my life.

"We did," I whisper.

"You should've accepted my proposal at the park," Ben teases. "I meant everything I said, regardless of it being satire."

I bite my cheek. "I accept now. Does that make you feel better?"

"Lots," he says on a breath. "Lots better."

He pats my hand with his bandaged fingers.

He doesn't say anything else.

"I can get your dad," I offer.

"I talked to him," he says. "When I first got here."

I swallow.

"He's said his goodbyes already," Ben whispers.

Almost robotically, I step back and drag a chair to the edge of his hospital bed. He looks confused, only for a second, before his face softens back to its usual expression.

He understands.

He knows I'm not leaving this room. Not until they drag me out. Not until that monitor goes flat or he goes home.

I grab his hand over the rail. Somehow, I've plugged my tears for time being, more focused on being here for Ben than myself.

"You gave me such an incredible day," I whisper. "I won't forget it."

He smiles, and another tear skates down his face. I lean forward and kiss his cheek, trying to memorize the way he looks.

"I love you," I tell him.

"You don't understand," Ben says breathlessly. His eyes flutter shut for a moment, and my chest starts to heave again but he keeps talking. "I didn't…not…"

"Ben," I say, but no sound comes out of my mouth. Now I'm crying, even though I said I wouldn't cry until after the fact, but I don't think it matters. I don't think there's an 'after the fact' anymore.

I think this *is* after.

Ben gives my hand a weak squeeze.

The monitor flatlines.

I drop my head, letting tears fall onto my blood-spattered skirt. I stand on wobbly legs and kiss him, right on the bruise on his cheek.

Then I fall to my knees in front of the trash can and throw up.

I let my tears go. All of them.

The doctors definitely hear me now.

# CHAPTER THIRTY-SIX

Unbeknownst to both Mom and I, Don invited Mr. March over for dinner *tonight*. This was discovered when Don asked what he should wear two hours before dinnertime.

That's when the chaos began.

Mom dropped the twins off at the neighbors, saying she'll pay double for the last minute notice. We ran to the store and tossed a bunch of random junk into the cart. I grabbed a box of pasta because it's a safe thing. Mom threw in some tomatoes and cream, so we called it good. She can think up something or other out of that.

We're in the kitchen now. I'm stirring the pasta while Don runs around and picks up scattered toys. Mom is messing with bottles of spice, trying to make whatever concoction she's invented even better. It smells good, but anything with garlic always is.

It's a quarter to six when I decide to make myself presentable. The grocery store would've been useless to get ready for—all the employees have seen me looking *much* worse than I did today.

I fix my hair and dab a little makeup under my eyes. It's not like anybody in this house will care—they've seen me at my lowest, all of them. I *do* look like a crazy person today, though, so I try to tamp it down.

When the clock hits six exactly, I hear a knock on the front door.

Mr. March is nothing if not punctual.

"CELIA!" My mom yells up the stairs. "GET DOWN HERE."

I do get down there. Quickly.

Both Don and Mr. March are sitting at the table, already laughing at something or other.

"I couldn't correct the girl," Don says, shaking his head. "I don't know. She looked like she was having an awful day."

"You could've done it nicely, though!" Mom sighs. She's still standing over the stove. Don looks at her, and I know he wants to help, but he's been banned from the oven. He almost burned our house down last year via Christmas cookies. "Sometimes they only need a little push."

I take a seat at the table across from Mr. March. "What's going on? Did Don do something foul?"

"As if he's capable." Mom gives a laugh. "No, he just got the wrong subscription for a paper, and he didn't want to correct the girl."

"I just felt awful," he says, and I grin. Don has the sweetest heart of anyone in this house, so this is no shock whatsoever. "The music in the store was so loud, I couldn't even hear *myself* talk, and I had repeated myself multiple times…I didn't want to make her feel bad."

"So what did you actually buy?"

"I was trying to get a magazine subscription for my mom. She's been complaining about boredom lately, so I thought a weekly magazine would fix her right up. But somehow, I ended up with a newspaper. Singular."

"The communication was that bad?"

"Downright awful," he comments. "But it's alright. I got it taken care of eventually, but she had to get her manager."

"I hate to say it, but that's somewhat comical."

He eyes me. "A hoot, I'm sure."

I laugh, then turn to Mr. March. "*Seinfeld* marathon keep you busy?"

A nod. "Until three, when I fell asleep. It was a good time."

"Food's ready," Mom says, waving to all of us. She unties her apron as we stand and go to the cabinet for plates. We don't serve food around a table; we serve it right out of the pot on the stove. Makes for less dishes and less waiting.

When we're back at the table, Don says a quick, textbook prayer before digging in. Mom glares at him, but he just says, "I haven't eaten since breakfast."

Breakfast was at eleven this morning, but I keep that to myself.

We all quiet down for a moment to eat what's on our plates. I think it's just a courtesy thing. That way, there are no hard feelings if you have pasta shoved in your mouth and can't respond.

Whatever Mom threw together in that pot turned out to be the best thing I've eaten all week. I've plowed through half of my pasta when someone speaks again.

"What have you been up to this past year, Celia?" Mr. March asks, adding his usual smile to the end of the question. "School? Work?"

"I graduated last December," I say, wanting to hide behind the fork in my hand. It's nothing against Mr. March; I just hate explaining this to people. "I finished up early."

"Really?" He asks, and I nod. "Wow. A whole year early?"

"Only a semester," I tell him. "It just seems early because I was put in preschool young."

"You make me sound awful!" Mom sighs. "She likes to tell people that I shipped her off to preschool as soon as I could."

"Didn't you?" I tease.

"I did *not*." She jabs at me with her fork. "But you were smart. It was the best thing for you at the time."

"It's true. I was a master finger painter."

"A regular Da Vinci."

I grin and stab a tomato on my plate.

"Are you going to college next year?" Mr. March asks.

For this question, of course, I stay quiet.

He glances around the table when I look at the floor, a frantic look on his face. "I'm sorry, sweetheart. Did I over-step?"

"No, it isn't that." I clear my throat. "I'm just not sure yet."

"Oh, well, that's alright," he says. "I didn't go to college until my twenties."

"I didn't even *go*," Don says, chuckling.

"You didn't?" I ask. "But you own a store."

"You think I got a business degree to run a *drug store*?"

"Well, not exactly. But still."

Mom sits forward. "Well, *I* went to college, and I can tell you that half of it isn't worth a dang. Get in, get out. It's simple."

"It's actually not that simple, but I love your enthusi-asm." I grab my water glass. "I'd have to like, pass. And get a degree."

"What do you want to do?" Mr. March asks, then quickly tacks on, "If that's an okay question."

I laugh. "All the questions are okay; I just might not have answers to them. But on that note, I don't know."

"You want to write, no?" Mom asks.

I glare at her, feeling my face heat. "I mean, yeah, but that's impractical to the max. I've gotta find something that will keep me fed and under a roof."

"You've got time," Mr. March says. "And anyways, it isn't so impractical. There are newspapers, magazines…"

"Anything like that would take ya," Don says, nodding. "I think you've got something."

I look at him. "You haven't read a word I've written, Don. That's the classic parent saying."

He shakes his head. "No. Well, you're right—I haven't read your writings. But I know you'd be good at it."

"How so?"

"Your heart." He says it so flippantly. "You feel things deeply. You're opinionated, and don't take that as a negative." He shrugs. "You *feel*. That's what you have to do, right?"

I gape. Don looks at me with blank eyes, as if he didn't just say something I'll never forget.

*That's exactly what Ben told me.*

"Thanks," I say, sort of awkwardly.

"Marcus said the same," Mom says, folding her napkin. "He actually did read your writings—told me he stole a notebook once and it was weighing on his conscience, but not enough to ask for forgiveness. He told me you're great, and that I should read it too."

"Thank you for that information. I'll deal with him later."

She grins, her smile lines deepening. "Don't. He felt bad enough when he told me."

"He should've considered that before stealing my book," I say, but Mom can tell I'm teasing.

We finish our plates. No one goes for seconds, probably because there's a cake on the counter. We each take a slice and stand near the stove while eating, still talking about random nonsense. I'm thankful the conversation has moved away from me; being the topic of discussion is *not* something I enjoy.

It's ten o'clock before Mr. March ever checks his watch.

"Good grief," he mutters, looking at us. "I should be going. I've got to teach in the morning."

I forget all the time that he's a teacher. It makes sense, especially after the topic at dinner.

"Bye, Neil," Mom says, stepping forward to hug him quickly. "It was so nice seeing you again. The door is always open."

"Thank you for dinner, Daisy. And likewise to you all," he says, shaking Don's hand. Mr. March gives me a quick wave right before he steps out the door.

After turning the lock, Mom crosses her arms and stops in front of me. "You're okay."

"Yes?"

"I was worried you wouldn't be. I didn't even think."

I pocket my hands. "I'm alright. I've missed Mr. March; I'm very grateful to have seen him again. And thank you for cooking."

She bites her lip. Before I know it, she's stepping forward to hug me, squeezing me hard. "I'm glad," she says softly. "I'm so glad, Cici."

I nod against her shoulder, hating that I'm lying to her.

The three of us clean up the kitchen but leave the dishes for tomorrow. We're stuffed and tired and ready to lay down. Nobody wants to do dishes on a stomach full of pasta and cake; it just doesn't work.

We all say our goodnights and go upstairs. The twins are staying the night at the babysitter's, apparently, so I don't have to worry about noise. Sleeping without fear of being jumped on sounds incredible.

I get ready for bed quickly. Heartburn hits me like a train when I sit on my bed, but I don't care enough to deal with it.

What I *do* care about is the unopened letter sitting on my nightstand.

*Save it*, I remind myself. *Save it for later.*

I wish I could.

I really, *really* wish I could.

But I can't. So I rip into the envelope.

*(October 9)*

*Dear Celia Louise Greene,*

*Hey, Cici. I'm writing this now, even though I'm seeing you to-morrow. I'm planning on offering you my hand in marriage.*

*Now, this is fake. Don't get me wrong. I know exactly how it will play out, too.*

*I'll ask you. You'll say we're too young, to which I agree. Then, you'll say something about Romeo and Juliet, and I'll act like I haven't got a clue what it means, because it's funnier that way, and you're <u>still</u> convinced I haven't read it.*

*Little do you know, I went out and bought a copy the day you said you liked it. But that's quite irrelevant.*

*You've brought a lot of good to me. It's only fair that I offer you a satirical proposal, obviously. Just to prove as such.*

*Love, Bennet*

And that's it.
The last one.
The last new thing I had of him.

# CHAPTER THIRTY-SEVEN

Mr. March came over for dinner nearly every day this past week. Him and Don have rekindled what scraps of friendship they had a year ago, only *now*, it's increased by tenfold. They've made arrangements to go golfing next week. It's comical.

It's also been a really good distraction.

Unfortunately, it isn't enough to keep my family from remembering my birthday.

It's gone from *next week* to *tomorrow,* and I don't think I could be less thrilled. I want to ignore it, but that won't work for anyone else. My parents have asked me over and over to give them ideas.

*What cake do you want? What gifts do you want? Where do you want to go?*

But I don't know. I can't think about that right now.

That empty feeling, it's here, and it's subtle. But it's enough to scare me.

I shift uncomfortably in my desk chair. I'm sitting in my room, a book in my lap. It's something I've been doing a lot more this past week—I start trying to sort out my thoughts, then end up reading a book to forget about them.

Every emotion in my head, every thought I have, it all feels so invalid. So wrong.

I had him back. Wouldn't people kill for that? Shouldn't I be *fine*?

It doesn't really matter, I guess. I've kept my shifts up at the store. My room is clean and my chores are done. I *am* fine, at least outwardly. That's good enough.

And anyway, my family is one for parties. I can't escape the celebration they've got planned.

"Celia." A knock on my door, followed by my mom's voice. "Your dad is calling you."

"Dad is calling me…on your phone?"

"Home phone," she clarifies, still talking through the door. "Come downstairs. It's ten in the morning."

Reluctantly, I toss my book onto the bed, accidentally losing my page in the process. I try to prop it open and find my place, but it's useless. I wasn't paying attention anyways.

"Celia," Mom calls again, firmly this time. I huff and drop the book onto the ground.

Slowly, I make my way down the stairs. Whatever is on the other end of that phone call is *not* exciting, given her tone.

I hear Mom sigh as my foot hits the bottom step. She walks toward me and puts the phone in my hand before I can say a word to her. The cord is stretched all the way out.

"Take it," she says, her voice clipped.

I do, because I don't want her irritation directed at me. "Hello?"

"Hey, Cici." My dad's voice is bright, and I can hear his smile through the phone. He's been like that a lot lately—brighter, happier with each call. I like to think it's because of what happened while I was there, though I'm sure more has happened since I've been back home. We've only talked a few times, just to catch up. Nothing too deep.

Nothing that takes longer than ten minutes, lest my mind wander back to what happened in that town.

"What's up?" I ask, checking the clock on the wall. "At *ten in the morning?*"

Dad laughs. "I am, for one. You seem to be up as well."

"I was. Is something wrong?"

"Not at all. I've just got a proposition for you."

I twist the phone cord around my finger. "Do tell."

"Your birthday is tomorrow."

"Ick."

He laughs again. "*And,* I just moved into my new apartment. I'm still finishing decorating, but you know. I thought you'd maybe want to spend the weekend with me? We could do it up real big, get a cake and everything. Ice cream, even."

I'm not shocked by his effort this time, and it makes me smile.

"That sounds nice," I say. "Have you talked to Mom?"

"It's all figured out," he says. "She's right behind you, I'm assuming?"

I look over my shoulder. Mom's ear is right by the phone, and she's nodding. "Hi, Carlos."

So she isn't irritated at *him,* then.

"Good to hear from you, Daisy," Dad replies.

I laugh under my breath before spouting off the usual things one says to end a phone call. *Can't wait to see you, okay I'll let you go, yep, yeah, all right, well bye.* All in that order, too.

When I put the phone back on the hook, I find Mom staring at me.

"What?" I ask slowly. "Why are you looking at me like that?"

She pokes my arm playfully. All of her aggravation has apparently melted away. "Why are *you* so intent on getting back there?"

I tilt my head. I figured she'd be surprised, but I didn't expect her to voice it. "What do you mean? I told you that I wanted to go back if I had the chance."

She shakes her head, and she seems…amused? Why on earth is she amused?

"You're eager," she says, crossing her arms. "You're never eager about anything."

It takes me two seconds to realize what she's implying.

"Oh, gosh. You think I met—"

"You met a boy, didn't you?" She blurts.

I crack my thumbs on my hips. "That is maybe the furthest thing from what happened, Mom. Is it so bad that I want to go back?"

"Not bad at all," she says sincerely. "I just expected it to be a little…more."

"I *knew* you thought I had a fling!"

"I did not!" Her wide eyes give it all away. "I did no such thing!"

I exhale. "I would've told you."

"I know you would've," she says. "I just thought that, perhaps, you didn't. That's all."

"I would've," I say again. "It's the same as always. I tell you everything."

*Except for the biggest, most insane thing that's ever happened to me.*

"I gotcha, sweets," Mom says, rubbing the back of my arm. "You'll leave the day after tomorrow, is that okay? We'll get your ticket again."

I nod. "That's okay, and thank you. I assume you've got some big party planned for tomorrow?"

"Not really, but I'll think of something." Mom steps aside so I can go upstairs. "You can start packing if you want. I've got to run to the store. Need anything?"

"Cheese," I say, then bolt to my room.

I'm sort of glad she lets me go at that moment, because when I close my door behind me, my eyes start to sting. I blame it on birthday emotions for now—it's the easiest out.

Before I truly start packing, I rifle through my crate of CDs and find one to listen to.

The first one I grab is *Rumors* by Fleetwood Mac.

I flick open the case and pop the disk into the player.

If nobody can fix me, Stevie Nicks can.

Ten or so minutes later, my floor is covered. I've got a pile of clothes to wash, and a pile that I *say* I'll fold, but really I'll just shove into my suitcase later. Most of the stuff I want to take is dirty from my last trip.

My backpack is still filled to the brim as well. The only things I've removed are the DVD player and my wallet. My copy of *Twilight* is still safely tucked away, buried under a cardigan and tangled headphones.

I still haven't read what Ben wrote to me.

I know I promised him that I would, but it won't be soon.

Mr. March being around and not having Ben with him has been harder than I'd anticipated. Not knowing if he's still out there somewhere, it's bittersweet. It's a completely different feeling from when I lost him abruptly, from when I thought I was at fault.

From when I wore his blood on my clothes.

That's a feeling I'll never forget, regardless of my want to.

But *this* is the opposite. This is tedious, a sense of comforting pain. It's the same one I basked in during those last days with him.

It isn't healthy. Never was. But I don't remember how I lived before this past month, and I have no idea how to go back.

The first night a week ago was the worst. When Mr. March left after dinner and I read Ben's last note, I tried to write. I tried to get words onto paper, for it to be something that wasn't tethered to me. But it was. It was tethered to me, just as it always is, and it came back to *that* night.

All my writings come back to that night. To us. That's why I stopped.

It makes me sick. Like I'm validating everyone in this town who told me I grieved for too long, that it was time to heal.

*They were so young. How bad could it have really hurt her?*
*You didn't even know what you felt. It was infatuation, not love.*
*It wouldn't have lasted anyways. You will be over it, over* him, *in months. This won't be a lasting impression.*

I prayed for it to be that simple. Begged.

But it wasn't. It *isn't.*

Furiously, I swipe at my under eyes. Packing my bags wasn't supposed to end in tears.

I huff and tie my hair back. I've got laundry to wash and fold; no time for tears, not today.

I stand from the floor and take the basket of laundry into the hall, tossing it into the washing machine with a capful of detergent. Hoping that I'm not about to completely destroy my clothes (I suck at separating laundry the correct way), I close the lid.

Instead of starting the wash cycle, I lift myself up onto the machine and lay forward in my lap. It's kind of nice, actually. My headache worsens—it's been my friend all week now—but it makes the pressure melt off my shoulders. I clasp my hands behind my back and stay there, curled up in a little ball. If Maisie was here, she'd deem me a roly-poly.

"Celi—" My stepdad's voice stops in the hall.

I realize that this is a strange way to be found.

"I'm fine," I clarify. I don't unfold myself, because the knot in my back has finally disappeared. "Do I need to move?"

"You're okay." He opens the dryer. "Just grabbing my work shirts."

"I tossed them in last night. Dryer sheet, too. Sorry if they're wrinkly."

"That's alright," he says, slamming the door closed. "I'm going to iron them anyways."

I sit up, my hands now folded in my lap.

"Hey," Don says softly. "You okay?"

Saying 'yes' while looking like this probably isn't convincing, but I do it anyway. "Yeah. Promise."

"You don't have to fake it," he tells me. "I get it."

"Get it?"

He nods and sets the shirts on a rack across from us, then lifts himself up on the dryer. I watch as he tries to cross his legs like mine. He fails miserably and eventually gives up. "I think so. Is this about him? Mr. March's house stir up some memories?"

I swallow. Don and I don't talk about Ben. We haven't since before he died. But the fact that he can tell, that he just *knows,* makes me want to tell him everything.

"It's about a few different things," I say. "But yes, mainly."

Don nods. "I lost someone too, 'bout ten years ago."

This has never once been mentioned to me before.

"Really?"

"My first wife," he says. "A few years after we got married, she was in a terrible accident. Car was messed up. Brakes didn't work, and she hit a tree."

My stomach dips. He says it so simply, like he's just telling a story and not discussing someone he loved.

"I won't tell you it gets easier," Don says, and his voice is quiet now. "It doesn't. You never really forget it, that feeling. But you find new things to focus on. For me, it was the twins." His face breaks into a sad sort of smile. "They were so young. They don't remember, but Maisie is just like her."

He sniffs, and it doesn't look like he's crying, but I wonder if this is as close as he gets.

"I'm so sorry," I whisper.

"It's alright," he says, squeezing my shoulder. "I didn't tell you for sorries. I just wanted you to know that I get it. I figured with Neil being around again…" His voice trails off. "Or maybe that's assumptive. Either way, I'm always here. Your mom is too, but if you don't want to talk to her, I'm here."

I laugh at the panic that crossed his face. "Thank you."

"You got it, kid."

My throat tightens, but I say, "I remember that day, when it felt like my heart was being torn out of my body. It hurt me physically. It still does, every now and then, and it makes me feel crazy." I pick at my bloody thumbnail. "He's all I think about, but somehow, I think about him less every day."

There are a few other variations of that in my mind, but I keep them to myself.

*I miss him so much, but he can't be here.*

*I want him again, but I wish he hadn't come back.*

*I just want to go back to the day I met him. None of this other stuff.*

My brain is like a broken record. I need a new focus. Maybe that's why I agreed to stay with Dad so quickly.

"That about sums it up," Don whispers, staring at a spot on the cabinets.

I hop off the washing machine and stand in front of him for a moment before hugging him. He seems shocked, and it's a fair reaction—I am *not* a touchy person. I'm the least affectionate in this house. But he pulls me into a tight hug, one of those dad hugs where you can't breathe for a second.

"I can't breathe," I say out loud.

He laughs and releases me. "Thank you for talking to me."

"Thank you for listening."

I start the wash, then walk upstairs to fold my clean clothes.

# CHAPTER THIRTY-EIGHT

Per the usual, my family turns my birthday party into an all-day thing. Granted, the *thing* was just ice cream cake and the twins gift-wrapping themselves, but still.

It was a good day. A really good day. One of the best I've had in a while.

This morning, they sent me on my way. Told me that Dad called before the sun was up and asked when I'd be leaving. I wasn't even sure what time my ticket was for, so it was a surprise when they rushed me around the house.

"Do you have a toothbrush?" Mom asks me, as if we aren't at the train station. She's the only one here to drop me off—the twins fell asleep promptly after hugging me goodbye.

"Yes, and just like last time, even if I didn't, I'd have plenty of funds to buy a singular toothbrush." I untangle my headphones as she adjusts my stocking cap. She yanks one side over my eyebrow, then the other over my actual eye. "Mother, what are you doing?"

"It's crooked," she says, scrunching her nose up. "Can it be crooked? Is that the look right now?"

"It was unintentional." I laugh as I straighten the hat myself. "I'll see you guys on Monday. I'm only leaving for two days."

"I know, but we just got you back!" She tugs me into her side. "And just because you're eighteen now doesn't mean you can go galivanting around, doing whatever you want."

"I barely leave the house, ever."

"Yes. And as a friend, I'm worried about it, but as your mother, *please* don't start now."

I laugh and wrap the drawstrings of my jacket around my hands. "I'll see you soon, Mom."

She waves goodbye as I walk toward the platform.

I hand the conductor my ticket and find a seat. The whole thing is so reminiscent of…what, only a month ago, tack on a few weeks? It's the exact same, but this time, I'm alone. No one to share this ride with.

"Excuse me," an older man says, grabbing my attention. "Is anyone sitting here?"

I eye the empty seat across from me. "No, I don't think so."

He smiles and sits down. "Thank you."

I nod. When I'm sure he isn't going to say anything else, I turn my music on and stare out the window, looking at the withered trees that are starting to bloom again.

I stay that way the entire ride.

Not good for my neck, especially because I fall asleep.

Hours later, someone taps my shoulder and startles me awake. I don't turn my head, mainly because I *can't*. There's a terrible crick in my neck that becomes obvious as I try moving.

"Ma'am," the person says. I'm guessing it's the conductor because I'm not old enough to be called *ma'am*. "The train has stopped. We're at the platform, please—"

"I'm trying," I say quietly, "but I can't move my neck. Give me a moment, please."

The conductor sighs but walks away soon enough. I try to pop the left side of my neck, and the attempt hurts worse than just about anything. How does this happen? I'm eighteen. I shouldn't be in pain from a nap on public transport.

The floor of the train rattles. I expect it to be the conductor again, telling me to leave or be forcibly removed, but I look up and find my dad smiling at me. "Hey, kiddo. You didn't come all this way to stay on the train, did you?"

"No," I say, shoving my headphones into my bag. "That would be horrid."

"Indeed it would," Dad agrees. He grabs my backpack and tosses it over his arm. "How's the old age treating you?"

"No differently. You?"

"*Me?*"

"How are you?"

"Oh." He sniffs. "I thought you were calling me old. I'm fine as well."

I laugh and zip my jacket as we leave the platform. It's cold and wet, and it's starting to rain, but this is still preferable to car rides with Nina.

"I don't live that far away," Dad says. "The apartment is close."

"I remember. I saw it with you."

"Oh." He kicks a rock off the sidewalk, just like I always do. "Right."

We walk for ten minutes and neither of us say a thing. I'm guessing Dad wants *me* to talk, but my conversation topics have run low. So we stay quiet.

The apartment complex is just as I remember it. This time, there are potted plants around the automatic doors, as well as new rugs. A little chihuahua is yapping at one of them as we walk past. The sound is earsplitting.

When we reach Dad's door, I find myself excited to see the place. Has he decorated, or is there a single chair and TV? It's an exciting roulette.

He finally gets the door unlocked, and I step inside.

It's a healthy medium of the two options.

Dad has decorated—well, *furnished*, at least—the apartment. There's a couch, a TV, and a singular coffee table in the living room. The kitchen isn't much better; it's got a table and two chairs, with a fruit basket in the center and a plate with half-eaten toast. I'm shocked to see curtains on the windows, but that's the extent of things.

"It's still very empty," he says, closing the door behind us. He takes his boots off by the door, so I do the same. "Kat is helping me, since I'm awful at decorating and she has to put up with it."

"Does she live far from here?"

He shakes his head. "No. She lives in this building, actually. She'll probably be over for dinner this evening, but you don't have to stay."

"I want to," I say. "I like Kat, remember?"

"I don't remember, but I believe you."

I laugh quietly, feeling another weight fall off of me.

*Distraction*, my mind whispers.

I see everything as a distraction.

*That. Isn't. Good.*

"Let me show you to your room," Dad says, walking toward a miniscule hallway.

I grab my bag and follow him. To the right, there's a wooden door, and it looks untouched. Inside is a cozy bedroom, themed with green and beige. The dresser is white and the bedspread is a jade color. There are little potted plants along the windowsill, and the curtains match perfectly.

And the shelves. He wasn't lying about those.

Three white shelves line the far wall. He's put a fake plant in one of them and a few books on another. I can't read the titles, but based off the spines, they're classics.

"Kat did this?" I ask, astonished.

Dad shakes his head. "No, I did this room. Knew you liked green. And those twinkly lights, too. There's some of those on the bedposts."

He motions toward the headboard, and sure enough, small Christmas lights are twined around the rails.

"Thank you," I say. "This means so much."

He just smiles. "Take the day to do whatever you want. Go into town or nap or hang around here, though there isn't much space. I've got some paperwork to finish today, but tomorrow, I'm all free. Okay?"

I nod, still taking in the tiny room. It's so perfectly done for *me*. Specifically. It's a nice feeling. "Okay. Thank you. I'll let you know if I decide to leave."

He gives me a thumbs up and leaves the room.

I'm hesitant to sit on the bed, given how pristine it all is, but I do it anyways. The room will look even better when it's been lived in.

I toss my bag down and dig through the front pouch. Three outfits are all I've got: today's, tomorrow's, and one for the ride home. Pajamas are nothing—only a big shirt and underwear, because I didn't have room for pants. My toothbrush is shoved in a sandwich bag in the front pocket, along with my underwear and socks.

The thing is about to burst. I brought too many CDs.

And the book. The book is still in my bag.

Reluctantly, I tug it out and run my fingers along the spine. Every passing day, it's more likely that I won't open the thing, and that's alright.

Whatever keeps me sane.

I stand and dump the contents of my bag onto the bed. I put the clothes and toiletries in the shallow dresser and set the CDs on the bookshelf.

I keep the book, my wallet, and my headphones with me.

"Dad?" I yell into the hall. "I'm going into town."

# CHAPTER THIRTY-NINE

I zip my jacket back up the second I step outside. April is cruel, and I forget that. It makes this very *not* fun. My shoes are already wet from the puddles on the sidewalk, so I don't bother dodging any more of them.

*Ventura Highway* is playing at nearly full volume through my headphones. I know it isn't wise to walk with music on, but I don't really care. It's helping my mind stay clear.

My goal is to walk with no direction, but that gets ruined when I see the bakery. Unsurprisingly, I end up with a croissant in one hand and a hot coffee in the other. It's bitter when I take a sip, so I sweeten it up with a few sugars.

Past that, I try to stick with my original plan. I let my feet go wherever, all while actively fighting the one place I *want* to go. I hit the game store down the block, the one Marcus raided. Then I go to the used bookstore and find six copies of *Gone With the Wind*.

And then, I realize I just can't avoid it.

I end up in the doorway against my will.

Jones's, of course. Where else?

I take a deep breath, my lips cracked from the wind, and walk in.

Somehow, the smell of the store is already nostalgic. Like paper and coffee, and today, the faintest hint of a fresh cigarette.

There are only a few people here today, and two of them are looking through the same crate. Another small group is gathered around a listening table, playing an album through multiple pairs of headphones. The cover is mostly peeled off the casing, but I can tell that it's a Billy Joel record.

I walk around and browse, anxiously waiting for Mickey to appear behind me. Part of me hopes she isn't here. I don't know what I'd even say to her.

I take a bite of my croissant and wash it down with my coffee. It's still much too hot to drink, but the bread leaves my mouth dry. I'd rather not die of asphyxiation per pastry.

"Celia?"

I jump at the voice behind me. The one I knew I'd hear.

Slowly, I turn around and take my headphones off, leaving them around my neck. I smile when I lay eyes on Mickey, and I can tell the expression shocks her. "Hey, Mickey."

"Hey!" She's beaming. "I didn't think I'd see you for a while. This is a surprise."

"Yeah, it definitely is," I admit. "I wasn't planning on coming back for a while, but…"

She doesn't urge me to finish my sentence, and I'm grateful. Instead, she asks, "How have you been?"

"Good, I've been good. You?"

"Busy," she says, looking around the shop. "I mean, it's not *crowded* or anything, but it's more crowded than normal. Four people is a mob."

"Better business is a good thing, mind you."

Mickey laughs and tugs at the end of her braid. "Agree. It's a little insane on weekends, though. Mostly kids. My brothers have been gone, so I'm here any time the doors are open."

I nod and don't ask any questions, mainly because my questions have nothing to do with her brothers. They have to do with someone that isn't here, all when I assumed he would be.

*Why isn't he with you?*

*Did you know about the photo? Did you guys figure it out?*

*When was the last time he said my name?*

I close my eyes.

"Hey, are you gonna buy anything?" Mickey asks, then holds up a hand. "Okay, wait. That sounded bratty. I just meant, like, I can check you out while everyone else is busy."

I take another look around the store. There's nothing I really *need* to purchase. I've got a lot of these at home, and Marcus has twice as many, but—

*Oh.* Well, I don't have that one.

I step toward the CD rack and lay eyes on the case. The album cover—which is a boy smashing a guitar over the hood of a car—looks back at me. If I squint hard enough, I can see my reflection in the plastic casing.

*The Adolescent: Headlights!*

As I read the words, I feel the roll of nausea over me, but it isn't as bad as it once was. I don't get the urge to cry or scream or bolt through the glass front door.

I raise my shaking hand and grab the case.

*It's literally just a piece of plastic.*

"This," I say quietly, setting it on the counter. "I'll take this one."

"Alright," Mickey says, opening the register. "Nine dollars even."

I hand her a ten-dollar bill and swallow, still shocked with myself as she puts it in the drawer.

*What am I even doing right now?*

I know exactly what I'm doing, I guess. I'm buying a CD, because I liked that band and I want to hear their voices again.

Maybe it's because I'm numb. Maybe it's because nothing *feels* real, so that's why I'm okay.

"Here you go," Mickey says, handing me the change and the bag she put the case in. "Oh, random, but have you heard from Bennet?"

I nearly drop my coffee at that.

*Maybe not as numb as I thought.*

"Have *I* heard from Bennet?"

She looks at the counter, her brow wrinkled in confusion. "I haven't seen him in a while. A week, I think. That isn't very long, but whatever. He said to give you this when you return." She hands me a piece of notebook paper, all crumpled at the edges.

Every shard of sanity I have threatens to break.

"Thank you," I say, my throat raw.

Mickey gives me a nod.

I need to get out of here. Now.

Unsure of where else to go, I bolt to the town park and drop down onto a bench, my knees threatening to buckle and send me to the ground. My hands are trembling as I unfold the piece of paper.

The handwriting itself makes my eyes blur.

-

*Hey, Cici.*

*I guess you're back with your dad now. How's he doing? I hope he's well.*

*I hope you're well, too. I hope you're doing better than you were before.*

*I don't know how to start this, so I'm just going to get into it.*

*The day after you left, I became less…here. The next, more so. As I'm writing this, I'm pretty much a shell of what I was a week ago, and even that wasn't much.*

*Maybe some ghost things are real in movies.*

*Anyways, I think it happened because you're gone. Because you're miles away.*

*I guess ghosts are a little clingy, huh?*

*Well, I can't…I don't know, Cici. I guess I could go back to you. But I think it's supposed to end this way. This was never some chance at changing the end, not like we first thought. I think it was supposed to end with your closure, and I think that Mickey was just a bump in the road that threw everything off.*

*Still, if that's the case, then I did my job.*

*I think it's the last thing I'll do.*

*PS. I read your note. Now, read yours. I know you haven't.*

*Love, Ben*

-

Okay. Definitely not as numb as I thought.

I fold the paper up, my fingers trembling. I didn't expect this today. I thought I had a stretch of blissful ignorance before this happened.

My stomach turns, and before I can stop it, I'm throwing up behind a tree.

Truthfully, I can't blame the note. My coffee and croissant weren't settling well, but the added nausea most certainly didn't help.

Of course, at this moment, some innocent passerby…passes by.

"Woah—hey," a voice mumbles, and I can't even afford to be embarrassed. "Are you okay?"

"No," I mumble, hands on my knees. I vaguely recognize the voice, but I don't turn toward it because I've got vomit in my hair and that's absolutely horrifying. "Who are you?"

"It's August. Are you okay?" He asks again. "Like, I know that you just said no, but—"

"My boyfriend is dead."

Silence. As one would expect, given what just came out of my mouth. Literally and figuratively.

"He's been dead for six months," I clarify, standing straight. I wipe my mouth on the sleeve of my jacket and resist the urge to chug the remainder of my coffee. I cover my mouth with my hand before talking again. "He…I don't know. I can't explain it. He's just gone. I don't know."

Poor August, really. I just threw up in front of him and dumped my emotional trauma on top. Every boy's dream.

"I'm so sorry," he stammers. "I had no idea."

"You wouldn't have," I say, taking a deep breath. Without looking at August, I take the book out of my backpack, fully aware that if I don't read the note now, I never will. Ever. "Sorry for…all of this."

"You don't leave a lady sick in the park," he says, as if it's a known thing.

I would normally laugh, I guess, but I can't find it in me right now.

Reluctantly, I open the front cover of the book, right to the dedication where Ben's handwriting has been waiting for weeks.

*Love again, Celia. Please.*

I slam the book shut.

And then I sort of lose it.

I'm crying into my lap, until my mascara is smudged on my jeans and I can't feel my eyelids. August doesn't leave, and I don't ask him to. I don't want to be left by myself. Not like this.

I thought I was fine. Really and truly, I thought I would be. I don't know when I convinced myself of that because it clearly isn't true.

*Love again.* What an open statement.

I have my family and the love they give me. I got that back, not that I ever lost it. And on that hand, I'll always have love. Maybe I'll be lucky enough to keep it.

But on the other hand, I can feel Ben's tears falling onto my shirt and his freezing hands gripping mine, and I realize it finally.

It was inevitable. Our end was never going to change.

And now, I've lost him twice.

# CHAPTER FORTY

"Breathe."

I am breathing.

"You've got to breathe, Celia."

*I am breathing.*

"You're alright." A different voice this time. A woman's. "You're okay."

It's Kat. Kat is here. So I'm at my dad's, by logic. I don't remember getting here. I don't remember taking my boots off, but they're by the door now. I don't recall a sitcom being on TV, but I hear a laugh track, loud in my ears.

I remember nothing but two words.

*Love again.*

Easier said.

He's not coming back. He never came back. He was never really here. He *never*—

"Water," I manage, blinking hard. I feel confined, frustratingly so. I want to thrash around, to scream or cry or *anything* but it seems I've stopped moving. "Please."

"And food," Kat adds, handing me a water bottle. "You're okay, Celia. Everything's okay. I think you had a panic attack."

"How did I get back here?" I mumble.

Before Kat can answer, Dad enters the room with a singular slice of bread. She eyes him, like that isn't the food she had in mind, but I couldn't care less. I don't plan on taking a bite. I don't think I can keep solid food down right now.

"Your friend brought you home. You were coherent enough to give him this address." Kat runs a hand over my hair, and it's the most comfort I've felt all day. I lean against her arm, feeling physically tired. It's a full contrast to my thoughts and emotions. "Honey, what on earth happened?"

"He's gone," I say simply, as if she'll get it. She knows about Ben, I know, because Nina told her. But she doesn't know what happened this past month, or what just happened in the park.

*Nobody will ever know,* a voice reminds me. *Nobody can ever know, nobody—*

I take a breath and dig my nails into my wrist, so hard I see red. Because I was right. My worst fear came true.

Not a single soul will ever know me again.

"Who's gone?" She asks quietly.

I wipe my eyes, and my fingers are covered in black. "Ben."

Kat makes an *Oh* sound under her breath, but she doesn't push further. She doesn't ask why I'm losing my mind over this six months later. Just opens another box of tissues and wraps an arm around me, whispering apologies that have no weight to them.

Dad walks in and sits in the chair across from me. He mutes the TV and just stares, looking heartbroken at the sight of me. Part of me wonders why he isn't the one comforting me, but I know why.

He doesn't feel worthy. And I understand.

"Celia," Kat says softly. "What do you need me to do?"

I inhale, and my lungs feel like they're about to pop. "I think…I think I need to talk."

"Okay," she whispers. "Go ahead."

I wipe my eyes again. Lick my cracked lips. "He was…I don't know. As horribly cliché as it is, I think Ben was the love of my life. I've just…it's been so *bad* lately, and I don't have an excuse. It's just been worse. Something set me off, and…" I exhale shakily. "I never dealt with anything, and it's all on me now."

Those are the only words I can really say, so I stop. Kat's eyes are watering now.

"Honey, I had no idea. I'm so sorry."

"You wouldn't have. Nina gave you no context with the situation." I tack a laugh onto the end, and she winces.

"Take a bite of that bread," she says, wiping her eyes. I do, because this has been enough ruckus and I don't trust myself not to pass out. The bread is dry and sort of stale, but I take another bite after the first.

Kat lays a tissue flat on the table. I set the bread on it and pull a blanket into my lap. I tug it up to my chin, suddenly realizing how hard I'm shaking. Not from the cold—I'm shaking from nerves, but I can't fix that.

"What can we do to help you?" Dad asks.

I open my mouth to speak, then close it immediately.

Because I don't know.

I haven't got the slightest clue.

"I don't know," I say aloud. "I never found out what there is to do. I holed myself up in my room for months. Didn't eat unless forced. Barely slept through the night but slept all day. The only thing that got me back to life was Marcus. He dragged me to my shifts and made me spend time with my family. And it all worked, for a time.

"Now I'm wondering if I should've done more. Therapy or something. Talked about it. But now it's all different. I can't do those things now because it isn't the same. It's been *months*, and thoughts and dreams of him shouldn't hurt as much as the funeral. But for some reason, they do. They hurt so bad that sometimes, it's all I can feel. And I know he wouldn't want that."

I swallow hard, giving either of them time to speak. They don't, so I keep going.

"He'd want me to go to college," I say quietly. "To travel. To write. To do everything I told him about two years ago, then gave up on the second I saw his headstone. He'd want me to live my life again. And I want it too." A laugh escapes me, weak as it is. "I want it *so badly*."

Dad coughs, and I realize he's crying, too. "You can, Cici," he says quietly. "You can. We'll help you. Your mom and Don will help you." He moves toward Kat and I, then sits on his heels in front of me. His shoulders shake as he lets out a quiet sob. "I should've been there."

"You aren't to blame," I tell him. "No one is, Dad."

He shakes his head, and my heart breaks as I watch him cry. Dad never cried when I was younger; maybe once, in the whole time he was around. I didn't think it was possible. I used to think he was bigger than tears. Bigger than sadness. I know that isn't the truth, but it doesn't make this any easier. To know that I'm the thing breaking him now, tearing down those cracked walls, hurts me more.

Kat, bless her soul, hands us both a tissue. I try to smile at her as I dry my eyes. Dad takes his and stands, only to sit on the coffee table in front of us.

"We'll help you, Cici," he says again, his voice muddled with tears. "Whatever you need."

"Thank you," I choke out. I can feel tears welling again, but I don't suppress them. I hug my knees to my chest and cry for at least twenty minutes. Kat sits beside me but doesn't say a thing. Dad goes to the kitchen, because apparently, there's a pie in the oven.

I stay like that for most of the evening. Neither of them tries to stop me, or console me again, or make me do a thing. And I'm thankful. I don't want to explain any more.

At some point, I end up back in my room, clothed in Ben's shirt that I deemed a nightgown long ago.

*Love again*, he said.

"I can't," I whisper aloud, to nobody at all. "I can't do that."

Some small part of me hopes that he hears it. Maybe that's selfish or wrong. Maybe my answer will change with time. But I clutch his shirt tighter to me, and I hope it nonetheless.

# ONE YEAR LATER

## April 29, 2010

"Daisies, please," I tell the florist, showing him the ten-dollar bill in my hand.

He glares down his nose at me, obviously aggravated. "Ten dollars can't get you a bouquet."

"Oh. Well, what can it get me?"

One exasperated sigh, apparently. The florist looks like he gets this question a lot, and I can guarantee that he doesn't. "I don't know."

"Can it get me three flowers?"

"Probably."

"That's a rip-off. Give me ten, please. Daisies."

Something like annoyance flares brighter in his eyes. And yet by some miracle, the florist disappears, then returns with a handful of white daisies.

"I don't think this is professional," he mumbles, flicking a few buttons on his cash register.

"Clearly, I didn't come here for professionalism." I hand him the bill and take the daisies, boldly assuming there isn't any tax. He takes the money and sticks it in the register before bidding me goodbye. I thank him and leave.

It's warmer outside than it has been recently. April has never been kind to us, but it's just sunny enough to make me feel alive. To make the flowers in my hand feel more like an adornment than a weight.

There's hardly any mud on the sidewalk, but some still manages to get on my new white shoes. I ignore it fully, keeping my eyes ahead of me. Nothing can rip my focus away from the rusty metal gate I've become so acquainted with.

I walk to the familiar corner of the cemetery and sit on the cold, damp ground.

"Hi, Ben," I say softly, to nothing. "It's me. Celia. I'm back again."

I set the daisies at the base of his headstone, making sure they stay untouched by the surrounding grime.

"Your dad is good. Just wanted to let you know, though I'm sure he's been here to tell you." I pause and wait for the lump to appear in my throat. It doesn't, so I keep going. "I'm doing well, Ben. Really well, actually. I'm letting myself heal. *Slowly*. My gosh, has it been slow, but it's working.

"I think about your last note a lot. And I want you to know that I have. Loved again, I mean. Not romantically, but not because I'm avoiding it. Just because it hasn't happened yet.

"I've healed a lot of relationships in my life," I say, and I feel myself smile. It's something I'm proud of. "The distance that I put between my family and me is long gone. Obviously, they still don't know everything. Marcus is here, reminding me every now and then that I didn't go insane. He's still my best friend, but I'm sure that's no surprise." I exhale. "I keep in touch with Mickey. August and I keep running into each other, anytime I visit Dad. We're working our way towards friends.

"Remember how I told you I wanted to write? For magazines, or newspapers, or whatever would take me?" I pause, the reflex of waiting for a response. When I remember that one won't come, I continue. "I got an internship. I'm writing for the local paper. It's not *The New York Times*, but I'm trying to get a transcript. I'm applying for college this fall to study journalism."

Silence blankets me, and the one-way conversation feels a little more *one-way* than usual.

"We miss you, Ben," I whisper. "Still. I don't think we'll ever forget the light that you carried. I know that I won't. But also, I think…"

I look at the clouds, taking a moment before I continue. "I think that I won't be visiting you as often. I'll still stop by, and I'll always bring you daisies. But I'm just…I'm trying to let you go a little bit more."

Those words. The emotions they elicit are undefinable. It sinks my chest to say them, but at the same time, it feels like a step forward.

"You'll always be a part of me. I didn't lie about that." I swallow. "I'll never let you go, not fully. Just…you get it. I know you do."

I stand and dust the back of my pants off. They aren't muddy or anything, but they're slightly damp from the dew.

"Thank you, Ben," I say quietly. "You taught me so much in life. I'll forever be grateful that I got to know you."

I stare at his headstone for a second before walking away. I jolt as my hand touches the cemetery gate—somehow, even after a year, I'm still not used to the cool metal.

As I walk home, I think back on all the words I said, even though they were only to myself.

Ben *will* always be a part of me, but not all of me. I didn't realize that the first time around. I thought the loss of him had to be all-consuming. Never-ending. That I wasn't *me* anymore.

I let the pain become who I was.

But Ben didn't want that. He never wanted me to view myself as a sum of the parts that came from him.

It still hurts. Of course it does. The pain is less frequent, less vile, but that doesn't make it any less real. Some days and nights are harder. Sometimes, all I can remember is the month when I had the privilege of holding him again. It was hard to move past that at first. Torture to accept the process.

But somehow, I don't think I can ever wish for another outcome.

Because it's our story. *My* story.

And I'd be selfish to try to change it.

# ACKNOWLEDGEMENTS

To be quite frank, I don't believe in ghosts.

I understand the irony, and truthfully, I'll never know what brought this story to my mind. I remember writing the first chapter in my notes app and falling asleep minutes later. I assumed I'd never touch the book again, but these characters had other plans.

Lucky for you, though, I'm not here to talk about the book you just read. That would be horribly boring and uncouth. (But hey, if you liked it, you should totally leave a review on Amazon and Goodreads. That's what all the cool kids are doing.)

Anyways, I'm here to say thank you to people who deserve it more than anything.

First and foremost, I want to thank Hannah. The front dedication simply isn't enough, so I'm going to dote on you here. Thank you for never telling me to shut up even when I deserve it. The amount of time I've spent talking about this book (and others) probably amounts to hours. And no, I'm not exaggerating. You'd probably agree. But really, thank you for being the first person to ever love this book. Thank for your encouragement, your friendship, and this absolute banger of a book cover.

Second, I must thank Rachel. Not only did you have to listen to my complaints while editing this book (there were a lot), but you edited alongside me. You are a *saint*. I'm being serious. Lord knows I have more typos than correct spellings. Thank you for telling me to keep going, even when I wanted to give up and scrap the whole thing two months from release.

To my family, all of you. Parents, I'll put you on the chopping block first. Thank you for not getting *too* mad when I'd stay up all night to write. I was groggy more days than not, I know, but look where we are now! And to my grandparents, each of you, for always telling me I could do whatever I set my mind to. I genuinely believe it's words like those that got me through 4+ drafts of this book. And of course, Addy. Thank you for letting me ramble about these characters for hours—HOURS—on end. I know you wanted to tape my mouth shut a few times. Or multiple times. It's a little insane what you put up with.

And to Ally! You thought I forgot you, hm? I did not. I could never, because honestly, I think you were the first to hear the idea for this book. I recall texting you in a sleep-induced haze and telling you I had an idea for a ghost story. Clearly, you must have said positive things, because I didn't scrap it. Thank you for being someone I can ramble to at any time of day, no matter the subject.

And last but CERTAINLY not least, I want to thank the person reading this. Whether you're someone I mentioned here or someone who just happened to stumble upon this book, thank you for making it this far. I pray that my words were able to comfort you, or to make you feel seen, or even just give you a few hours of enjoyment. Any of those things are positive to me.

I love you all. I'm grateful for you all. Thank you so much for letting this be a possibility for me. Even though it's just another silly book to most people, it truly means everything to me. I hope you'll stick around for more.